# WHEN YOUR BEST FRIEND WANTS TO EAT YOU

*by*

Winston J Smith

# Table of Contents


Introduction....................................................................................6

Chapter 1: The Bell Tolls for Thee .......................................................8

Chapter 2: Seeds of Destruction..........................................................24

Chapter 3: No Going Back...................................................................35

Chapter 4: Of Dead Soldiers and Wedding Cake ..............................44

Chapter 5: Chinese Whispers Beijing 2022 .........................................49

Chapter 6: It Begins! Thursday Bloody Thursday..............................60

Chapter 7: Fostering the Fear ..............................................................67

Chapter 8: Signs and Wonders.............................................................72

Chapter 9: A Fairey Story of Brass Bands and Brass Necks ...........76

Chapter 10: The Man with a Flowery Crevice...................................83

Chapter 11: Ostriches and Flamingos (April 2024) ...........................97

Chapter 12: Big Farmer (Around six months later).........................104

Chapter 13: Baked Beans and Brylcream .........................................120

Chapter 14: Dressed Up Like a Dog's Dinner
Late October 2024..............................................................................127

Chapter 15: The Slippery Slidey Stone .............................................144

Chapter 16: Heroes and Villains ........................................................ 155

Chapter 17: Becoming History........................................................ 171

Chapter 18: From Barnsley to Paradise .......................................... 173

Chapter 19: Dust to Dust ................................................................ 186

Chapter 20: Grave Warnings ........................................................... 189

Chapter 21: The Mayoral Banquet.................................................... 205

Chapter 22: A Great Awakening....................................................... 213

Chapter23: Cover Up and Carry On ............................................... 224

Chapter 24: Alternative Ending - Remorse and Restitution......... 233

# Preface and Disclaimer

The story you are about to read is mainly fiction.

Resemblance of characters to people living or dead is uncanny.

Only the names have been changed to protect the author.

It contains no intentional full-frontal nudity.

Those of a nervous disposition should proceed with caution, as this tale is provocative, and in many places, in very poor taste.

No animals were knowingly harmed during writing. Fictional deaths, animal or human should be treated as such, however barbaric.

It contains bad language, horror, and bloodshed. The bad language is solely for authenticity and is included to reflect the vernacular of the town in which the tale is set. To illustrate, a true story:

*Around twenty years ago, a young Scotsman asked a passing pedestrian if he could help, explaining he'd just arrived from Glasgow and was unsure of his directions. The stranger simply replied: "Fuck off!" The young Scotsman still made the town his home and testifies little has changed.*

# Introduction

Almost every child once turned over a stone, to be appalled by creepy crawlies writhing and wriggling and trying to escape back to the cover of darkness. Some children recoil in horror. Some lift even more stones to see how many other creatures are working unseen in the darkness, and what they are up to. The most fearless pick the creatures up to take a closer look. The stranger children even put them in their mouths to see what they taste like.

In life we all respond differently to the same information because our perceptions are shaped by our experiences and prejudices. This is healthy and normal. What is unhealthy and not normal, is that for possibly the first time in peacetime history, politicians and news organisations speak with one voice, even using identical words and phrases about controversial and unprecedented events. Contrary opinions are ridiculed, even presented as some new form of blasphemy.

Many are reassured, whilst others are uneasy and a little suspicious. The reassured leave the stones and the creepy crawlies in place, free to go about their business without being dazzled, interrupted, or eaten. The more suspicious, or inquisitive, are far from reassured. They are lifting more and more stones, to see how many other creatures are working unseen, and what they are up to.

Not many of the characters in this story were prolific stone turners and consequently few of them make it to the end. If they make you smile along the way, and even better think, then it has been worthwhile.

*"The liberties of a people never were, nor ever will be, secure, when the transactions of their rulers may be concealed from them."*

*Patrick Henry (1736-1799)*

# Chapter 1

## The Bell Tolls for Thee

October 25th in 2024 was an unexceptional day in Stockport, although many say every day in Stockport is unexceptional. The grey slate rooves of the old town's buildings mirrored the unforgiving sky, and the familiar, persistent drizzle was interrupted only by heavy showers, or the occasional deluge. Whether they were hungry or not, the rain fed the town's three rivers, as it has for centuries.

A young local man by the name of Adam Woodhouse flicked disconsolately through the tv channels, hoping to find something that could distract him from his waking nightmare at least for an hour or two. He avoided the news channels, as it seemed inevitable, he would see images of the ongoing horror that would serve only to catapult him back into despair, and his incessant dark thoughts of suicide.

No one could blame him, Adam had always worked his socks off,

the one exception being school, where every report included "could do better." There, he'd used his sharp good-natured wit to amuse his friends, and hopefully catch the attention of certain young ladies. His teachers were over lenient with him, partly because they too were amused by his witticisms, and charmed by his good nature and disarming smile.

Unfortunately for Adam, the crown of class clown robbed him of the qualifications and opportunities that would have eased him more comfortably into adult life. Even so, around ten years later he'd made the best of a bad job. He was on the first rung of the property ladder. He'd married his childhood sweetheart and was happily raising two young children, a textbook route to contentment, or so he thought. He was a typical Stockport lad, if there can be such a thing in the melting pot of a large and growing municipality. This was an old and upwardly mobile northern conurbation with its bustling masses and cultural cocktail.

Adam had worked four ten-hour shifts a week since the children were born. This way he could make the most of their early years. He had blocks of three days off, which felt like weekly Bank Holidays without the crowds. Suddenly at the tender age of twenty-seven he had nothing, no wife, no children, and no prospect of ever being truly whole again. All was taken in one dreadful afternoon.

Just seven short days earlier Adam's last shift for the week had ended, like so many others, with coarse but good-natured verbal jousting. The work's bell sounded for the end of the shift, and the customary resounding cheer went up, echoing in the exposed metal rafters of the factory roof. The four-shift fraternity had finished for the week, so were especially chirpy. They took the obligatory opportunity to gloatingly remind the "fivers" they were back in the next day, and the joys of weekend were not theirs yet. The gloating was a hollow and pointless exercise, as they all ultimately worked the same hours. Most had the option to choose shifts too, but it always felt good, and it was tradition. It was also mainly the younger men, as the old boys and the ladies didn't seem to feel the need to heartlessly insult their friends. Even so, they enjoyed watching the soap opera and listening from the sidelines to see if anyone could land a knockout blow.

Adam had a particular line of attack in mind that day for one individual, with the year's most critical bi-annual event imminent, the Manchester derby. In this period of history Manchester City were in the ascendency. With a change of owner or manager however, things can quickly flip so no quarter could be given. Adam believed two decades of mockery and derision from the red half during their own good years still required atonement.

Through Adam's school years United had been reaching for the stars, whilst his beleaguered but beloved City had been yo-yoing between divisions and seeing more false dawns than a battery hen. Adam said he was now merely making hay while the Blue Moon was shining. Wearing the smile of a newly released prisoner he launched his opening salvo:

'See you on Monday everyone! Oi, see you Ahmed you rabid red muppet, or probably not, after we give you another spanking. Are you faking another Facebook ban for a week and pulling the usual seven-day sickie? You don't want to be wasting your sick pay on that shower of shite!'

Onlookers or readers might be forgiven for assuming Ahmed was of Asian descent, but it was just a nickname. His real name was Denis Whittle, and any apparent dark pigmentation was just the effects of a bedsit, and forty years of nicotine. His yellowy brown stained skin was decorated with faded home-made tattoos. Working class would-be alpha males historically opted for indiscreet messaging on their knuckles to assert their dominance. Alternatively they might have references to family members, especially parents to proclaim their softer side. Having said that, the latter was generally a pretty insincere exercise and mainly done in the interest of pulling birds.

Ahmed couldn't decide which characteristic would serve him best. He was torn between two old favourites, "Fuck Off" or "Mam and Dad". Neither are particularly good choices given the maths of the letters and available knuckles. Eventually he chose the daft option of having both. His younger brother George did them for him while he watched old Eric Cantona and Christiano Ronaldo videos and drank himself from starry eyed to glassy eyed. His brother thought it would be funny to switch the tattoo order while he was distracted, so the finished product read "Fuck Mam" and "Off Dad." Consequently, Ahmed was being called "Mother Fucker" well before it became an acceptable term in semi-polite society. It cost George a pummelling, but he counted it an excellent deal for the years of amusement it gave him.

In time, Ahmed had Pamela on his arm, not literally, in fact women were not his strongpoint and the Mam and Dad tattoos flopped. Pamela was just an imaginary liaison expressed in India ink rather than emotion or commitment. It was Pamela Anderson, not a girlfriend or daughter, and he only wanted to drown in her dairy pillows, not die in her arms.

Above each of his thumbs were childlike attempts at swallows in flight. The swallow on his right hand looked like it had been throttled and plucked because he'd done that himself with his wrong hand. On his forehead was inked a very strange and mysterious word, "DETINU". However, DETINU was not chosen to express a special quality or idiosyncrasy cast in an exotic language. Nor was it to lend intrigue or mystery to his persona. Rather, it was just the fruit of eight cans of Stella, a drunken attempt at tattooing UNITED on his noggin in his bathroom mirror. In his defence it wasn't entirely legible anymore as one of his pals had helped in partially removing it using sandpaper and Savlon.

On top of his head was perched a terrible attempt at a wig, in orangutan auburn. It looked like it had been woven by sausage fingered scoundrels as part of their community service. It also clashed badly with his remaining lank and lifeless hair of dark brown and grey, but it was cheap, the air mail was free, and he liked it.

The origin of his work nickname is a somewhat convoluted story. A local and legendary Asian immigrant businessman once had a huge clothes shop, next to where the old open-air market used to be held. Legend has it that when this Mr Ahmed first came to these shores, "without a pot to piss in," as they say in this town, he used to sell rugs which he displayed on factory steps. The shop was something between a modern high street store and a market, as fixtures and fittings were pretty rudimentary. However, all shortcomings were easily forgiven when you could be dressed like a Carnaby Street disco peacock for just over twenty quid. The quality may have been more Skid Row than Savile Row, but Mr Ahmed knew his market and Primark clearly stole all his best ideas.

In his heyday Mr Ahmed sold a million and one gaudy nylon trouser suits and cheese cloth shirts for lads or lasses. The lads queued for two tone parallel trousers whilst the girls bought unfeasibly wide culottes to drape over lethally high platform shoes. The local girls' combos led to many a stylishly acquired sprained ankle, pissed or sober! Brutus penny round giant collared shirts also flew out, appropriately as a strong tailwind could render the skinny 70's boys and girls airborne.

Hopefully, by this point you have solved the riddle of the nickname. Mr Ahmed once sold rugs, a cruel euphemism for wigs, though it is doubtful he ever did an orangutan auburn shag pile number. Personally, the original Mr Ahmed stuck to the classic swoop, the Bobby Charlton style comb-over debacle so popular with balding middle-aged men of that generation.

It's uncertain whether Ahmed, or Denis, has ever fully understood his wig related factory moniker. The shop has been closed down for decades, standing derelict, apparently due to subsidence. The signage however fittingly remained like a kind of cut-price epitaph to the great man. Adam only knew the story from his dad and an older work colleague but decided it was a good enough fit, certainly a better fit than the ninety-nine-rupee toupee. Denis responded to Adam's derby goading with a smirk and two raised middle fingers and hit back with the rapier-like subtlety forged in the Manchester overspills:

'You're a cheeky blue bastard you are Adam Shithouse! When the camel jockeys get bored, you'll be back in our shadow where you belong, if the 115 charges don't get you first you Emptihad empty head. Come and talk to me when you've got twenty titles and your own stadium. Anyway, have a good one Bitter, see you Monday.'

'Ha ha that's pretty good for you Denise. Your best yet actually. See you a week on Monday mate. Hopefully it won't be sunny so you don't get dazzled when you crawl back out from under your rocks! If you scrawp a win I'll look forward to hearing 20 20 20 five minutes after the final whistle.'

It was short, not overly sweet, unrefined even, but a necessary release valve for the pent-up boredom of a week in low skilled production. The happy herd stampeded from the factory, heading to the freedom of the sodden Stockport savanna and Adam identified his next victim, shouting to make sure it was heard far and wide:

'Hey, Wally you nonce, don't forget to bring those gruds I lent you back, and make sure you wash your skid-marks out first this time you tramp!'

Gruds as a local name for underpants is an example of the evolution or regression of language. Bill Grundy, probably most famous for his Sex Pistols interview, hailed from Manchester and lived in Stockport. His local popularity and name recognition was sufficient for him to be a victim or beneficiary of some rhyming slang. Undies became Bill Grundy's with a few of the next generation opting for Tim Grundy's after Bill's son. Both were shortened to gruds though many still go with the equally concise "Bill's". Adam's dad being a champion of the hideous string Y front and string vest combos was unimpressed all round. He was already annoyed at the adoption of the American usage for pants. He said you wear bloody underpants underneath your pants and we all know where we're up to. He was probably right but it was hardly a reason to get his knickers in a twist.

The aforementioned Wally, real name Pete Wallace, was not really a nonce, nor had he actually borrowed any underpants then, or previously. He responded matching the eloquence of Ahmed moments earlier:

'Suck my arse Woody, they all know your specialist subject is talking bollocks you wazzock!'

Wally glanced around vainly hoping for some visual signs of support. He didn't get any, then again it was home-time, and everyone knew the score and were still chuckling at the daft accusation. Wally was floundering but just when all seemed lost, he managed to scramble a better response:

'Hey, Woody you Shedhead, look after that little lady of yours. Tell her I'll see her again on your next shift. I'll put a smile on her face alright pal.'

Unperturbed, unoffended and laughing, Adam replied:

'Dreaming as usual Waldo, the only skirt you ever see is on your computer, and if you turned your webcam on, they'd bin you off too you ugly spud.'

'Jog on Woody you cockwomble, I'll be on Tinder later locked and loaded, lining them up like ducks at the fairground. Just because you gave up your freedom for the first bint who looked twice at you!'

'Haha course you will Wally. I've heard Tinder admin changed your username to Swipe Left? Stick to Brail Bunnies, you might have half a chance there! Anyway, take care my mate and I'll see you next week.'

'Yeah, see you Woody you twat, be good our kid.'

This was all pretty crude and basic stuff, but it was all the situation demanded. Adam Woodhouse was well accomplished in the verbal joust and could hold his own in far more demanding settings. If he lost, he took it on the chin, he always tried to laugh along, acknowledging the prowess of his opponent. His father was of the "sticks and stones may break my bones" school of thought, and the fruit had not fallen far from the tree. Adam had learned at the knee of his father like a Socratean disciple:

'Taking the piss is the right of every Englishman son. It sharpens your wits and thickens your skin. When people stop talking, even arguing, lies can grow legs. Never get so busy you don't have time to think, or when the time comes, you'll have nowt to say, and someone will have your kecks down. If a politician speaks, keep in mind nine times out of ten it's shite with sugar on, and if you ever notice governments wanting to stop people talking, look out! They are far more dangerous than even the most obnoxious and loud-mouthed piss taker. Old George Orwell said: "Free speech is my right to say what you don't want to hear." I wish I'd never told that to your ruddy mother mind.

'Don't be afraid of titles or reputations and train that snout of yours to sniff out deceit and trickery. Horse shit smells the same whether it's from Shergar or an old nag in a knacker's yard. In the pub or on the shop floor, I warrant you'll hear nigh on as much truth as you will in any posh lecture theatre once minds are focused. If you've no great reputation to protect, or you're more concerned with truth than appearance or acceptance, you'll more likely ask the questions that need asking, and not be looking for a pat on the head.

'There'll always be more we don't know than we do, so never fret so much about what you're going to say, that you say nowt. Sometimes you have to go against the crowd and remember, unless you're a Christmas tree your balls aren't just for decoration. Always fight your corner but if someone's argument is better and makes more sense, take it on board, even if the person making it is a pillock. If you find yourself digging for dirt on someone because their arguments are better, when you look in a mirror there'll be two clowns in the room. With so many like that around these days, it's little wonder so many halls of learning have become circuses. Some set too much store by experts with their theoretical papers, but never forget, everything has to be tried for purity in the furnace of the real world, or it may crack and fail under pressure like badly forged iron.

'At least half of what's been written by experts has turned out to only be good for bog roll, and all too often it has been enacted by careless politicians to the peoples' cost. Don't get me wrong lad, experts have their place and at the top table too. Having said that, if you forget everything else I've ever said, never forget this: He who pays the piper calls the tune! Burn that deep in your mind and always find out who that is before you put your dancing shoes on. In everyday life lad, most want to be liked, few are controversial just for the sake of it. Truth and wisdom young Adam, evolve naturally, as the language of life is expressed, even by the gob-shite!'

Adam had said his goodbyes to his workmates and made good his escape and was about to leave for home. He saw one of the foremen caught short, relieving himself in a bush at the edge of the car park which was an opportunity he couldn't pass up.

'Oi Tony! That's a criminal offence!'

'What, having a piss in a bush? No one can see anything!'

'I meant an adult holding a child's penis, but thanks for proving my point mate.' Tony processed the comment, then they both laughed and said their adieus with Tony still chuckling as he got into his car.

Unbeknown to Adam, Susan, one of his "fiver" work colleagues had clearly not understood the dynamic of the banter with Wally and reported him for bullying to the shift manager the next day.

'Can I have a word please Mr McNally?'

'Of course you can Susan what can I do for you?

'I assume you heard all that last night, but Adam Woodhouse should be disciplined or sacked for swearing and bullying.'

'Shut the door please Susan and take a pew. Do you want to put your complaint in writing?'

'I already have, there you go.'

'Ok, first off if I sacked everyone who works here for swearing I'd have no staff, including you, would I?'

'Well, what about the rest of it? What he said to Peter Wallace was a disgrace. That kind of talk shouldn't be tolerated.'

'It sounded like banter to me Susan but do you know who won't be complaining, Peter himself!'

'But that's how bullying works isn't it Mr McNally? He's probably not spoken up because he's intimidated.'

'I heard it all Susan, it was earthy I'll grant you that, but there's something you almost certainly don't know. I assume you're aware Peter Wallace has a little girl with cerebral palsy?'

'Yes, I did know. I put in for the trip that was organised for her.'

'I'm glad to hear that and well done for contributing. Between you and me, Adam arranged that trip and the collection anonymously with our blessing. Even Peter doesn't know it was him. Adam also takes little Esme out with his family quite regularly because she's in between the ages of his own kids. He thinks it's good for her and for his own nippers to help them appreciate how fortunate they are. Apparently wee Esme says aside from birthdays and Christmas those are her favourite days. As for Adam, from all accounts that lad hasn't got a malicious bone in his body.'

'Oh fu, excuse me, oh I didn't know all that.'

'Do you still want me to proceed with the complaint, but I will say to you that this is North Reddish not North Islington. I'm not sure it will get very far once everything is put into context.'

'No, obviously not. I would need Peter to be in agreement.'

'Well, here you would, but obviously not everywhere is here. I'd think twice in future before going nuclear if I were you. That lad has a family and a mortgage, and, in another setting, this could have caused real problems for all of them way into the future.'

'Yes, yes, I understand. Maybe I'm upset about something else and wanted to let off steam. Can I withdraw the complaint then?'

'Yes, I'll put it in the shredder for you. No one else will hear about this, from me at any rate. One other thing. Mr Arkwright likes solid people. He said that has been the backbone of the company since he founded it. He told me he's been impressed with your work over all so keep your nose clean and who knows. He was already moving

Adam up even before Adam put in some written suggestions which will boost production and save money without negatively affecting any staff. He is earmarked for promotion to management any time soon so he would be a better friend than an enemy.'

'Oh, right ok I'll keep that in mind. Thanks.'

'Not a word though, Let's make this a teachable moment or whatever bollocks they're saying nowadays. Ok you get back to your team, and remember, silence is golden.'

Unaware of any of this back story Adam had jumped in his car, put on his seat belt, and fired off a quick text to his beloved wife to say he was on his way home. There was no need to call to see if he had to pick anything up for tea. It was Thursday night, the Woodhouse family's unorthodox takeaway night. Even though it was school the next day, the kids were allowed to stay up an hour or so later to watch a movie. Thursday night had become special for both Adam and the kids. The rules were simple; their room must be tidy, and any homework done and dusted before daddy returned with the week's chosen banquet. Play the game and share in the pig out, don't do your homework or tidy up, and watch the dog eat your share. The system had worked perfectly so far for all except the dog, who was yet to share anything besides the odd chicken bone or boring leftover crusts.

Adam's dad never approved of movie nights:

'They're films not movies! You were raised in Stockport, not bloody San Francisco. You'll be buying take away pizzas next!'

Needless to say, pizzas were a firm favourite with the kids on either movie or film night, despite grandad's insistence pizza is glorified cheese on toast. On the other hand, or paw, it had traditionally and unsurprisingly been the dog's least favourite. The kids loved the dog, not least because it amused them their dad had named it Kevin, and he featured in all their stories. They loved Kevin just short of sharing special film night food with him. There was a time he stood with hopeful eyes, his long pink frilly tongue hanging out optimistically, ready to seize on moments of generosity or weakness. He eventually learned Thursday night begging was futile, and their love for him wasn't quite unconditional. In time Kevin resigned himself to settling down and curling up with the children and enjoying the show, to avoid further disappointment. As will later become clear, in the last few months he'd had no interest whatsoever either in what they ate, nor what they left.

Ruthie was eight years old and was her mummy's mini-me. Ethan was five going on six. He was as fair-haired, fresh-faced and as happy and contented as his big sister. Mummy Jenna was a young twenty-five and had never regretted the unplanned baby that temporarily curtailed her education. Ruthie had been such a blessing that Ethan was inevitable. All three had elfin features and loved nothing better than family time. Ruthie had done her spellings and Ethan had produced yet more disfigured images of his family for his teachers. Daddy would be home soon, and anticipation began to fill their modest but happy home.

On his way home the customarily slow traffic was of no consequence to Adam on Thursday evenings. He was as happy as a pig in poop, and at ease with the world, anticipating the long weekend. Alongside him the big orange double-deckers moved freely, whilst in contrast the motorists and truckers made only glacial progress. It was as though the bus drivers were captains of great many sailed schooners, whose sea craft helped them catch invisible gusts and currents that quickly thrust them out of sight of the lesser vessels. There were no wells of wisdom at work however, just the effect of the grotesque, fine revenue generating bus lanes. Before devious councils and governments had recognised more elaborate opportunities to fleece motorists, the bus lanes were introduced to "encourage" people to leave their cars at home. It was part of a strategy known locally as *Stockport Clean Air Management,* or SCAM for short.

It would be good for people to walk the parts of their journeys not on the bus route, however long or dangerous, and whatever the weather. It was such a visionary and optimistic view of the future, and of wintertime in Northern England. Curiously, those booking the mayor for an event will see a parking space for the mayoral car is a pre-requisite; as the saying goes: "Rules for thee, but not for me!"

Boomers will remember when the bus lanes were introduced, the prevailing international scare story was quite different. Then they spoke of an impending, civilisation-crushing ice-age. Crops would fail, energy would become increasingly scarce and expensive, thanks to the inevitable exhaustion of natural resources. The CO2 demon had not yet even been imagined, let alone released. Oddly the remedies for fire and ice are identical.

For around forty years, bus lanes have been an unmitigated triumph for council coffers across the nation. Millions of pounds in fines have been raised and squandered. Traffic moves slower than ever, turbo charging pollution as vehicles are forced to perform at their least efficient. Commerce and pleasure alike are delayed, simultaneously choking economic growth, lungs and enjoyment. Best of all, it seems there are less people on the buses now than when the lanes were introduced. It has proven to be a total nonsense, just like ordinary folk predicted. The remedy, double down, screw the people and their opinions, then lecture them on their moral inadequacies.

Adam was more than gratified he no longer used the bus lanes. After all he was a veteran of the 192 bus which covers a roughly eleven-mile stretch between Manchester Piccadilly and the great misnomer of Hazel Grove. For decades, after its imaginative rebrand from the 92, the bus has travelled, one every ten minutes, in a kind of languid loop for the lobotomised. Hazel Grove is a large village a couple of miles south of Stockport. It may well have been a grove of hazel trees once, maybe the leafy grove is still tucked away somewhere behind the Superstores, KFC or Maccy D's but if so, it has been hidden well.

What was hidden until a social media post went viral is a spectacular gravestone in the local Norbury Parish churchyard. It reads:

*"In loving memory of Harold Fidler, also his wife Fanny."*

As for the Hazel Trees, John Wesley might have been able to shed some light. Over two centuries ago, the fabled Christian preacher and hymnwriter visited Hazel Grove, which in his day still bore its old name of Bullock's Smithy. Upon leaving, Wesley branded it:

*"One of the most famous villages in the country,*

*for all manner of wickedness."*

Upon hearing this, rather than taking offence at Wesley's snipes, most "Grovers" smile and say: Little has changed in three centuries! Wesley never rode the 192 or he might have been even more damning in his assessment. No-one can claim to have truly plumbed the lower reaches of human behaviour, until they have travelled on its all-night incarnation. It is where an unsuspecting traveller might encounter implausible swearing, where f or c words outnumber all others, even being inserted in the middle of words of more than one syllable. There are standoffs, actual fighting, drunken relationship guidance from strangers, in-transit urination and occasionally, copulation. In truth these activities tend to be nearer the Manchester end. Many who complete the entire expedition are often by then asleep, shoe tread deep in urine, or comatose. Two quid well spent!

Daytime bus journeys are on the whole a different kettle of fish. For the budding anthropologist eager to learn the ways and speech of the chav, it is well worth the bus fare. Chavs are more commonly referred to as "Scallies" across Greater Manchester. They are a subsection of society heavily overrepresented in many SK postcodes. Fashion wise, they are well catered for by the town's many sportswear shops. They flaunt their finery aboard the borough's generous bus fleet speaking loudly in fake Salford accents. The truly hardcore Scallies disdain bus travel, preferring stolen or unregistered motocross bikes. On these machines they pull wheelies all around town without a care, or a helmet. They scorn PC Plod and his futile attempts to catch them. They willingly mount any kerb or central reservation and gladly chew up well-tended lawns or flower beds to make good their escape.

When the scallies are present on the buses, leg room for others is sparse. It is essential their legs are splayed, and trackie-pant drawstrings are not tied. Waistbands must be loose enough to allow at least one hand down them to nurse the precious family jewels. No wonder then that Adam was more than pleased to enjoy the tranquillity and comfort of his car, with the choice of who and what he listened to. And for sure, road-rage is infinitely preferable to bus-rage, as at least you can wind your windows up and bugger off.

# Chapter 2

## Seeds of Destruction

For now, we leave Adam and his homeward trek, and go back in time. Decisions were being made that would lead to events beyond his darkest dreams, but could he have stopped the useful idiots who brought such terrible destruction to his town and home?

In 1983, a now deceased British crooner by the name of Frankie Vaughan, recorded a good-natured mickey taking parody about this town, a town whose residents regard their borough with equal measures of pride and embarrassment. Those who know of the song or seek it out on YouTube still sing along, fully aware urine was being gently extracted. Those unfamiliar with Stockport and its glorious dullness would doubtless benefit from watching and listening before proceeding. If that is not possible the first verse goes something like this, in fact it goes exactly like this:

*"I've travelled up and down this country, From the Pennines to Lands-End,*

*But if you ask my favourite place of all, the answer isn't hard to comprehend.*

*I'm going back to Stockport, there's nowhere that can beat it.*

*That's right I tell ya Stockport! Do you want me to repeat it?*

*Well it's S-T-O-C-K-P-O-R-T! Stockport, Stockport's.... the place for me!"*

This joyful self-deprecation also finds expression in the range of merchandise on sale in the town centre. Inspired by terms evoking the essence or spirit of a place, such as Rome the Eternal City; Paris the City of Love; or New York the City That Never Sleeps, some marketing marvels in Stockport's Merseyway Shopping Centre settled on: "Stockport Isn't Shit!" It is a window on the soul of the town and is printed on mugs, bags, table mats, cushions, and other goods, soft or hard. Shit or not, this old former railway and mill town, which might be described as Manchester's even uglier little sister, had been studied from afar. It was not observed from some timeless worlds of space, nor scrutinized as someone with a microscope might study creatures that swarm and multiply in a drop of water (as someone once wrote).

It was not mal-intentioned aliens bent on war between our worlds. The so-called Peoples Republic of China knew much of the world held them responsible for the pandemic and would like to punish them with a dig in the spare-ribs. China had been seeking an opportunity for bridge building, to restore their reputation. They had a technology that had been long in the making, which offered an opportunity to pour sesame oil on troubled waters. If they could pull this new scheme off, it had the potential to please our politicians and enrich the Chinese economy, their favourite formula. It would rival even their discounted supply of other barely green technologies. All they needed was the right place at the right time. Stockport, it transpired, became an unfortunate victim of its own unexceptionalism. It would soon be known the world over, but only as a byword for tragedy. It would become the setting for blockbuster movies and mini-series but would yearn for its days of obscurity in return for the restoration of its loved ones.

Students of international politics are well-aware little escapes the penetrating eyes of the Chinese Communist Party. With a population of almost 1.5 billion, there are many minions who can be assigned to every task of espionage, be it hostile or benign. Tourists, students, embedded agents and Tik Tokkers alike, all feed-back an endless stream of data and information to central command. Many volunteer this information without ever knowing it. It is quite possible that CCP artificially intelligent surveillance has captured the unique features and expressions of millions of British faces. It is equally possible even our individual DNA is known and stored in the near infinite server capacity in the Land of the Dragon. Such information falls under the authority of the Chinese Military, and of course, the Dear Leader. This includes your most personal and intimate information, including medical, and that of all your family, dear reader.

Somebody, somewhere in that great and ancient land will likely be well versed in the affairs of every locale, including the Borough of Stockport in Greater Manchester. Bureaucrats and bots alike will have probed and perused every penetrable conversation. Social media posts are stored, along with who liked, and shared them! Particular attention will have been afforded its leaders. What are their appetites and motivations? What is in their personal lives that may be useful now, or in the future? Leaders can be bought, blackmailed or seduced, though as often as not, simple dastardly appeals to vanity are enough.

It is only pragmatic for a nation like China, intent on international supremacy, to take account of everything and everyone. If there is a skeleton in a cupboard somewhere, they seek them out. When they require international co-operation, they call upon those skeletons. In the legend adapted for the good old Christmas Day classic Jason and the Argonauts, the one we all spent trying to explain to Grandma, the skeletons were seven bony savages with swords. They had a kind of human form, and the army the CCP call upon, is little different. They cast the Hydra's teeth, of secret affairs, corruptions or perversions, and a craven army of enablers arises. These are living people who have looked the other way so often, been compromised, or pretended not to understand, they have betrayed their own humanity, maybe even, humanity itself. Such a political cesspool is an ideal conduit for China to advance, seen but unchallenged.

Our politicians plan for the next handful of years, always with one and a half eyes on their own re-election. The Chinese meanwhile plan by the century or even millennia. Like ants or bees, their common purpose eclipses all, though its leaders are thought to be as ruthless as any who have ever lived. Never before though, were their enemies so stupid, greedy, politically suicidal or treacherous.

China has an endless stream of international leaders willing to sell them their souls or their countries for cheap Chinese goods and a cut of the proceeds. The Chinese are great chefs and they help other governments cook their net zero books by making everything we used to make. In return, our leaders have dished up our manufacturing industries. The biggest take-away is their secret ingredient is no longer sparkling white mono sodium glutamate, now it is glistening black coal. Ninety percent of the world's solar panels are made in China, using mainly coal fired power, now that is sweet and sour at best. To leave us even more jaded, close behind are the very pale green inventions of wind turbines and EV batteries. Vast mining operations are undertaken in liberal paradises like Congo, to source rare earth minerals such as cobalt and lithium. The cost is offset to some extent, as slave or child labour is an unmissable bargain compared to conventional mining. The children get sick, and many die, but the green aims are so noble, and the profits so great, their short miserable lives are deemed a price worth paying.

The turbines' failure rate is as monumental as they are, but in relation to their subsidies and backhanders, it is small fry or dim sum. Fund managers for ethical investors know they will soon be so enriched by carbon credits, they could decorate the minor miners' graves with the most exquisite bouquets and wreaths. Should they last twenty-five years the turbines have reached their life expectancy and are ripe for scrap. The untold story is they will have outlasted many of the innocents who dig, often with bare hands, sacrificed to the glory of the green god of the new religion. When turbines are worn out, they have to be dug out of the tons of concrete holding them up, more costs and emissions almost beyond comprehension. A simple soul might think it is a giant con trick, but they are quickly reminded not to think.

All the green revolution shares a similar story but try and find a British king or politician to tell it. It has all done wonders for China's balance of payments whilst British green subsidies propel us relentlessly toward a most honourable bankruptcy. Meanwhile the burden is piled onto the working people in new and imaginative taxes.

China as always, waited patiently for our next kamikaze crusade, devising new plans to separate us from our wealth and security. They, like many nations across the world, have always marvelled at the elevated status of the family pooch or moggy in the West. Some are offended we condemn them for considering the creatures a delicacy. But, as with "fossil fuel", one man's poison is another man's meat, and they intend to eat our lunch. So, as we flagellate ourselves like nuns who misused the soap, China gorges on coal. Every two years they surpass the totality of Britain's coal and steel production in its entire history. It isn't a game, they have 1.5 billion mouths to feed, and survival is serious for people and Party. If Britain sank into the sea tomorrow it would not even register on the CO2 scale. If we did start sinking, China would be throwing us a cash cow sized life jacket. In the meantime, a dog sized one was readied.

It suddenly became important people were told a third of UK households own at least one dog; that they number around thirteen million, almost double the dog population of 2010. Carnivorous canines gorge themselves almost exclusively on meat and emit gases like fleets of Soviet era Ladas. A large dog has a similar carbon footprint to an SUV, but as dogs are now human in all but name, just getting rid of them would be murder. It is hardly their fault in any case. China knew we would embrace this new guilt trip. They had prepared for it, and even nurtured our self-loathing and were quite willing to celebrate their own Year of the Dog out of sequence.

Thus, our national deliverance became possible, thanks to a new cohort of wise men from the East, the Far East! These Magi came not with gold, frankincense or myrrh but with magi-cal green dog food! It was the answer to a dog driven disaster. As with most modern emergencies, nobody thought or even knew there was one, at least not until we were advised, persuaded and nudged by our betters. In many ways it was obvious, if humans are the enemies of the planet, then so must their best friends be. The message was clear, dogs, like cows, are unwittingly complicit in a fart fuelled fiasco. They are frying our fragile sphere with their flesh fetish and their foul and fetid sphincters.

China's solution was a revolutionary formula, an elixir, literally a world saver. They could help us to shrink at least a part of our anthropogenic assassination of the Earth, the bit caused by our obsessive dog worship. At a stroke, we could moderate the effects of the meat laden menus of our mutts. We could nullify the noxious discharges and carbon paw prints of our four-legged emission factories. It was an inspirational idea, irresistible to all but the coldest of heart, or for those fashionably identifying as cats. Man's best friend was to be enlisted to defeat man's worst enemy. Striding heroically together, Roger, Rita and Rover will save the planet.

There would be no need for neutering or mass culling, or at least, not for the dogs. Thanks to skilful, genetic manipulation of bamboo, normally the least nutritious of plants, a solution was found to the dog problem. China had created a plant-based dog food irresistible to every mangy mongrel and pampered pedigree pooch on the planet. The wonder food would add gloss to their coats and calcium to their teeth and bones, even moderating mood and increasing affection and obedience. It turns even the most rancid dog fart to the fragrance of a femme de France and dog dirt into fertiliser fit for grandad's rhubarb.

It was worthy of national celebration. The nations of the world will gaze with envy once more on our tiny island. The land of hope and glory will be born again, but this time not a bastard child deformed by avarice and disdain for nature. It would help us to feel good about ourselves again. We could at last celebrate that we are once more the champions of progress. As banners are run up the flagpoles and ripple in the wind, our backs will stiffen, shoulders thrust back in pride. Our hearts will swell with joy, rather than with myocarditis, as once more we embrace our national identity. We will be better than our wicked ancestors. We will be more righteous than they, because our hearts are purer, cleaner, not consumed by reckless self-interest. Our hearts are not just pure and clean; they are pure and green.

We will no longer be hamstrung, weighed down by phobias and guilt, for a history we did not imagine, influence or even inhabit. A new unordained priesthood has re-written our theology. They preach that we must after all not just be punished for our own sins, but also the sins of generations of our fathers and forefathers. They have laid a curse upon us, and we've let it bind, then crush us. At a stroke, China could help us cover a multitude of those sins with a dog food deliverance. China was in the Garden of Eden and barking up the right tree. Repentance will be marked not with baptism in the Jordan, but in the mighty Yellow River, with a heavenly hope to share in the resurrection of the right thinkers.

Maybe one day, we may even be lifted up on angels' wings, to Davos. There we may gaze upon the world's leaders as they grovel and debase themselves before Heir Schwab the Hairless. There they become witless and intoxicated with pride, being honoured, and feted as visionaries in that most elevated of company. They writhe like swollen maggots amidst the sewer of the self-righteous. Their egos are massaged and engorged, until they mindlessly sell out their own peoples whose taxes pay for their vacuous, vainglorious, VIP visits.

The precise science of the solution the Chinese geniuses concocted, is to this day a secret, but that is a trivial point as this marked an historic international accord. It was a cause so virtuous it transcended small-minded concerns of busybodies, or even public or parliamentary scrutiny; and was protected by the strictest observance of commercial confidentiality. Still, they claimed in time everybody will know everything, apart that is from potential risk, or an exhaustive list of the active ingredients or financial beneficiaries. But when the planet itself is under threat, and an emergency has been declared, then no explanations are necessary for plebs.

No-one could deny this was a flawless plan, the government and media would see to that. This was critical because everything was underwritten by government to avoid delays. Liability for harm, including mass death was nonchalantly nullified. All liability rests on the heroically broad shoulders of taxpayers. It seems almost negligent that councillors and politicians forgot to tell this to their electorates. That wasn't bad news for everyone as the manufacturers, select advertising agencies and distributors are in dog's heaven with the arrangement.

Obviously though, there had to be a trial! Probably! Maybe! We couldn't trust China to run that because they don't make their trial data public. Even if they had a system with freedom of information statutes, they wouldn't just let people with a right to know, have the right to know. They would delay and obfuscate. They'd give vacuous responses failing to address the specific questions asked. After several requests for information, and several non-responses they would label concerned citizens as serial pests and end communications.

Thank goodness we don't have that problem here; or at least not until we ask difficult questions of officials, either in government or those supposedly overseeing safety, such as the MHRA. They claim to monitor the voluntary, passive yellow card warning system on harm from pharmaceutical products. It appears it is they who are passive and also firmly in bed with big pharma. They show scant interest in spiralling death counts in the young, yet are laser focused on speeding new products to market and streamlining critical safety trials. From reports of vax injured citizens seeking redress, it seems they have effectively given the yellow card reporting mechanism the red card.

Meanwhile, in Stockport, everyone in power, or on the payroll, agreed to a mass 'cynical trial'. It would be carried out in real time on real dogs. In days of yore, when they at least pretended that safety mattered more than profit there were strict protocols. Only the deceived or deceitful could entertain an untested universal solution. No formula, be it ingested or injected, could be tested on every dog's body without safety trial data open to all. In that way would lie madness, as no two metabolisms or immune systems are identical.

A mass experiment was needed on some unwitting populace to prove it is safe and effective. Where could such a legion of lilliputian lab rats be located? A town densely populated, all levels of wealth to ensure all breeds are reached. A council eager to embrace modernity was required but not known for excessive greenery to date. After all, they had to quell the fears of neanderthal science deniers. Agents of the CCP scoured Britain for such a place. Where could they find a posturing moron? Was there another Matt Smallcock? Could they unearth a new buffoon, another Drakefoot? There surely must be another low octane 20mph non-descript grey man in a grey suit and grey shoes; another Divali dancing dimwit bent on a legacy.

The North-West England observer said she knew of a definite maybe. A town of which she knew of the Yin but feared the Yang of the actual townsfolk. She advised of a council, expert in obscuring its landmarks and winning architectural booby prizes, an outstanding candidate. An unlikely boomtown where house prices are rising, where businesses are investing and where nothing is too precious to be preserved over a vanity project. They had it! The diminutive Chinese delegate said,

'If it please most honourable ladies and gentlemen, I will present my case by medium of song:'

*'I've travelled up and down their country, From the Pennines to Lands-End,*

*But if you ask my favourite place of all, the answer isn't hard to comprehend.*

*We are gonna use Stockport, there's nowhere that can beat it.*

*That's right I tell ya, Stockport! Do you want me to repeat it?*

*Well it's S-T-O-C-K-P-O-R-T! Stockport Stockport's.... the place for Xi!'*

They would make Stockport an international phenomenon, sung of by the likes of Elton St John and Ted Sheeran. They would be filling in for Frankie Vaughan but with the global reach of Frankie Sinatra! Elton's St John's private jet will be resprayed declaring: "Stockport Saves the World". It will herald a new dawn as it makes its multi-millionaire's carbon offset way from L.A. to Ringway. If you're rich enough to have enough dosh to plant a forest you can be as dirty as you like and still lecture the trolls. This was just another a Rocket Man's jet set journey, powered by hypocrisy, with special guest tiny dancer, Loose Lips Shamilton, the preening Petronas prostitute.

First, a publicity campaign to cajole and convince the gofers the greater good coming to Stockport was groovy. Wheels were quietly put in motion whilst the people went about their own business. utterly unaware of the plans and schemes their betters had for them, or of the death and ruination soon to overwhelm them.

# Chapter 3

# No Going Back

At the foot of the hill where lies the soon to be internationally famous Mersey Square, the lights turned red, interrupting Adam's progress on his mundane homeward journey. As he waited, still only halfway down the incline, he glanced over to his right. This was an opportunity he never passed up. He could gaze again upon the majesty of the twenty-two yawning arches of Stockport's magnificent railway viaduct. It is a glorious sight and testifies to human ingenuity to overcome the natural barriers that would pen us in our burrows like timid woodland creatures.

The viaduct is visible from every approach to the town, despite eternal efforts of town planners to hide it with soul sapping multi-storey monstrosities. Its towering piers straddle the vale, thrusting up a hundred feet or more. The artisans who built it did not imagine carrying on trying to reach heaven. They had no designs on divinity, like the Tower of Babel brickies and their heavenly minded hod carriers. They just had to get the railway track from 'ere t' theer,' fillin' gap in between wi' as few bricks as possible! Having said that, the Victorian architects instinctively understood utility should not be divorced from beauty. The functionality of their constructions lives in perfect union with their underpinning understanding and appreciation of classical architecture and its ratios and symmetries. These principles are apparently either not understood or despised by modern murderers of the aesthetic.

The humble masses seldom ventured beyond the borders of their towns and villages before that great railway age of liberation. In those days the world suddenly shrank. The natural limitations of the land were subdued by the genius of the great architects and engineers of iron, brick and stone. In the space of a generation, it came within the grasp and budget of the great unwashed to at least see the seaside for a week or so, or traverse their green and pleasant land, most of which they had never seen in real life.

Stockport Wakes were when the town's factories and mills would close for a couple of weeks. The working people and their families crammed the trains like sardines in tins, sardines with buckets and spades. They were fleeing en-masse to exotic paradises such as Blackpool and Rhyl. They could escape the monotony of seeing the same old people in the same old shops and factories. Instead, they would see those same old people in the queues for the deckchairs and funfairs by the seaside. They had no need of Dior or Versace. The ladies put on their cotton sun-frocks and the men rolled up their trouser legs. Work boots and clogs were exchanged for brown leather sandals worn over white socks. Flat caps gave way to knotted handkerchiefs. If they were really lucky, they would all soon be smothering themselves in calamine lotion to soothe their newly purulent pink skin.

Never tiring of the sight of the viaduct, Adam rehearsed under his breath, for at least the thousandth time: 'The largest brick-built structure in Western Europe'. He'd heard his own dad say it countless times, and they were not exceptional in this. No stalwart of Stockport worth their salt would fail to proudly announce the news to anyone making their first (or fiftieth) visit to the town. Estimations of the bricks alone number them well above ten million, each one skilfully and artfully laid by masters of their trade. Stone architraves decorate the piers and matching stone facings adorn the walls enclosing the tracks. Many hardy souls perished during its construction. Tragically most of them fell to their deaths from the giant wooden scaffolds, platforms and vast timber arch formers.

Beneath the arches today are several roads, the River Mersey and even the M60 motorway pass underneath. Several old buildings still nestle in their protective shadow too. Adam's pride was not misplaced. Over a century on, this brick and stone beast still stands proud, such was the skill and precision of the men who raised it; skill matched only by their hardiness and unflinching courage.

The traffic lights changed again but nothing moved, not even the buses. Horns were sounding at half-witted amber gamblers who had darted out from the side road, only to find their escape route up the hill was like a car park. Still unflustered, Adam waited for his next green light, in daydreams this time not featuring his dad, but his grandad.

'Sometimes Adam you'd be taken aback on the railway platforms from huge blasts of steam, pshhhhh! Heehee it made you jump alright. Then there were the hairy-arsed engine drivers. How they'd fill the air wi' sounds of their mighty whistles. They'd wave, like Biggles bound for a dogfight. Their great iron monsters rumbled and hissed along the tracks high above the town with clouds of steam billowing behind.

You also had the Idle Jacks, the old station porters. Most of the time they'd be second place to a snail, but by Godfathers when they were running away from work, they were faster than Roger Bannister on roller-skates. I once saw one kill a full fifteen minutes rearranging a small pile of fag ends and rubbish he'd swept up. We were all watching him from behind us newspapers. He was a right scrawny beggar in a wrinkled uniform that fitted where it touched. He needed a bloody good haircut cos he could hardly keep his cap on. He had no idea he was the main feature, the day's matinee like. There must have been a hundred people waiting for trains. We all watched fixated. We were witnessing a master skiver at work and he didn't disappoint us. As we anticipated his great and climactic act with his shovel and bin, he bowled us all a wrong 'un son. With the speed of a rattlesnake and the wrists of a gunslinger, he just brushed the bloody rubbish straight onto the tracks below. Then he re-lit the dimp from behind his ear. Bone-idle bugger!

'Ha, then you had bloody station guards bellowing out instructions like tin-pot Sergeant Majors drunk on two minutes of power. It was their kids who would grow up to be pool attendants or traffic wardens.' Adam remembered his pride when he suggested football referees, much to his granddad's approval. Very good son, you're a chip off the old block you are! Anyroad, my dad used to say Walter, if you don't like hard work, get a job on the railways.'

Needless to say, Adam the infant often had no idea who some of the people were in his dad's and grandad's stories. They didn't worry though and told him to learn how to ask, and also to learn to discern the wise from the fool. The lesson was usually clear enough if he had his thinking cap on.

Like his dad and granddad, Adam empathised with those who had no notion of the exotic or the far away. Today such confinement is seen as a curse for even a circus or zoo animal. Distant mist covered hills and mountains, glistening rivers and streams, rolling fields or baking deserts only ever experienced in books or on screens, was the stuff of nightmares.

Even more inconceivable is hearing that in towns and cities up and down the land some devils in flesh are planning a re-run. Officials, who surely also sprang from the loins of the old porters and guards, want the commoners to regress to those days in the so-called interests of saving the planet. Doubtless such luminaries imagine they will secure exemptions for themselves, unaware they will also soon be disenfranchised, just a little later than the friends, family and voters they betrayed.

Adam was grateful no such notions had yet been publicly floated in his town. He was for now, free to direct his wheeled carriage where he chose, unrestricted by tracks or the lofty prescriptions of others. The newly emerging open prison zones will never be accepted in Stocky. This had been established by detailed, high level diplomatic talks in the brew room at work. The consensus was Stockport's MPs and councillors would find out quickly and personally, they are public servants not overlords. They agreed that if they tried it in Stockport the officials would go the way of the Persian emissaries in the Sparta legend. Lead plotter was Andy Shawcross from packaging.

'Hey Woody, I know what we need to do. Remember in that film 300! Some big Persian prick was giving it the big I am with the King of Sparta. "We want gifts of earth and water as tokens of your submission." The muppet was in the king's gaff surrounded by psycho killer Spartans and starts mouthing off. That's like some scouse bastard singing You'll Never Walk Alone in the Stretford End, or me singing Hillsborough songs in the Kop. What a knob-head!'

'Innit mate. I bet those screenwriters couldn't have imagined that western leaders would start acting like Sultans, telling us where we can and can't go, planning quotas for days out? They're 'avin' a laugh mate. Top-down government and central digital bank currencies is bullshit too! It's time people woke up and started fighting back.'

'I know. That stuck up Tory tosser Adolf Ellwood was an MP, yet he's still in the military and has been spying on citizens with his regiment. 77th Brigade spying on us, what's all that about? Those units were set up for counter terrorism and foreign threats, but it turned inwards on all of us. The cretins were monitoring anyone speaking out against official policy. I thought it was just during Covid but this Russell Brand stuff makes me think it's still going on. That Tory cow who sent a letter to tech firms trying to get Brand demonetised is married to a Major General and deputy commander of 77$^{th}$ Brigade. Looks like the jokers are still pissing on our freedoms.'

'Makes me sick Shawshank mate. They're using the power of the State to get dirt on people speaking out. Elwood should have been sacked before he quit. They hounded him out in the end for saying the Taliban were doing a decent job since Biden's balls up. Spying on us should be what he got the boot for the slag! It shows though that they can act like the Taliban themselves but they daren't praise them, in public anyway.'

'I know what you mean Woody. To be fair, I doubt they'd spend much time spying on us two though. They'd do us a favour anyway, getting us sacked from this shit-hole.'

'Tell me about it mate but it's one thing getting sacked for skiving off or calling your boss a prick, but having the wrong view about summat has got sod all to do with them or anyone else!'

'It was funny how Andy Burnham's arsehole got inverted when they kicked off about his ULEZ plans for town. He didn't think the Mancs would be so militant. Round Wigan, woollybacks were cutting signs down with grinders. It shows, if they think they'll get kicked out before they've climbed far enough up the greasy pole, the old sheriffs badge gets rusty, and they bottle it. It was a strange one though, Burnham seemed one of the better ones, then he came up with that crap. I just hope he isn't backing off with a view to doing it later, only I was told they already bought the cameras and signed the contracts. And there are under review signs all over the place!'

'That's the trouble, it's like snakes and ladders. They go down but keep rolling the dice to get back up again. They know their only way to the top table is for them to toe the globalist line, so they screw us over. Fucking snakes alright!'

'I'll tell you what though Woody. If they start that here, I'll be in that public gallery giving 'em shit. They'd be like: "Sir, please be quiet, or we'll have you removed. We will not have you speaking like that in this chamber. Please, from now on, choose your words carefully!"

'I'd stand up and give it full Gerard Butler: Oh, I have chosen my words carefully Mr Chairman. Perhaps you should have done the same!

**"THIS - IS - STOCKPORT!"**

'Then I'd kick the bastards down the well like Butler done with them Persians, though I suppose down the stairs might have to do.'

'What about a stair-well Andy?'

'Haha, top one mate, they need a size ten up their arses either way.'

All those present at the staffroom summit agreed, but lamented they appeared to have no voice and couldn't really affect anything even if King Leonidas himself was with them. This whilst everything they'd grown up with was being changed and they seemed helpless to stop it. All political parties seem to be on the same page and listen to the same people so what could they do?

Recalling that conversation stirred Adam's emotions and got his blood pumping. Yes, this is Stockport! The White Rose County might be putting up with it. Leeds city centre might be awash with intelligent cameras tracking the faces of its citizens and even using AI to monitor how they move and walk. But our rose is red like the blood of the martyrs who fought for our freedom. It appears that

Yorkshire now has not just a white rose but also a white flag. Too much bone in their heads and not enough in their backs. He heard himself saying:

'Awake, Awake O House of York! The enemy is within your walls!'

He gripped the hilt of his sword firmly for the taste of battle was upon his lips. I will raise an army and ride to York, then even to Liverpool and we shall lay old enmities aside, and fight as brothers in arms against our common foe. In truth, he was gripping his hand brake and the taste on his lips was some Irn Bru he kept for the odd sugar boost, but the fighting spirit was real enough!

Feckless trouser dropping is to be expected of Londoners although they seem to have woken up at last. Until lately they seemed to enjoy being pushed around by Mr Punch their despotic dwarf of a mayor. He probably breathes most of London's air in anyway with that conk. Any kind of creeping climate lockdown policies, however strict or lenient elsewhere should be stored where they belong, up the politicians' jacksies.

Anyone who says we need to be made uncomfortable if we don't reduce our car use, should be in the driving seat with voluntary bans from all car travel for life, along with their families. Those getting the needle over lack of population controls should volunteer to take one of those one-way tickets to Switzerland. Either that or be sterilised along with all their family members, or better still just shut the hell up.

Adam saw the lights on the road to his right were changing yet again. Jerked back to reality he noticed his phone was illuminated. He took a quick look before his traffic light turned to amber. He'd missed several calls from a withheld number. He wasn't perturbed as he always ignored id withheld calls in any event, assuming it was slippery salespeople after his hard earned. Less than a mile now and he would be entering an area called Heaviley, where all his favourite people awaited. In his mind's eye Adam saw Ruthie and Ethan's sweet little faces. He felt the surge of emotion, known only to parents, when their very innards long upon their children. The mingling of unconditional love and burden of protection has cemented families and honed fatherly purpose for centuries beyond count. With a lump in his throat and a tear in his eye, he smiled and drove on.

# Chapter 4

## Of Dead Soldiers and Wedding Cake

Suddenly, the traffic cleared as if up ahead, some metropolitan Moses had raised his staff, parting the traffic like a divinely appointed lollipop-man. The drivers, seeing the promised land of open road, surged ahead in hope, only to discover the sounding of the Shofar was premature. There were chariots everywhere!

Another bottleneck had begun with a minor bump just beyond the town hall thanks to a numpty jumping the lights at Greek Street. Adam often wondered about Greek Street. Who came up with that name? Stockport is as far removed from Greece as you can get, in every way, even kebabs were unknown in the town back when the streets were named. In those days the mainly flightless folk of Stockport could only dream of Grecian beaches, and most who did escape wouldn't entertain foreign muck like moussaka if there was an English chippy on the island.

Suddenly, as if Zeus himself was eavesdropping, the grey sky was riven. Beams of dazzling sunlight illuminated an extravagant white Greco Roman style building to his right. Woodhead you plonker, he said to himself, that's probably why. In all his years going up and down the A6, he'd never made the connection. His feelings of stupidity were compounded, as he noted anew the elaborate white stone recessed bus shelters, complete with striking white stone pillars. This was less embarrassing for as long as he'd known of them, the bus shelters had stunk of urine, not Greek, mainly English or Scottish. In his childhood they housed tramps, but nowadays only homeless people, at least there has been progress with their occupants' name. With fresh eyes he gazed at the elevated and imposing white edifice gleaming in the sunshine. It's four great pillars, each with its ornate capital, support a portico bearing the inscription:

"IN REMEMBRANCE"

It was originally built to commemorate those who fell in the First World War. Later years have seen it expanded and it doubles as the Stockport Art Gallery. Even though the art is generally excellent and mainly local, for some, this doesn't sit quite rightly. They feel some kind of permanent Great War installation or even a small museum housing photos, mementos or artefacts of Stockport's fallen would be more appropriate; especially since the old, actual museum was shut. A historically attuned councillor might say: "We could house the art gallery in the beautiful library building we've been bent on closing, despite widespread public opposition and protest. There, art and literature could sit in perfect harmony like the ebony and ivory keys on Paul McCartney's racially pure piano. Oh Lord, why can't we?"

The War Memorial is built diagonally opposite the town hall. Was this so the spirits of those being memorialised can stand on eternal and silent sentry duty? They could keep a close eye on those shifty buggers over the road. Watching the voters' representatives, they could help guard the very liberties they gave their lives to protect. If only they could nudge the councillors to never forget the sacred oaths they've sworn? Their oaths are to serve their intended masters, the hoi poloi, as of course the Greeks say, or in plain English, The People!

It must be said, there is nothing obvious to suggest malice lurks in the chambers of Stockport's town hall. It is an almost fairy tale, English Baroque style masterpiece. Its many pillars and architectural flourishes are elegantly accentuated by its white stone façade. It is an aesthetic triumph, or as locals say, 'kin gorgeous! It more than deserves its nickname of the Wedding Cake. Given its grandeur, if it was to be built today, only an Indian wedding budget could cut it. Surely no devilry could be brewed in this self-same building that once hosted Harry Corbett, with his glove puppet sensations Sooty and Sweep. They were the very embodiment of British childhood innocence. Mr Corbett enchanted children and adults alike, with his cheeky humour, skill and innocent fun filled antics. He brought those bits of felt to life with his magical imagination, ably succeeded by his son.

In 1998 when Matthew Corbett retired, the franchise passed to evil genius Richard Cadell. It is unreliably reported that Cadell wickedly cloned Sooty and friends in his underground laboratory in Switzerland and continues the legacy, leaving original Sooty and Friends to fend for themselves. Whilst no-one can vouch for this being true and could be a ruse to allow a wacky storyline in this book is anyone's guess. Let us just say Cadell is a magician by trade and much like the puppets, his show is suspiciously ageless!

It was a gentle irony that when the original puppet duo adorned Mr Corbett's hands in Stockport, the town hall was itself sooty, blackened by a century or more of domestic and industrial coal fires. In those days the factories were in and amongst the dwellings and clean burning technologies were not yet invented. In time, the residue from the fires coated everything that didn't move in the same black soot that was the inspiration for the little yellow bear's name.

Around a decade later, yet more enchantment was afoot. Sooty had long since married Soo, his leading lady puppet panda. They had their own litter of cubs having taken out injunctions against the Corbett family and their cold intrusive hands. One day, hosts of astonished Stockport folk rushed home with eyes shining, asking if anyone else had seen the miracle happening on Wellington Road. After overcoming their shock and rediscovering their tongues they cried:

'The Town Hall is being cleaned, and it's WHITE!' Generations had grown up assuming it, and most other old buildings were black, as that is the only state they had ever seen them in. It was a marvel akin to a weeping statue of the Virgin. For local architecture enthusiasts it was the icing on the cake, THE WEDDING CAKE! Being in Stockport this particular cake was always out in the rain, but it had been remade. The head of maintenance had after all, found the recipe, again. Oh yeah!

***Public Notice***

*"As Sooty and Sweep, in part owe their careers to coal, they have asked people be reminded its discovery saved the forests of Europe and lifted millions out of poverty. The one-sided negativity surrounding it has been detrimental to their emotional well-being, and as fully paid off fact checkers might say, "lacking context!" They draw our attention to the fact billions of poor people in the third world still live without any electricity in their homes. Coal fired power stations remain the only viable and affordable option for them.*

*Sooty, Sweep and friends also wish it to be known they are available for local events such as the opening of fetes and supermarkets.*

*They are not however at this time able to fulfil any public speaking events; that is unless Matthew Corbett is willing to overlook the previous injunctions, and the bitterness and resentment it generated."*

Sooty has a point. We should pray our elected officials be involved in nothing more sinister than the petty squabbles and one upmanship of local politics. May they be free from seduction into grandiose schemes, of saving or upending the world, or being manipulated by more pernicious puppet masters than the noble Corbett family. Most townsfolk wish their representatives would just represent them! The majority don't want them to champion quixotic fantasies of ideologues. Well meaning, small-scale visionaries are too easily fascinated, then just as easily, swallowed up, regurgitated, spat or shat out and forgotten. In the meantime, they unwittingly aided the schemes of corporate titans who were all along focused solely on their own interests. Sooty says:

*'Just make sure the bins are emptied and fill the pigging potholes!'*

# Chapter 5

## Chinese Whispers Beijing 2022

The serious account of subcommittee deliberations without music.

A senior ranking official name Xu Guang convened a meeting of a subcommittee on behalf of the Party. Xu Guang had risen through the ranks and his loyalty was unquestioned. He once informed on two teenagers who had mocked Chairman Xi by repeating the highly accurate accusation that he looked like Winnie the Pooh. The evidence provided by Xu Guang was damning and extensive, with internet posts, handwritten comments and cartoons. It was decided on his recommendation the teenagers be executed. Xu Guang even volunteered to carry out the execution himself such was his zeal for the Party. This was despite the desperate pleas of his son and daughter who were also teenagers. In fact, they were the very teenage dissidents in question. Xu Guang was a hero.

*Notes for those unfamiliar with the Chinese system.*

Chinese citizens must perpetually prove their loyalty, and as in all totalitarian societies, speech must therefore, be guarded. It is taught from childhood that Party loyalty exceeds all other, including family. Citizens may be betrayed by their friends, even their own offspring, siblings or parents. Proving loyalty to the Party increases status and benefits through a social credit system. Social credit scores are like normal credit scores and have a range of values. Everything a person says or does is monitored and ranked by party officials. People with high compliance to Party policies are considered good citizens and enjoy more freedoms. Those who upset the government and have a low score, cannot buy a car or a house. Nor can they leave their district to visit friends or family. The digital credit system won't allow them to purchase any goods or services their leaders exclude them from. Resistance leads to loss of access to healthcare or education for themselves or their families. Every service and system is linked, so control is absolute. During Covid, Justin True-dope, disciple of Heir Schwab the Hairless, flirted with all these concepts, as did certain Australian World Economic Forum vassal states.

Such societies cannot operate without informers to establish and maintain control. In the days of the Soviet Union, most KGB agents were no James Bonds or Jason Bournes. They were more often just pathetic weak-minded tell-tales eager to boost their own status. They hid in the shadows and snooped from behind curtains for titbits with which they could betray their friends and neighbours. Such people emerged in Britain during Covid lockdowns. Hitler had his Brown Shirts. In the west the tittle tattlers of social media are our Brown Noses. They are unwitting regime enablers. The Party has fact-checkers who are part of the system and well briefed. Only one truth, only one narrative is permitted. There must be no debate as it only causes confusion and encourages the enemies of the people.

Lao Bai Xing, the ordinary Chinese people, look westwards in hope, but weep to see us taking a path that may soon converge with theirs. Recent depositions and freedom of information requests in the US Congress and Senate, reveal direct involvement of the CIA and FBI in virtually all social media. UK freedom of information requests show similar deep government activity even here, in the birthplace of parliamentary democracy. There are behavioural change agents embedded in our government and media. Mindspace and the Behavioural Insights Team warp our minds to accept and promote globalists policy. Once we put the latest trending badge or colours on our profiles, we are captive to the cause. They know from experience most will never thoroughly investigate the issues, not least because half the information is hidden or censored. They also know those people will be fiercely loyal, as they have emotionally invested, and have a feel-good-factor and a sense of being part of a great and noble crusade.

In China, absolute obedience to The Party has some fantastic benefits. The unusual longevity of senior CCP officials has long been suspected to be due to their organ donor programme. It is believed that if one of them has organ failure, then replacements will quickly be found from among the living and healthy. Disobedience or dissent is a fast track to the top of the donor list. You must serve the Party with all your heart, liver and kidneys.

Individualism is not a thing and free speech does not exist. What the Party says is true. If the Party says up is down, then up is down until further notice. If you are told to stay home to protect granny, then home you must stay, or expect drones or secret police. Your word for the day, every day, is COMPLIANCE! Most western governments trumpeted allowing China full access to the world economy, meant they would in time become more like the free west. The exact reverse has happened, and currently free citizens need to wake up and smell the oolong.

The following committee meeting "translation" attempts to China-fy the discussion. As the articles 'the' and 'a' are not used in Chinese, they will be omitted for effect. It is not intended to be offensive in the 'Me velly solly sense,' but if it does offend, then me velly solly.

The meeting was held in a sparsely furnished office with windows high enough to let light in, but not low enough to look in or out. The only decoration was an unfeasibly large picture of Chairman Xi whose benevolent fatherly face watched over proceedings. For extra back up, banks of CCTV cameras and listening devices did too.

Dissidents among Lao bai Xing also have private pictures of Chairman Xi, but theirs include his friends Piglet, Tigger and Eeyeore and all their friends from the hundred-acre wood.

**Xu Guang**: Comrades, before we begin, let us say Communist Party of Peoples' Republic of China Oath. Stand and speak:

**All**:

- It was my will to join Communist Party of China.
- Uphold Party's programme.
- Observe provisions of Party Constitution.
- Fulfil a Party member's duties and carry out Party's decisions.
- Strictly observe Party discipline.
- Guard Party secrets.
- Be loyal to Party, work hard.
- Fight for communism throughout life.
- Be ready at all times to sacrifice all for Party and people.
- Never betray Party.

**Xu Guang** 'Loyal Party members. Everything now in place. Chairman has sent important message, but first I gather your final thoughts, in case we have overlooked anything. If bees are within dǒu lì, please speak now, better honey than sting. Comrade Ding Disung you have question?'

**Ding Disung** 'Yes comrade Xu Guang. I have studied their social media. Many Stockport people strange! Have dog on profile picture, not own face. Dog picture actually help, their own face all look same to me. I fear they won't obey restriction on dog getting meat if they love dog as much as it seem. Will poorer people pay premium on wonder food? Won't there be uproar and riot, tanks on street?'

**Xu Guang**: 'Comrade, have you been sleeping since 2020? For two year they robot. Do whatever they told, however silly. They follow feet painted on floor and walk round supermarket in same direction like toy figure on novelty clock. They obey man without comb, and man with funny face. When they learn man without comb is also man without values, they get angry at him instead of at self. Pay day will be China's. They too stupid to copy secrets even as we ride roughshod over pitiful patents of west. They send us premium brand, we send them snide knock off, they big clown show! Western leaders left path of wisdom long ago. Like everything else, they fund for us with own taxpayer. Right people will receive cut of favour, dirty money or public profile. Only currency is ever question. Please now, deputy sub-committee leader Dou Wei Dong, address meeting with explanation of why we win big.

**Dou Wei Dong:** Thank you Xu Guang. Comrades, scheme faultless! Politician, media and activist ignore coal and oil of China. Our so-called human right abuse safe because West is compromised with hands of blood. They say technology save planet, but as with dog carbon pawprint, no politician or media question energy use of giant tech server. Big computer server produce big emission at unimaginable level, like many volcano. These server also true lever of power. Like us, their governors harvest data on citizen. They point finger at China, whilst copying our method to control population like we copy technology of west. Brazenly they ignore fact that necessary gigawatt to enable total control, centralization, and monitoring of everything make cow, car and dog irrelevance. However, as we know, control not achieved via democracy or truth. We hand a few wealth or prestige, they hand us country in return. As for local leader, they usually good people, mainly sincere and honest, but naïve, like infant. They learned two plus two equal four in primary school, but now wait nervously to be told new answer by new "expert," as if truth change. They think they adult and wise but they just toddler in shitty nappy. They unable to trust evidence of own eyes or understanding of own mind, think they have wisdom of owl, but only have big eyes like owl and small wisdom like pigeon.

Greatest fear is not loss of own country or liberty but fear of being put in community of foil hat. At least for now corporation and centre of learning do bidding of China. Many perversion and corruption of elite and academic filmed and filed. We see also championing causes drive them, however irrational cause is. We know UN invented climate disaster lies in 1990's as tool to control populations. We pretend to cut emission but commission new coal mine and coal fired power station at least one a month.

Many clever fool protest in England and say no oil please, only wind power. They must know all wind power backed by coal or oil plant or when wind stop, economy stop too. They pretend big battery near, knowing it no nearer than building house on moon. China soon eclipse USA with help of American politician. Britain same, once world's powerhouse now only pimple on backside of China. Here is conversation when their leader call to order Chinese:

"'Harro, is that Beijing Palace?'

'Yes. What you want?'

'Windmill, many windmill. Will they contain nut or wheat?

'No nut, and windmill is gluten free. Ingredients are billions of tons of steel, alloy and copper. Make in sweatshop with billion ton of coal we mine and import. We have special offer. If you devastate beauty of British coastline and hillside ruining landscape and vista enjoyed for century too, we throw in job for life for family member and free bag of prawn cracker!'

'Ok that's fine. Do you deliver?'

'Yes, no problem. Transport using monster truck with gigantic diesel engine and rivers of hydraulic oil. Have to charge for delivery, colossal machines shipped across continents in diesel driven ship, then loaded on diesel truck and train, and you are outside 3,000 mile free delivery radius."

'Their leader pat themselves on back and preen like peacock Never tell people vast turbine blade kill bat and bird of prey by million. RSPB never tweet complaint, instead say domestic cat kill more bird. That true but domestic cat kill sparrow and robin, not osprey and albatross. Blade made from fossil fuel triumph of fibreglass. Every turbine need at least 80 gallon of oil every year for lubrication so if they just stop oil, they just stop windmill too. Mining necessary for millions of tons of iron and copper ore for huge turbine motors and almost infinite miles of cables. Finally, they embedded in thousands of tons of emission rich concrete. They filling countryside with concrete people don't see, like ancient conquering army sewing fields with stones. Lamb to slaughter all of them. China's plans many decade in making, and they cannot understand our mind, it is child's play.' Yes Lixui?'

**Dang Lixui**: 'Honourable committee leader and sub-committee leader. As you know, I study England at close quarter, embedded in education and government at many level. I once envy Fang Fang, our spy who date Epic Foulsmell from US Senate for two year. Even after all exposed, he still sat on Senate Intelligence Committee. They so corrupt! Had to be more careful in England though not much. Nobody ever asked me difficult questions, especially Comrade China Dave.'

**Xu Guang:** 'You jealous you too not sleep with Epic Foulsmell, Lixui?

**Dang Lixui**: 'No, no, no comrade that make me feel sick. He greasy man-pig. I mean I always nervous, afraid of being caught until I realise, Britain still fast asleep.

**Xu Guang:** People who matter to us are not asleep Lixui. Their eyes wide open and do as told. Rest are in Land of Nod. I sense you have reservation about Stockport!'

**Dang Lixui**: 'I would never question wisdom of Central Committee Xu Guang! I'm sure you know it was me who suggest Stockport based on all criteria given. I just want to say fears in case bad thing happen and I did not tell all mind.

**Xu Guang**: Very well comrade I understand. Now tell all mind!

**Dang Lixui**: Thank you dear comrade. Stockport people what they call northerner and stubborn like mule. They proud of industrial heritage. Glory in blood and sweat of ancestor. Celebrate pretty, cast-iron façade even though forged in unforgiving foundry, ornate elaborations of First Industrial Age everywhere. Mills that in day were comparable with our own prison factory looked upon fondly as stepping-stone for later generation. They enjoy ornately laid park bearing name of benefactor who sponsored them, knowing well, often they just vanity project or guilt offering of those who abused forbears. Can't change past they say and carry on.'

**Xu Guang**: 'You speak well comrade, but we using past to advantage. Mighty ship change direction by rudder, though rudder tiny fraction of whole. Only need control those who control rudder. No elected government ever obeyed will of governed. Sunak and Starmer follow Schwabb and Soros. They rule as we do but lack our discipline. Critical mass to lead people small if right inducement and punishment applied in right place, especially if done secretly. Establish big lie in mind, smaller lie willingly swallowed. In fact, as we know and they learning, they expect them and believe them whatever evidence of own big saucer eyes. They say they want to be free, yet we see they want to be led, they trust wealthy leader despite countless lesson of history.'

**Dang Lixiu** 'I agree comrade, but these people one with Manchester, home of railway, rooted and grounded in past. Proud guardians of birthplace of industrial revolution. Stockport not Brussels, not Davos or Geneva. Know ancestor live in squalor, every day battle to survive, dependent on forgiving harvest. Families toiled in heat and cold, nature best friend and worst enemy. They know coal, oil and gas set them free to live life of comfort, wealth and length. Won't quickly toss that away. Not children of People's Republic. Believe have inalienable rights not given by Party or State.'

**Xu Guang**: 'I believe you are beguiled Lixiu, that history now hidden from all but a few. Population of West now as docile as ours. Create monster, scare pants off, then be Youxia on horse with glittering lance. Bigger lie is, greater its power, truth irrelevant! Churchill now ghost, they will have no saviour. Many decade they tell people about great firewall of China, whilst at same time building own, and deceit is password!

They just pass Online Safety Bill. Safety really mean control. Say new bill is to protect children, same children they know are in sex slavery for years and do nothing. New Bill is Trojan Horse for surveillance state. Don't care about children, weep over Schindler's List but ignore Epstein's list.

Some dissident voices allowed but only for show. People dream of distant paradise but accept elite plan to imprison in hovel and ghetto. Those who control politician in West learned from us, and very soon will have same power over masses. They right now handing sovereign power over to World Health Organisation for next pathogen release response without consulting people. If Tedros announce emergency for health or climate, they lockdown. Many changes in wording necessary to hide intention but day will come.

They jettisoned history and foundations for illusion. Their leader denounce meat for masses, prescribe bug and lentil and thing foreign to them. This done when field green and livestock flourish. We sit with them in G8 and Davos, watch them eat caviar, Wagyu fillet, lobster and delicacy of whole world. After they eat food enough for many African village, and guzzle fine wine and brandy enough to float battleship, sing "Food Glorious Food" then get in private jet. Have less shame than Blair and Bush at Middle East Peace Conference. Make people ignore own wisdom tales and sell inheritance for bowl of crickets. British leader becoming like us, just as their people are becoming like ours. Turkey they love to eat at Christmas, they will become.'

**Dang Lixiu** 'Very well, I yield. Comrades, maybe having studied their empire for many year, I have more respect for it than they.'

**Xu Guang**: 'Lixiu, you have heart as pure as spring water from Huashan Mountain. Head may have been turned being with people of such town too long. Maybe forgotten Communist plan. Maybe you remind all of us of Communist Masterplan, especially for British.'

Lixui was nervous knowing the kind words were just as likely to be a snare, that she might go the same way as Xu Guang's children. Anticipating her loyalty might be in question, she had prepared her statement in advance, with bullet points, which once more was very helpful to readers of this tale. She stood and controlled her nerves speaking steadily and clearly.

**Dang Lixui**: 'Honorable Comrades and loyal Party Members.

- Bring glory to Party and victory to China.

- Conquer world without bloodshed, not like West.
- Complete long march through institutions.
- Capture elite by all means possible.
- Wise man say: "When have man by balls, heart will follow!"
- Work in secret behind scene. Infiltrate school, university, government, all organisation and boardroom
- Undermine confidence in national history and culture.
- Undermine parental authority over children.
- Divide society. Make many group fight each other.
- Make people hate own country and flag.
- Country divided and lacking confidence easy to conquer.
- Country united and proud of history will resist overthrow.
- Build only in interests of China and glory of Party.
- May China be victorious and may Party rule for ever and may Chairman Xi live forever.'

**Xu Guang:** Well, Ding, Dang, Dou! All spoke well. Lixiu put mind at rest. Plan for Stockport in place. Will report meeting to committee. If they happy, all will be implemented. Before conclude, one more item. Historic concord with Stockport deserve fitting celebration feast. Who fancy fish and chip supper with mushy pea? My shout! Can have Holland's pie or steak and kidney pudding if prefer! One last item, message from Chairman. Anyone having fish and chip, no ketchup allowed, only salt and vinegar! Chinese people not vulgar!'

# Chapter 6

## It Begins! Thursday Bloody Thursday

For the final time we return to Adam and his languorous Autumn journey home. As often happens the traffic cleared, and in only the time it took to push a stranded Vauxhall Corsa into a safe space. Very soon Adam's adoring wife and his two little angels, would be sharing the stories of their day with him. His heart would be full, as would his belly be, an hour or two later. Adam had that TGI Thursday feeling and who was going to spoil it? At this stage he had begun singing his reworking of Friday On My Mind. When he was alone, he would sing the old Easybeats version. For the kids he performed the David Bowie rendering because they loved the weird intonations and Adam was their favourite entertainer. The children never found out it wasn't really about Thursday.

Adam loved nothing more than pulling up and seeing two excited little faces at the window. There were three if you include Kevin the Labrador, although he would keep disappearing for a few seconds as he completed deranged dashes to the kitchen and back. If there were no parking spaces outside the house, Adam would try to sneak up and crawl under the window and surprise the children. Jenna wasn't sure who enjoyed it more, him, the kids, or the neighbours.

As he pulled into his narrow street, Adam could see commotion up ahead. A couple of police cars were being maneuverered to cordon off the street at each end. Officers were in the process of taping off one of the properties. Adam swallowed hard, realising it was his house. He parked up in the nearest available space and ran over. His heart was racing upon noting the ashen faces of all those around, and seeing neighbours in tears, apparently comforting one another. A blood covered policeman was being helped into an ambulance. His face contorted with grief and compassion as he saw Adam running toward the house, guessing who he must be. As Adam approached, a female officer took his arm and asked if he was Adam, from number eighteen and said they'd been trying to reach him.

'What's going on?' he asked. 'I can't let you go in there sir. Your neighbour has offered his house for us to talk to you' she said softly, her voice breaking slightly.

'What do you mean I can't go in? It's my bloody house!'

Tragically, truer words were never spoken. Around half an hour earlier, neighbours had heard terrified screams from inside the house and called the police. Two officers, both in their early twenties were nearby and arrived quickly. Sensing a dire emergency, they kicked the door open and rushed inside; only to be rocked back on their heels in horror and disbelief at the scene that greeted them. A dog was in the corner of the room, gnawing at the corpse of a little girl, flanked by his other two fresh kills, her little brother and her mummy.

Though horrified and shaken, the policemen moved quickly into gear, drawing their batons and reaching for their tasers. Nervously, they approached the dog as quickly as they dared. It was a sturdy and well-favoured creature, its coat having a reddish gold tint. Up until this point, admiring dog lovers would pet him saying he was a big baby, a beautiful honey blonde softie. On this day however, his mantle was blood red, being soaked in the life's essence of those he once charmed and entertained, and who loved and trusted him the most.

The once gentle and docile family pet was somehow transformed into a ferocious killer. With fangs bared and blood and drool dripping from its murderous jaws, it wheeled round snarling viciously at the officers. Before they could react, the beast leapt high at them, sinking its cruel teeth deep into PC Danny Andrews' arm as he sought to fend it off. Its lower jaw locked on his funny bone, and searing pain made him gasp and stumble. Its upper teeth pierced the soft and nerve laden tendons in his inner elbow causing his senses to swim, and a sickening nausea threatened to overwhelm him. He was dragged toward the floor calling out in agony as the dog's primeval instinct made it try to shake him as it might a rat or a rabbit. However, PC Andrews was no rodent or easily spooked burrow dweller. He was fit, fearless and surely not yet ready to die easily. He steeled himself, breathed in deeply and pulled his arm tight to his side as best as he could.

His colleague PC Craig Brown followed his own impulses, smashing his baton down on the animal's head. It barely flinched, continuing the attack, and if anything, biting deeper and harder. With his hands trembling, still reeling from the shock of seeing the carnage, his stomach convulsing as he fought back the urge to vomit, PC Brown drew and fired his taser. The dog yelped, before falling to the ground limp and incapacitated. 'Kill it Browny, don't let it come round!'

He didn't need telling twice. He rained down blow after blow, until eventually, after nine or ten hefty baton strikes, he heard the unusually welcome sound of skull bones cracking.

'Keep going,' PC Andrews shouted, 'Don't leave anything to chance like idiots in films do, smash its fucking head in and make sure it's stone dead.'

Seeing Adam's stricken family from the corner of his eye, PC Brown, despite experiencing shock, and now with anguished tears streaming down his face, carried on for two or three minutes, pounding on its head until the creature was unrecognisable.

Eventually, he fell to his knees, at once relieved and frustrated, then heaved, until his stomach gave up its contents over the dead animal.

Regaining his senses, blinking away his sweat and tears, he asked,

'How are you Danny mate? That arm looks like shit?'

Danny replied, 'I think it's broken, but fuck that, what's happened here? You'd better call in and get some ambulances here quick!'

He hadn't fully processed the scene, nor was he entirely aware of the extent of the carnage. His view had been slightly obscured by his colleague before he was attacked.

'We're only going to need one Danny my mate, and that's for you.' Danny then looked over, before he too sank to his knees, distressed by the sight of the mangled and half eaten little family. He momentarily forgot his own terrible agony, then he also wept, then wretched repeatedly until his vomit sprayed and spattered everything within reach.

What the two young bobbies had seen would never leave them, not least because they were soon to experience many similar scenes, along with the rest of the force.

A week later, a distraught and broken Adam Woodhouse, could be found in bewildered solitude. In keeping with the habits of many men, especially northern ones, he chose to face his grief alone. He existed in a daze, in his private wilderness of desolation. His parents and friends told him he could stay with them, but he was too raw. Even kind, well-meaning words only stirred sickly unquenchable emotions of sorrow and anger at his fate. He had no desire to vent on those who loved him, but nothing could console him. There was no solace to be had. He knew his loved ones did not die quickly or painlessly, or without knowing. He was powerless to stop his mind replaying the dread and terror that would have gripped them.

His wife Jenna was only slender, standing just over five feet tall and weighing not much more than a large child. What could she have done, especially from a sudden and unforeseen attack? The children took after their mummy, nimble and agile, but slight, and no match for a dog even half the size and strength of theirs.

Adam cursed his fate. No father wants to face the reality he could not fulfil his first duty, to protect his family, so what could anyone say? There was no light to pierce his darkness, no words of hope promising happier days to follow. Adam sat uneasily, helpless and numb. The minutes, hours and days flowed into one another in a formless swirl of hopelessness. The tv was no comfort. Every scene seemed to contain children with their parents and a family dog. Adverts, shows, trailers, they jarred his spirit and seemed to mock him. Unbearable reminders were everywhere. Watching football gave some trivial respite, as long as he skipped any preliminaries to avoid seeing the young proud mascots. Adam averted his eyes when the cameramen sought out satisfied dads with their kids, sharing the spectacle in the modern arenas.

He yearned to join his loved ones in his own restful sleep of death but knew he would only add to the suffering of those who loved him. Besides, he didn't even have a date yet for the funerals. His mind was in perpetual torment with recurring visions of three coffins, all three small, but two of them far too tiny to be comprehensible. He lived minute by minute, contemplating the most considerate way he could end it, should he fail this horrendous test. He was settled on an overdose, so nobody would have to find a disfigured or bloated corpse. A note and a phone call just before should do it he reasoned, as he struggled to put up his own fight for life. One grotesque reality helped him in small measure. He knew his was not an isolated incident, just the first. Like PCs Danny Andrews and Craig Brown, Adam would in time see barely a family left untouched by the deadly chain of events quickly unfolding.

In the land of the living, it was approaching noon. For the first time that morning Adam looked at his phone to see if he had any messages, despite having no stomach to answer them. He squinted at the small font giving the mundane date and time as absentmindedly he wondered what day it might be. Suddenly, he saw it. His breathing became erratic, he trembled fitfully with the realisation he should not have looked. It was Thursday, their special day, their family day! It seemed as though the room darkened but it was only a new depth of despair enveloping him. At the top of his lungs, he cried out as his pain and grief soared to unbearable levels:

'IT'S THURSDAY, IT'S
BLOODY…FUCKING….THURSDAY!'

Adam spluttered and choked, trying to fight back the bitter tears that flowed uncontrollably stinging his eyes like fire. He wept as his broken heart fluttered but would not stop to end his torment.

'I'm sorry, I'm sorry' he cried out, but there was no one to hear him.

'I'm sorry Jenna my angel, I'm sorry Ruthie, I'm sorry Ethan! I'm so sorry I wasn't there when you needed me most! Please come back. Please don't leave me here without you!'

For hours without count, his convulsing body writhed and trembled uncontrollably. At last, his eyes were red and sore, and he had neither tears, nor strength, to cry any more. Alone he grieved, in a barren, meaningless existence, in which he would likely be imprisoned for ever. What was left of the little broken bodies of the children and of Jenna had been removed before he ever went back in. Their blood had been cleaned away and everything replaced as it was before.

Adam never knew where precisely their slaughter had taken place. This was so he could attempt to recall the many blissful, carefree days they'd enjoyed together in their little home. His resilience and emotional skin, though thicker than rhino hide were pierced, though not with cruel words nor deadly dart or bullet. His quickfire tongue was still, with no reason to stir. He was fractured and exposed, laid bare to heaven and earth without the three people whose existence made his very heart beat, and lent his life form and purpose.

Adam looked around the now cold and silent house that was once warmed as it rang with joy and merriment beyond measure. He didn't want to move out because he wasn't planning to move on. Adam reasoned that if he was going to go anywhere, it was to be with them!

# Chapter 7

## Fostering the Fear

Six months before Adam's ordeal, the plans were ratified. Well-rehearsed final preparations swung into gear. Every bus stop, placard, local paper, leaflets, automated text messages, and localised big tech algorithms were in overdrive saying dogs are deadly and dangerous! Your best friend is really your worst enemy. This canine catastrophe, this peril of pooches, hazardous hounds and malignant mutts will destroy the ecosphere.

It was important to undermine and shake age old traditions. It would be the ultimate challenge driving an emotional wedge between owners and their pets. As the weeks passed, a looming and threatening spectre of punitive taxes began to grow in the minds of the dog owning population. Canine carbon charges, levies on dog compounds, the prospect of dog ownership challenging horses as the preserve only of the wealthy. The fear and panic grew. The modern distress cry went up: Can't the government help us? If only good people would realise that is always the wrong question.

Once the fear was firmly established in the hearts and minds of the by now, emotionally battered and bruised population, the dissenting voices had to be dealt with. They were pleading on behalf of the dog population and begged instead for remission for their emissions. However, leaders of all stripes have learned well from political gurus and paymasters how to persuade and nudge their people. They don't get bogged down by open debate. Rather, they belittle and besmirch contrary contentions and slap on derisive labels.

Clumsy weapons have been developed. The billion dollar think-tanks have conceived eugenically perfected twins. These twins go by the names of Misinformation and Disinformation. They are not identical but are deliberately difficult to tell apart. They have arisen like characters from a dark medieval fairy-tale and comparison to them is intended to intimidate and threaten our confidence. They also have a remedy however, guardian angels guaranteed to keep us safe. Funded by the same billionaires spinning the news, these angels go by various names such as Trusted Sources, The Trusted News Initiative (TNI) etc, who offer us a dot gov deliverance. Their methods are crystalised in the words of the ghoulish, former New Zealand Prime Minister: "Trust your government! We will be your single source of truth!" Were more chilling words ever uttered, this side of Stalin or Mao? The Trusted News Initiative has received over $8 billion in funding from big pharma, which gives eight billion reasons not to trust them, yet most still do.

So called official sources attempt to mimic the other scary twins Tweedle Dee and Tweedle Dum. Mainstream news outlets try to never contradict each other on the big narratives, even as truth itself is eviscerated. They mess up often but cover their tracks with blatant lies or claims of new information coming to light, information so called deniers or tin hatters were warning about all along.

One day the populations may see through this malign mist, for it is the fog of war. Many believe it is a psyop, psychological warfare waged by our own leaders against their populations. When almost every institution and public service is a total shiz-show, the same people overseeing them say, listen only to us, and our experts. Misinformation and Disinformation are but phantoms and shape shifters. They are intentionally vague and versatile and thus malleable to suit almost any situation. People feel in their bones subconscious unease, but propaganda is potent when it is repeated ad infinitum and woven into every storyline be it news, soap operas and even sport! This is now possible because super elites pushing the narratives also own every mainstream media outlet and streaming service. Once great universities, and their less well-endowed offspring now hide from public intellectual sword play. They ban truth before it can impale them.

When little Adam Woodhouse imbibed his father's counsel things were different. His father likely never envisaged a world where academics and scientists refuse to debate critical subjects affecting us all; subjects like man-made climate catastrophe, Covid truths, vaccine harms and even the natural boundaries of human biology. The science is settled is the great deceit of our time. The very nature of science is that it is never settled, and all evidence is always couched as a theory lest new evidence comes to light. If someone refused to debate in the old days, it was considered an admission of weakness or of having something to hide. Today the position is defended and accepted by a certain class of people Adam's dad would have given their technical name: Bloody Educated Idiots!

Our once free media is as nostalgic a notion as the steam trains that once spluttered and chuffed across Adam's beloved viaduct. Orwell and Huxley spin in their graves like prop shafts in a pair of dragsters duking it out at Santa Pod Raceway. Meanwhile, mealy mouthed newsreaders do their spinning like rotary engines by Wankel, or similarly spelled names. They denounce all alternative narratives as conspiracy theories. Once fiery journalistic instincts are tempered by timidity or subservience. To hold on to jobs, they sacrifice integrity. The days of the scoop are all but over. Conformity will be their career lifeboat, no matter how catastrophic the ratings collapse as people tire of the homogenisation of every story.

This was only phase one of the dog dilemma fear programme. Scare the people until they cry out for a saviour, then heroically present the solution, which upon close inspection, often pre-dates the crisis. For the dog food trial, distribution contracts were issued to those with lips for the teats, and financial directors examined potential profitability with the precision once exercised by pharmaceutical regulators. Though the sirens of doom wailed most loudly across the wards of Stockport, word spread far and wide. As with many a radical policy float, most assumed any serious risks would be remote and our government and councils would have our backs.

Unfortunately, mental and emotional manipulation is now standard government methodology. Behavioural change techniques have replaced the soap box and the stump. The stubborn streak of the north would not easily yield to accommodate herbivore hounds, but spiralling costs are another thing. Mixing financial anxiety with relentless assertions of "wrong think" knocks people off balance. It is never intended to align with reality, only to achieve the ends of the powers that be!

Over six straight months the fires of fear were kindled. Prices for everything were still rising precipitously, there seemed no escape. Energy costs were crushing small businesses and households. Well-heeled green gurus and political power brokers for years said energy needed to be far more expensive to "encourage us" to use less. Hey Presto, crisis after crisis coincidentally brought previously unimaginable energy price hikes into being, under the cover of plausible deniability.

For those with seeing eyes, such tricks are as crass and predictable as the bunch of plastic flowers produced by a sideshow conjurer for his amazed audience. To complete this performance the magician's assistants picked the spectators' pockets as they watched in awe.

Those who say this is part of a plan, even pointing to the description of the conjurer's intentions on his advertising leaflets and website, are mocked as conspiracy theorists by those who count themselves wise.

Some of the wise had seen his show before and paid top dollar, this despite a good few of them and their fellows later noticing missing wallets and purses. Not only did they pay to watch again they still applauded, and even invited friends and family to the show. Others who had previously been rinsed and reported the crime to the police without response, warned those queuing it was quite literally a criminal act. They were shocked to be accused of being anti vaxers, racists or even Trump supporters.

Financial pressure was ramping up, even those who once thought themselves insulated from cost of-living rises were making cutbacks, so why should fears of unaffordable pets be proven wrong? Many prepared themselves mentally for a final trip to the vets. Old schoolers packed bags with bricks for Lassie's last trip to the lake. The dog rescue shelters prepared for financial ruin, their charity exhausted.

Then, just as unexpectedly as the fear had begun, deliverance was at hand. Word was systematically leaked out that there was no need to fear. The most naive in the borough anticipated a new miracle to eclipse even the town hall's facial scrub decades earlier. Others simply recognised the script. Even so a tremor ran through the foundations of the town and far beyond, a misguided glimmer of hope. Animal instinct had also made the dogs nervous, but now they sensed the burden of despair departing their owners and barked their approval in every quarter.

# Chapter 8

## Signs and Wonders

Far, far away, in a village in the wilds of the West Riding in Yorkshire, Sooty was in his local enjoying a pint of Guinness (what else but the black stuff)? He looked quizzically at Sweep.

'Do you feel anything Sweep? Something is astir in the kingdom. Something wonderful is afoot. Last night I couldn't sleep. As I lay awake gazing at the constellations, I fancied Ursa Major shone more brightly than in times past. I believe the Great Bear in the sky told me that something wonderful is about to unfold among dogkind.'

Sweep, the cute but mischievous little grey glove puppet dog could only squeak. His voice was a saxophone reed Harry Corbett's brother had fashioned as a substitute for the traditional bark. Sweep squeaked loudly and enthusiastically, so loudly in fact, the landlord asked him to leave, assuming he'd had one Brewdog dog brew too many.

Sooty noticed a mysterious old grey man at the next table. He was shrouded in a long dark coat with a huge hood, within which his face was but a shadow. Sooty wondered how the old man came there unseen and unheard. The old man muttered something barely audible. Sooty asked,

'Friend, did you just say you are Gandalf, heading west to Rohan? The old man slowly raised his head and his bright blue eyes seemed to illuminate the confines of his shroud. He fixed Sooty in his stare. Though it intrigued him that this mere glove puppet was moving independently and consuming alcohol like a living being, he let it pass. Sooty was about to repeat his question but was cut short as the old man suddenly replied:

'No, I said I'll have half, and then I'd best get going!'

Sooty was devastated, he had always prided himself on his keen hearing. He suddenly felt old, and noticed his reflection in his glass, and the tell-tale grey hairs in his once jet-black ears. He longed for the days when British children tuned in especially to see him and his friends. He knew those days were never coming back and time was marching on. Right then he would just settle for once again merely seeing the bikini girl on the card of peanuts behind the bar, as she was slowly revealed with each sale of the nutritious crunchy treats. He sighed a deep sigh of the burdens and disappointments of life. He was about to bow his disillusioned little head, when the old man unexpectedly leaned forward, and beckoning Sooty toward him spoke quietly as if speaking of deep secrets:

'Sooty, today the circle is completed. In the days people call the Sixties, a little yellow bear with black fluffy ears enchanted the children of Stockport. He had recently met a cute young Panda named Soo, whom he instantly began dating. But these things are known to you. Sooty and Soo the panda, exchanged interracial, nay, inter species kisses. Those kisses were seen in glorious monochrome on tiny goldfish bowl shaped tv screens across the land. Today the town hall prophecy is fulfilled, and the metaphor finds fruition. Listen well and understand: You, the fossil fuel bear despised by modernity, have lived many years in the shadows. You have been ashamed and afraid of being ridiculed and blamed, for not repudiating associations with the filthy fuel. Stockport Town Hall was the ultimate wedding cake, sealing and symbolising this union with Soo, your panda from China. This union, as if forged in the heavens, heralded these days when redemption will come for Sweep and his kind. As you know better than any, he was always a naughty, bone obsessed, intellectually challenged dog. He will not be a vestigial memory of one sweeping chimneys henceforth, but for sweeping away the wicked emissions of humanity. This is what you feel in your heart Sooty, as it is felt in the very bones of the earth.'

Sweep meanwhile was eavesdropping by the window and all the talk of bones caused him to become very excitable again. He tried to regain entry to the pub, and a brawl with the landlord ensued, spilling out into the car park. Sooty meanwhile, had closed his eyes in awe and contemplation for a moment. When he opened them, the old man had vanished, as if into thin air. Sooty rushed to the door, imagining he heard the clattering of hooves of some noble steed on the cobbles outside. Hoping to learn more from the old man, whose half pint of stout sat untouched on the table, he rushed outside to stay such steed and beg him to tarry a while. It transpired the clattering was nothing more than bins being skittled by Sweep and the Landlord as they were grappling. Bemused, Sooty cried aloud to all who would hear:

'From whence did the sage spring, and to what new destiny is he called? And how is he borne, per chance upon the wings of eagles?'

The landlord looked up from the headlock Sweep had him in,

'If you mean that old fellow with the big coat, that's him just exiting the car park in the back of that Uber. Locals say he knows things and tells of matters hidden but always has folly amidst his utterances. Some call him the soothsayer, others a storm bird, but most just say he's just a nutjob.

Sooty wondered at the day's events and what it meant for the earth, and for all mankind. He finished his Guinness, and as the landlord was still engaged in his battle with Sweep, Sooty looked around him before downing the old man's untouched stout thinking waste not, want not!

These are strange days' thought Sooty. Days where truth is become stranger than fiction. Maybe truth has been replaced by fiction, by guile and deceit, but to what end, and to whose benefit? Even now people are reading these words as if they are real, but such is the power of narrative. May people remove the masks of the storytellers before it is too late.'

# Chapter 9

## A Fairey Story of Brass Bands and Brass Necks

Back in Stockport, the air was still heavy with expectation. The very atmosphere itself was excited, and it drove the grey clouds from the sky, for the best part of an hour. The gathered throng murmured among themselves wondering what lay in store after the campaign of doom.

The Mayor and Mayoress, no relation, stepped forward triumphantly, golden chains glistening gloriously in the newly liberated spring sunlight. The great public proclamation of the wonder food from China was to be made. The two mayors personified the new inclusivity of their office with equally shared magnificence. One male, one female was a huge step forward for diversity and equity. Even so, some pointed out that the two mayors lark was already outdated, and that soon multiple mayors would be needed to fulfil ever expanding quotas.

Holding the fort for now, the current pairing were well versed in their task. They had long since learned to signal virtue with every pronouncement; and this despite the crushing, overbearing burden of their unconcealable white skin. The famous Fairey's Brass Band, surprisingly booked over a year in advance, struck up triumphal notes of deliverance. The uplifting sound of the horns and trumpets rang out and echoed throughout Mersey Square. The echoes fled, darting even among the arches of the distant viaduct, surprising a couple of pedestrians and a passing cat. The cat paused briefly, before continuing about its business, with customary disinterest in the affairs of either man or dog.

To all non-cats, it felt as if heaven itself had come to Stockport. People in the many two up, two downs, rooted through outhouses, searching optimistically for old maypoles. These outhouses were useful storage areas that once housed outside lavatories. The events hastened their spring clean when garden chairs and tables would be hosed down to be rid of the cobwebs and the tiny black slugs that wintered in them. People found forgotten bags of cement that had turned to stone, and more curses were uttered realising another parasol was ruined due to failing to keep the placky bag it came in.

But on this day, nothing could dampen the spirits of the town that gives damp its meaning. Little girls skipped and danced merrily in their summer pinafores, and threaded daisy crowns which they wore in their hair with joy. The man mayor and lady mayor meanwhile, cast aside for a moment the blue and yellow. They wrapped themselves instead briefly in the colours of their own nation.

As if by chance, or by a less than subtle literary device, an elderly, downcast local Russian legal immigrant of many years, happened to be walking by. She felt her heart leap mistakenly thinking it was the red, white and blue of the Russian Federation, that they'd finally remembered her fifteen million countrymen who died fighting Hitler's hoardes. Realising her error, the tired old lady sank back into the fear and apprehension recent times had saddled her with. She said in her heart:

'They say no minority should feel marginalised or oppressed, yet they have me living in fear with their blue and yellow town hall flag, and blue and yellow coloured lights. I know I'm sometimes a bombastic, even belligerent Babushka. I know Putin is no pussy cat and the reason I left Mother Russia but it's a bit rich saying the invasion was totally unprovoked. The regime in Kiev have been shelling my relatives in the Donbas for nearly a decade since the American led coup that overthrew the democratically elected Russia friendly government. Banning the Russian tongue which for 15 million Ukrainians is their first language was poking the bear too. In their own words this is usually called ethnic cleansing. They should fly a flag of black and white, for that seems to be the simplistic way they see the world.

'For many years I have counted myself blessed to be adopted by this country which I now love as my own. Oh England, Oh England, why can you no longer just fly the flag of St George and keep your political statements in your parliament when there are so many competing sentiments and arguments? If you must feign compassion, just fly your flags at half-mast? My God knows what is truly in your hearts.'

Completely unaware of her malevolent presence and highly controversial thoughts, the mayors, with the ambivalence of the aforementioned cat, embraced the occasion. With the poise and presence of two medieval town criers, they declared:

'Hear ye, Hear ye, oh noble Stopfordians. Listen well, dog owners of this ancient settlement! On this first day of April, in the year of our Lor, ahem, erm, 2024, salvation is at hand! Oh Stockport, lowly Stockport, for so long despised amongst the cities of our land. Today, other conurbations kneel in shame and astonishment. For this day you, O Stockport, do take one small step for man, and one giant leap towards net zero. Today we declare: Au revoir Bezier! Stockport is henceforth twinned with Beijing, formerly known as Peking! If you own a Pekinese, it will now be called a Beijinger. Let all put aside doubts and fears that would consume you. Come ye into the light. Today in this town a hope is born. All ye who are weary and heavy laden, come, and follow the science!'

They revelled briefly and undeservedly in the attention generated by this auspicious dog food launch. Other officials revelled in their own boundless sense of importance as they jostled to share the limelight in the photo op charade. Soon the brace of British burgomasters would be whisked the quarter mile back to the town hall in the mayoral cars. The lesser lights likewise scorned both bus and bike, even e-bikes, as they knew Stockport weather can change in a heartbeat or a stroke. Their publicly funded taxis ferried them back to the celebratory meat laden banquet with a vegetarian option. If only politicians would guarantee this menu choice to the people.

In fairness there was nothing else for them to do, as the wonder dog food was long since harvested, processed, and awaiting dispatch. Countless tons of nutritious, sustainable, protein laden bamboo-based nourishment was ready and waiting to delight the tastebuds and physical function of every hound in Stockport. The government and local council had heavily subsidised it. Dignitaries basked in that sense of achievement and lack of personal anxiety, only derived when spending other people's money.

Relief among the pet owning populace was palpable. Some with several dogs even had house parties. One or two discordant voices aired fears of possible long term side effects of the novel technology. Somewhat confusingly, they were called granny killers. The authorities have perfected a communist technique of getting the people to unthinkingly police and enforce their propaganda, using shame for batons and ridicule for pepper spray.

Meanwhile, a cascade of reassurances from every on-message official, government approved academic and uncensored scientist, allayed fears surrounding its safety and efficacy. It was basically bamboo they said. Don't worry about the other ingredients. There was no need to worry about the undisclosed chemical content. There was no possibility of DNA modification, no honestly guv, on me muvva's life! Nobody is making anyone use it....yet. It's everyone's free choice, at the moment. We foresee no mandates! This is not China or North Korea, trust your leaders.

And so, Stockport was bamboozled into belief. As it was rolled out the experts seemed to be correct. The pooches loved it and thrived. Regarding absent stock of traditional dog food in the supermarkets, the big chains explained that they only respond to local demand. This much was true. The local council had demanded they carried no stock and they responded. They concentrated instead on expanding their range of plastic dog toys and other tat, ironically also made in China. They didn't advertise these toys and gifts are almost universally fossil fuel by-products. This was reasonable in fairness because after all, virtually nothing we use or wear and drive or are driven in or on, is free from fossil fuel or animal husbandry involvement.

*Hey kids, make your own lists of things in your everyday life to see if this is true.*

These are indisputable yet seldom aired facts that hold true for almost everything we use or wear, either at home or at work, even if work is in any hospital or sustainable development facility. It is also true of every computer, and all climate modelling equipment used by scientists for the Intergovernmental Panel for Climate Change. The acronym of IPCC is a sly trick in itself. Most assume the 'I' is for International rather than INTERGOVERNMENTAL! The fact it is 100% politically motivated and governmentally funded is right there in the name, like everything else, hidden in plain sight! Its brief is to only look for evidence of potentially man-made contributions to planetary warming.

Given the cost and upheaval for everyone, a taxpayer might assume similar research looking for evidence of hitherto unknown natural causes might be being undertaken too, just in case! In the honest world this research is being done, but its findings are hidden and censored by compliant mass media and big tech. Even founder member of Greenpeace Dr Patrick Moore is ignored, since he became a climate heretic; just like the jovial beardy David Bellamy was disappeared from our tv screens for the same crime. For those interested in lifting a few stones, records and programs must be published by law, for now at least. This includes funding streams. Councillors and MPs should be the first to follow the money to see who is funding what. If all roads lead back to Western oligarchs and banks and corporations set to earn trillions, they should end all association immediately and pull all public funding!

On a lighter note; as with all great occasions or disasters, pop stars rushed to produce a tribute song, hoping to celebrate or cash in on the publicity. A Song for Stockport was written, winning nominations for Eurovision, despite vociferous but warranted protests from London and Liverpool:

## **A Song for Stockport**

*On a warm spring day in Stocky, all the Mancs weren't quite so cocky.*
*And the Scousers looked with envy from their slums.*
*It was China's finest hour, every Great Dane to Chihuahua*
*Barked in unison we'll see your kingdom come.*

*With the bells of heaven ringing, and with angel voices singing.*
*Dick Whittington looked down with tearful eyes.*
*He regretted going to London, but what's been done can't be undone.*
*We all know Cockneys can't help telling lies*

*He could have brought his cat to Stockport, bought himself a pair of Rockports,*
*Gone to Sports Direct who'd dress him like a king.*
*Smoke some weed in Stockport Precinct, thank the Lord he'd had a rethink.*
*Chug some pints of Robbie's Ale then start to sing!*

*Stockport's streets will now be golden, like the feet of Philip Foden,*
*And we'll see the people flock from far and wide.*
*From the Highlands down to Devon, to a Crufts show made in heaven,*
*Stockport isn't shit; the people cried! Stockport isn't shit; the people cried!*

# Chapter 10

## The Man with a Flowery Crevice

Eric and Brenda Donnelly were in their narrow kitchen, where Brenda was wrapping potato and carrot peelings up in a sheet of newspaper. It was a habit formed before the days of recycling bins, and it's unlikely she'll grow out of it as she recently turned seventy-five. In her heyday she was a real head turner and won Miss Pontins of Prestatyn three years straight. Being in Wales, that ancient land of myth and fable, a tale arose of a certain Booby Brenda, a beautiful mermaid who once warmed the bitter waters of the Irish Sea. Local historians believe the legend most likely arose in the caravan site social clubs after too much Brains Skull Attack, to this day a most favoured tipple amongst both tourist and Taff.

The Irish Sea in which Brenda frolicked, is a murky, frigid body of water between Ireland and Wales, so cold that generations of holidaying children have had to be cheerfully flung in by their dads to get a true seaside experience. Once in they are told to move around to get warm, not be standing still and shivering like little nesh sparrow legged southerners.

After Brenda's third walkover Eric decided she should give the other girls a chance. Secretly it was because he'd gradually become more aware of the other blokes ogling her and a little resentment was overpowering the sense of pride he used to feel. It made little difference in truth as if they needed a competition to notice her top heavy charms; they simply did their viewing more discreetly.

Eric and Brenda were inseparable. They married young, rumour had it that it was a shotgun wedding. They had three kids and for years, when asked about them, Eric had always joked: we've got three, one of each! Lately he'd dropped that gag because of the complications of recent times. None of their kids lived in Stockport, but they saw them all fairly regularly, though not as often as they would like, especially as there were six grandkids (one of each). A secret fear they both held, concerned who would be the one left to cope when death finally came to their household. They couldn't remember much of their past life without each other, never mind imagine a future alone.

It was early evening, Brenda was making a pot of tea with tea leaves, how they both liked it.

'Make sure that water's boiling properly before you put it in Brenda, I don't want tea leaves in my dentures.'

'Do you know Eric, you're a cheeky beggar. How many cups of tea have I made you over the years? It's about time you got off your behind and made me one.'

'Nobody makes it like you love, you're the brew queen of Edgeley.'

'You're a right one you are Eric Donnelly. You know how to get around me don't you, with your forked tongue. Oi, keep your hands to yourself you dirty old man.'

'You're still my bathing beauty Bren, even if I had to work hard to woo you. Lucky my forked tongue was a silver one. Give us a kiss.'

Eric, even at seventy-six, still stood well over six feet tall. He had a prodigious bought and paid for beer belly, which though vast was firm to the touch. It enabled the gargantuan gut to hang several inches higher than Brenda's bazookas which were continuing their relentless journey south. Although now a little bowed from carting his beer and pie belly around, he still looked like he could pack a punch. However, despite his burly appearance he was a gentle soul. He was more likely to stop a fight than start one, which many an Edgeley landlord was grateful for. More than once he'd carried brawling yobbos out, one under each arm like a farmer with a pair of piglets.

He was a big Stockport County fan and he'd had a season ticket for the Hatters for more than half his life. Like a lot of local lads, he didn't need match tickets or money in his younger days because wily youths gained entry with peg ups to conquer the fence at the Railway End. They didn't have much in the way of stewards back then, and not much call for police. There were a couple of exceptions, the visits of the wild heath dwellers and forest folk of Burnley, and that of railway town neighbours Crewe Alexandra. Crewe was a fair chance of fisticuffs and with Burnley it was guaranteed, it was a fun day out for them, with their bare knuckles and bare chests.

Back in the day, outside of cup ties and the fight days, the crowds were only two or three thousand, because the main battle was staying in the football league. It was easy to sneak in because County played Friday night to avoid clashing with the two big Manchester clubs, so it was usually dark. A lot of fans used to watch all three clubs, a rarity nowadays.

Eric still had a match day programme signed by Jim Fryatt in his career golden year spent with County, when his athleticism may have been waning, but his magnificent sideburns were at their most abundant. Fryatt once scored a quickfire goal that brought him many years of fame in the Guinness Book of Records and the epic Charles Buchan Football Monthly. County fans reckon he was more famous for his year with the Hatters of Edgeley Park, than for his four second goal for Bradford which brought him fame. Eric kept the programme on the mantlepiece as a conversation starter. Brenda was fully supportive of Eric's passion as she said it got the big lump from under her feet while she tidied up.

'Has that Chinese dog food turned up yet Brenda?'

'Yes pet, it's next to the toaster. Do you know I thought we'd be able to just get it from the shops, not have to put in a blinking application for it.'

'I know love, but we've got special dispensation to stop those buggers from town or Liverpool jumping in.'

'Special dispensation? Flippin 'eck Eric, Prince Charles will be visiting us next to see our special dispensation. Can't see the big posh sod coming to Stockport though to be honest.'

'Give him a chance Brenda love, he's our monarch now; His Royal Highness King Charles III!'

'Well, it's the right name for him! He's got ears like a ruddy King Charles Spaniel. It's a shame for him, he's always looked a gawky object. They say he never had many friends and got bullied at school. I don't wonder he took up talking to plants and trees. Do you know what I worry about Eric, there have been all sorts of stories about strange kids that were bullied, then wanted to get their own back when they grew up. I mean look at that little red-haired boy in the film the grandchildren were watching at weekend. He was a right dangerous and nasty little swine when he got all that power.'

'When you say film, do you mean the Incredibles love?'

'Yes, that's the one. I enjoyed it, especially when that little sod got his comeuppance!'

'Aye Brenda, but it is only a cartoon not a documentary.'

'Yes, well maybe someone was trying to tell us something. You've got Charles and that other funny little American fella that makes computers. They were all Smurfs those interweb people, but now they've got a lot of money and power.'

'Smurfs love? Oh, you mean nerds. I hope you're wrong, given the influence they've got between them. You're right though, Charles is an odd one and no mistake.'

'Eric, do you think they'll have to make the stamps wider so they can fit his ears on?'

'No love, they'll just make his head smaller I expect, but they'll need to be careful not to make the stamp look like a wingnut jamboree!'

'Do you know Eric I still miss our Lizzie. We all grew up with her, we all knew where we were up to with her, and don't forget she did come here in 1977 was it not?'

'She did that love. It was for the silver jubilee celebrations. Have you still got that tea towel you bought?'

'No, you ruined it didn't you, you big daft 'a'porth. I had to throw it away thanks to you wiping your big oily hands on it after you'd been messing with that damned car you were so proud of; before you scrapped the flipping thing that was.'

'Aye Brenda, looking back that was a mistake. It would probably be worth a fortune now.'

'I doubt it Eric. Don't you remember it was made in China, like this blinking dog food.'

'What was made in China?'

'That flipping tea towel, what do you think I meant?'

'I was talking about my Cortina Brenda. 1966 Mark 1 with a Lotus engine. It was only a 1600 but it went like snot off a stick.'

'Oooh hark at you with your locust Cortina. You were ahead of the times weren't you? Fancy having a car running on insects in the 1960's. You always were a Fancy Dan weren't you, with your blonde hair and your flowery crevice.'

Eric knew she meant cravat but didn't always correct her if he didn't think it was likely to crop up that often. As for the locusts he just couldn't be bothered explaining. The things he loved about her far outweighed any embarrassment at her special talent for mangling the Queen's English, or the King's in more recent times. She was a simple soul but had a heart of gold. She was always first to volunteer in any major or minor emergency amongst family or neighbours, yet as Eric often remarked, she still had her knockers.

'Do you know what I liked most about that car Eric? It was those lovely rear headlights. They were round weren't they, then split into three. They used to remind me of Kalashnikovs.'

'Kalashnikov rifles?'

'Don't be so bloody daft I wasn't talking about guns you whoremonger! I mean those little Kalashnikov telescopes with beads in them that made lovely patterns when you turned them round. I've never seen any car lights like that since.'

'Believe it or not I know what you mean love. Those lights were standard but they looked custom. The only snag was bloody students thought it was the symbol for those Ban the Bomb pillocks.'

He sipped his white-hot black tea and pictured himself hurtling down the nearest country lanes. When you were getting your foot down in those days it was advisable not to go too far afield, as most cars were about as reliable as a manifesto pledge.

'Are you going to stop having premonitions about that ruddy car and give Oscar some of this new bamboo meat? Do you know Eric I always thought bamboo was made from canes, not flipping dog food. I don't know why they make it so confusing.'

'Nothing wrong with reminiscing Brenda. Especially nowadays when the body won't do what the head is telling it. Come on Oscar, we've got a treat for you.'

An aging but still sprightly Jack Russell sprang from the living room sofa and sprinted into the kitchen wagging his little stump of a tail. In truth, he was more wagging his backside than his tail, his feet were skidding from side to side on the linoleum floor in his excitement. Oscar was a pocket rocket and he'd seen off more rodents in Stockport than Rentokil.

'You'll have to read this packet for me Brenda, I can't see past the end of my nose today?'

'Give it here sweetheart. Now then, it's called Super Doggy. I wonder who came up with that flipping name. Oh ey up there's something here on the side. Right, it says: knock-out, happy bark, good smell bottom, run fast, very obedience, yeah bamboo.'

'Bloody hell Brenda, what's that all about? I really meant how do you mix it though? Do we need to use boiling water or owt?'

'No love it just says mix it with cold water until it's a firm constituency. Three heaped tablespoons and tap water.'

'I'll mix it up shall I Brenda? I think we probably want something like a thick porridge.'

'Porridge? He's a Jack Russell not a Scottish Dog. Don't go putting salt in it then. We don't want him with blood pressure like yours. Do you want the syrup?'

'Syrup? No, I'm making it with the consistency of porridge that's all. No salt or syrup. Anyway, they said it's a special formula and we shouldn't muck about with it. Pass us a tablespoon love. Now then, one, two, three, I presume it must swell up or this won't last long. I hope it doesn't upset Oscar's stomach or we're all in trouble?'

'That leaflet we got from the council said it's good for their guts Eric. It said it will help stop smells. That's probably what that good smell bottom was about.'

Eric mixed up the food doubtfully then crouched down with a few creaks, cracks and bloody Noras.

'Come on then Oscar, get some of this. You could do with this couldn't you? You're a smelly little bugger aren't you!'

Eric stroked Oscar affectionately, placing the bowl of the greyish brown mash in front of him.

'Don't upset him Eric, he can't help it, he's 12 years old.'

'Don't upset him? He doesn't understand English love, he's a clever little sod, but he's still a perishing dog. He just hears tones.'

'Oh, he understands alright Eric. They say dogs have a seventh sense; they know what you're thinking. I sometimes think he knows more about what's going on than I do.'

'Aye, well I'll give you that one Brenda.'

'Shall I put a bit out for you Eric? After all you've hardly got room to talk with your backside. I have to light my New Yankee candles when you've had one of those foreign curries you like so much. You smell like the store's horse.'

'Let's see how Oscar gets on first. Come on lad what do you think of this Chinese banquet we've got you?'

Oscar looked at the plate of mush suspiciously. He looked at Eric then Brenda in turn with a pained expression suggesting betrayal.

'Come on Oscar, give it a try, don't be a faddy little beggar!'

Oscar sniffed at the food and licked it cautiously, before surprising them both, by demolishing the whole dishful in a matter of seconds.'

'Steady on lad you'll meet yourself coming back. I think he likes it!'

'Doesn't he just Eric? He made shorter work of that than your mother used to when she ate all they'd got at the Chinese buffet. Bamboo must be like rabbit. He loves rabbits, they're his favourite.'

'It's meat free love, that's the whole point remember?'

'Yes, but rabbits only eat grass so they're vegetarious. It can't just be canes and leaves the way he scoffed it all like that. Maybe he's got some koala in him, they love their bamboo, don't they?'

'Koala? Do you mean pandas love?'

'I don't flaming know! What do koala bears eat then?'

'Eucalyptus love, but to be fair it's as daft a choice for a diet as bamboo. They have to eat their own body weight of it every day because there's so little goodness in it.'

'You're a right clever-clogs you are Eric. How do you know so much about everything? You're like a walking talking paedophile!'

'I beg your pardon Brenda?'

'You know what I mean. Like a dictionary but with pictures in and not just all long words.'

'I'm guessing you mean an encyclopaedia love?'

'I don't bloody well know do I? Anyroad Eric, you should go on Mastermind with that Magnet Magnusson.'

'I'd have a job love he's been dead about twenty years.'

'Yes, well I've always said too much knowledge is a dangerous thing. You want to be more careful, you can only fit so much knowledge in your head before it bursts, it stands to reason. By the way, I always thought a eucalyptus was one of those little guitars George Foreman used to play when he was a window cleaner; you know before he started buggering about with beefburgers and bacon on QVC! 'He was probably a rum'un too, all that hanging around lamp-posts on street corners waiting on young ladies. Our Richard said they'd have him for stalking nowadays.'

Rather than unpick Brenda's tangled ramblings, Eric turned the conversation back to Oscar who was still on cloud nine over his Super Doggy experience.

'I'll tell you what I do know Brenda. If we let him, Oscar would eat his own body weight of this stuff. It's a grand start but we'll keep a close eye on him to see how he goes.'

'Are you taking him for a walk soon chuck, they've forecast rain?'

'Aye I'll nip out after I've finished this brew. Vesuvius seems to have stopped erupting now, I can drink it.'

'Who's Vesuvius, another foreign devil County have signed?'

'Mount Vesuvius, the volcano. It was a joke about how hot the tea was.'

'Oh, very funny Eric. I've no idea what you're talking about half the time. Have you decided where you are taking Oscar?'

'I think I'll just walk down Castle Street way and see how I feel.'

'Yes, well don't pretend Oscar dragged you into a pub because I'll get us tea on while you're out. You can't pull a wolf over my eyes Eric Donnelly.'

'Don't worry I won't hang about Brenda; my belly already thinks my throat's cut. By the way have you got some of those little bags? I've none left in my coat pocket.'

'What little bags?'

'You know for Oscar, those little shit bags!'

'Well, if you're going up Castle Street, I'm sure there'll be one or two knocking about. They'll be hanging round near the bookies or the boozer seeing as the dole office is shut.'

'Haha you might well be right love. Oh ey up, I've found a couple after all. By the way, I hear Stan from number 25 used one of those perforated food bags. He didn't know they had holes in them the daft bugger. He had to throw his jacket away because his dog is worse than Oscar. It had the runs n'all. The dozy sod was covered in it.'

'Yes well I don't need all the details thank you very glad.'

'Right love, I won't be long, If I do nip in the pub I'll only be having half anyway. Come on Oscar, walkies.'

Oscar did his Tasmanian devil impression, spinning round and round in circles in excitement, and panting out little breathless barks.

'Keep still you nutcase, let me get your lead on.'

'Blimey Eric look at him spin. We should buy him some ice skates, he's like ruddy Orville and Dean doing a silhouette!'

'Ok love I'll see you in about forty minutes or so. What are we having?'

'Corned beef hash pet, and I've already peeled the spuds and carrots, so don't take forever.'

'I won't Brenda love. Come on Pongo!'

Eric and Oscar set off into the gathering gloom. It wasn't dark but rain clouds were low and ominous, and the snug was beckoning. They walked down near County's ground by the terraced houses. Oscar liked to have a mooch on the grass embankments on Mercian Way thoroughfare. The old houses there stand out because the builders added pattern and detail using yellow tinted coloured bricks as accents. They were touches you rarely see today on homes built for the working classes. Eric's dad told him some gypsies had done some tarmacking for the Wizard of Oz and repurposed the old yellow bricks they'd rifled. Luckily, Eric never shared that story with any of his friends. Dads can be dangerous.

He crossed at the pelican crossing and walked up Castle Street to his regular. There wasn't anyone in there who he knew well, or at least not who he wanted to talk to, and the landlord was busying himself moving barrels. As a result, Eric did more walking than he'd planned so he had a good day's exercise, as he'd been out with Oscar earlier when another "swift half" was consumed. A swift half is the male equivalent of ladies sharing a bottle where "a" could be equally written with the infinity symbol.

On the way home, Oscar dutifully did his business. Eric noted it was obviously too early for the odour killing enzymes to have kicked in.

'Poof, I said you were a smelly bugger, didn't I? You and me both.'

He chuckled to himself. Having picked up Oscar's deadly deposits, he paused and looked around furtively like a burglar by an open window. Seeing the coast was clear, he cocked his leg, then unleashed a long and rasping brassy old man fart into the cool evening air. The fart was harsh and dry, and slightly painful, but well worth the discomfort. He thought it sounded like the Smartie tubes or fag packets kids wedged in their bike wheels to make motor bike sounds as they rubbed against the spokes.

'Get out and walk! Good arse eh Oscar? Pick the bones out of that. I'll tell you what lad, if Brenda had been here, she could have knitted you a winter coat out of that one. Phwoar that's ripe is that.'

Oscar looked up, admiringly and knowingly. Eric could have sworn he even gave him a cheeky smile.

'Bloody hell Oscar, Brenda might have been right about you after all little fella.' He crouched down and patted Oscar's head and stroked him firmly with his big shovel like hands. Then home they went like brothers in arms, bonded and content. He enjoyed his tea, as he usually did, because Brenda was as good at cooking and baking as she was at brewing up. The only question remaining is would anyone in the household be taken soon, alone or otherwise.

Similar stories played out right across the borough (fart excluded in most cases). Barely a single pooch was not enthralled with the new wonder food. To the human nose there was no smell, no imitation meat aroma, no hint of anything to entice any dog to salivate over a bowl of bamboo-based blandness. All appeared well with the world.

As the weeks then months passed, not only did the canine population continue to be enraptured by the food, but everything about them also improved. They were healthier, their coats took on a gloss only dreamt of by the finest grooming salons. Their teeth were whiter and stronger. They were faster, more robust and energetic. At the same time, their obedience and affection markedly increased too. They were less prone to chasing squirrels and cats, but remained inquisitive, and noticeably more attentive to their owners and handlers. Super Doggy was a triumph.

# Chapter 11

## Ostriches and Flamingos (April 2024)

In the leafy Stockport suburb of Cheadle Hulme, handsome couple Simon and Yolanda Hart were lukewarm participants in the scheme. They could easily afford prime cuts for their dogs, or their children as Yolanda called them. However, decades of continuous climate curation made them amenable to at least share in the experiment.

Yolanda and Simon were both doing well without being what one might describe as rich. Each had successful businesses, and their fees and services were sufficiently attractive for their clients to repeatedly choose them over the competition. They were engaged having met online, initially intrigued by them sharing the same surname. They planned to marry when they had a window for a nice long honeymoon. In the meantime, the name match was convenient for letterheads and minimising gossip, other than from insidious incest insinuators. They planned a simple wedding, probably on a Mauritian beach or some such earthly paradise.

Yolanda was independent and confident. She always planned to keep her maiden name but was disappointed she couldn't now have impressive double-barrelled one, like other posh birds in their neighbourhood. There was spare money in the bank, that is to say, they were not of the fur coat and no knickers brigade, like quite a few of their neighbours.

Simon in particular employed people from all walks of life. Despite generally paying his staff above the average rate, he was nonetheless on occasion, accused of being a "stuck-up Porsche driving prick". This despite the fact he has never actually owned a Porsche. Tory Scum is another epithet which doesn't suit his non-aligned political views, him being libertarian and independent and his small property portfolio being transparent and fully declared.

They both gave generously to charity, but only after checking carefully how and where the money was spent, along with the remuneration packages of the charities' executives. They were happier to give to causes they liked and verified, than trust the government to take their money in tax and spend it on their own priorities.

Either way, they were still living the life of Riley in the teeth of national financial uncertainty. And so, to their part in this tragedy.

'Simon, fabulous news,' our first delivery of Super Doggy is here.'

'My word, is that really what it's called darling? I've never understood why they don't hire better translators to overcome such linguistic incongruence. Some languages can be transposed far more effectively than others, and Chinese must be among the most difficult. Just think of all the take-aways trying to engender positive imagery with their names, then ending up with the crass banality of a Lucky Lucky House or Happy Garden and so forth. Still, it's appropriate in our case, as our two are pretty super.'

Simon and Yolanda had two impeccable, chestnut brown Doberman Pinschers with all the paperwork to testify to their purity and provenance; though their strong, sleek and supple appearance bore its own testimony.

To accommodate the dogs, Yolanda had sacrificed her M3 soft top with its metallic gold option paint. Coupes and convertibles are always looks over reason, but who apart from Nerds or even Smurfs uses reason when buying a car? Yolanda perused Porsche Cayennes, Range Rovers, BMW X5's and the other usual suspects, but finally opted for a Tesla Model X. In terms of comparative styling, it was a pig in lipstick. Its saving grace was sexy rear gullwing doors, which when open, transform the pig into a flamingo. More to the point they were perfect for getting the dogs in and out.

Yolanda was well aware that the already iconic T on the back gave her instant social credit. It cemented her membership of the eco in-crowd, so the compromise was a good one. Simon on the other hand, was perfectly happy with his Range Rover Autobiography. His white ostrich leather seats ensured a total dog embargo, much to Yolanda's disappointment. In these days of moral finger pointing and immoral joy riding, Simon had wisely, if reluctantly, had the Autobiography's emblems removed to conceal its monster performance. For a red-blooded petrol head, that was tantamount to plucking a peacock, even castration.

With a herd of over five hundred gee gees under the lid, he didn't think it likely little Greta would be asking him for a lift any time soon either. Greta's new musclebound pal, Arnie the amphetamine addled Austrian, and latter day pretend ecowarrior, apparently let her drive his Tesla during one of her many world tours of conscience. None of us know if she drove, or even knew, of his fleet of other vehicles, which includes a Bugatti, a Hummer and an actual tank. His collection has been valued at over $4 million but it proved more difficult to put a price on his hypocrisy. To be fair, it is difficult to discern when Hollywood elites are acting or not, bearing in mind Arnie played multiple roles masquerading as a bulwark against tyranny and oppression. When asked about vaccine mandates, he followed his fellow moustachioed Austrian megalomaniac's lead by bellowing: Screw your freedoms, a very forthright, fourth-reich view.

Simon claimed Yolanda was trying to make him feel guilty, by parking her automotive equivalent of Nelson Mandela right next to his Range Rover every evening. Not long after her purchase, Yolanda tentatively enquired:

'Have you ever thought of electrifying Simon darling? Tess is so quiet, she's amazing, and must be as light as a feather the way she moves so quietly and effortlessly. She's like you isn't she baby!' she said cuddling Beau who was affectionately brushing her toned torso against her leg. Secretly she hoped Simon would buy something he would let the dogs in, as when they went on trips involving stayovers, they always put them in kennels. This was because the Range Rover was a boudoir on wheels.

'They are a technological triumph darling I must admit, but your Tess the little Tesla weighs nearly the same as my Solihull CO2 machine. She's anything but light. I'm sure we will all be driving something similar in the future. Hopefully they will have resolved those ethical issues they keep quiet about some time soon.'

'You're such a killjoy Simon.'

'Yes, I know darling, but you've experienced Donnington Park and Silverstone. Could you imagine it without the screaming engines, not to mention the intoxicating perfume of petrol and hot oil? It's the original men's fragrance.'

'It must be a man thing Simon; it just gives me a headache.'

'I think that probably has more to do with the champagne darling.'

'Haha, you may well be right. I will admit I secretly enjoy the sound of your supercharger when you're being naughty on the motorway.'

'Yes Yolanda, that is my idea of electrification. Mind you, Tony at the office was telling me he'd been listening to that Joe Rogan chap who says his new Tesla Roadster does 0-60mph in a shade over two seconds. That's more like a catapult than a car. Rogan said the technology makes his other cars seem stupid by comparison, so never say never.'

Yolanda's car was more of a luxury in truth, another e-irony as many if not most electric cars are only occasionally used, or are second cars. Her successful part-time consultancy business was almost exclusively conducted on-line, but it was important to look good, even when only taking the "children" to the park.

No one could dispute Simon and Yolanda cut quite an impressive sight, in and out of either car. They were both tall and athletically built. In Dog World they might say Yolanda and Simon were the perfect accessories for Beau and Captain. They certainly looked the part, exercising the handsome hounds whilst sporting waxed jackets, high quality denims, closely matched but not identical, and smart brown leather boots, a Barbour shop duet. Yolanda's long blonde luxuriant hair was usually restrained by a fashionable silk scarf. Simon's outfit was completed by selecting from his collection of leather or tartan tweed caps. His caps had the side benefit of covering up an ever-growing sunroof he wasn't so proud of. They looked every inch a gentleman and his lady on a country estate. Only a shotgun was missing, but being a townie why would he ever have need of a shot gun outside of the shooting range? Yolanda removed the Super Doggy from its packaging.

'This seems rather counter intuitive Simon.'

'What's that darling?'

'They've sent this emission saving product in a box which also says 100% recycled green product; yet inside its protected by dozens of pieces of this turquoise polystyrene!'

'Well, it's almost green,' Simon replied.

'Hardly darling, it's a contradiction in terms!'

'I meant turquoise is almost green!'

'Simon, you get worse!'

'What are the instructions Yolanda, is it straightforward?'

'Yes, it seems to be. One simply mixes it with tap water, according to the packet. It looks positively repulsive. I can't see them taking to this, especially when they know there is a chicken in the Aga.'

Yolanda was mistaken. Beau and Captain made as light work of their helpings of Super Doggy as Oscar, the little working-class Jack Russell from Edgeley. They licked their dishes enthusiastically. After checking each other's bowls contained no overlooked morsel, they gazed at the box of food tantalizingly out of reach on the polished Italian marble work top. It seemed they had experienced a taste of heaven. They had lost all interest in Yolanda's free-range foul. This despite it being a corn-fed specimen from Waitrose, whose enticing aroma was now permeating their exquisitely appointed kitchen.

'Settle down you two!' Simon said sternly.

'Oh I say, you sounded just like Emma Strawbridge then Simon,'

'I am flattered Yolanda. Emma Strawbridge is a wonder the way she controls her animals. She's a female Dr Dolittle, although she looks and sounds like Julie Andrews don't you think? Maybe she has some of that Mary Poppins magic?'

'Haha, now you come to mention it, you're quite right Simon, I can definitely see that. However, if she'd been in The Sound of Music she'd have been the governess of seven dogs rather than seven children. She's a good friend though, and I love her company. Next time I see her I will find out how many octaves she can sing in.'

Beau and Captain had indeed followed Simon's strict command. They had settled down again and lay on the floor looking at Simon and Yolanda as if awaiting their next instructions.'

'Well, I say, you two beauties enjoyed that didn't you? Give mummy a kiss.' Beau and Captain raised themselves on their front legs licking Yolanda's face enthusiastically.

'Good girl, good boy, look mummy has a special treat for you.'

She dropped a couple of their favourite treats in front of them. They showed not a glimmer of interest before turning their attention back to the cupboard where the Super Doggy was now stored.

'That's strange Simon!'

'Very strange Yolanda, they usually beg for those treats! Never mind, it may just be the novelty. I'm sure it will wear off.'

Beau and Captain were as satisfied as the cat that got the cream. In fact, they were almost purring as they retired to their princely, blanket laden wicker baskets. In such a salubrious and cultured environment, it was fitting they didn't share Oscar's special talent.

# Chapter 12

## Big Farmer (Around six months later)

'Apart from your usual big thick fatty steaks is there anything you'd like from the Farmer's Market Simon? I'm popping over to Knutsford tomorrow then meeting Emma again for a spot of lunch.'

'I don't think so darling, I'll place myself in your capable hands. Any grilling steak will do, especially if it's dry aged for at least a month; letting enzymes eat it first cuts down on my chewing.'

'That sounds disgusting Simon.'

'Essentially darling it's the initial stages of decomposition, but it's also where the succulence and flavour comes from. We should never be slaves to sell by dates, while we have eyes, noses, and brains.'

'Don't worry I know you like your meat one day this side of rancid. I'll make sure it has some good cover and marbling how you like it.'

Simon was a steak connoisseur and always sided with Mrs Spratt the fat loving lady from the nursery rhyme. He stopped short of licking the platter clean however, unless he was home alone.

'I must say Simon, it's a lot easier around the meat stalls with Beau and Captain nowadays. Before Super Doggy it was an ordeal trying to control them but now, they are completely disinterested, and as good as gold. Who would have thought all these months on they would still be enjoying that awful looking mush?'

'I know what you mean Yolanda but look at them both. Goodness knows what that secret formula is, they look like Crufts champions of champions. Something is at work we can't see. They are as strong as lions yet as gentle as kittens, aren't you now, hmm, aren't you?' Simon was stroking and cuddling them, and they licked and nuzzled him excitedly.

'Ok that's enough' he laughed.

The following morning was cold, but unusually bright. Tess had plenty of charge and Knutsford's charms were beckoning. On days like this Yolanda kept the radio off and her windows down despite the chill. With no engine noise she chose to drive with just the sounds of the countryside for entertainment. The performance nature laid on was exhilarating, as the morning sunlight vividly animated the countless green hues of Cheshire's fields and hedgerows. The still plentiful leaves in the overhanging canopies were a thousand shades of gold and purpley brown. The leaves danced and sparkled as the breeze and the sunlight coalesced to produce a shimmering light show on the lingering dew. It was a lumiere extraordinaire that would have Jean Michel Jarre wringing his little French hands in envy.

Ever industrious squirrels were busy collecting the last of the nuts to bury in local gardens, most of which they would forget about, having ruined many bulbs for the gardener's spring flowers. If only they had the memories of elephants, although a forgetful squirrel is preferable to a reliable elephant in the flowerbed or running along the trellis.

For the enterprise to which Yolanda was bound, the sheep and cattle thronging the fields were a living advertisement. She shivered, not at the cold, but at the thought of the countryside without the animals. Wild flowers are nice in their own way but farmland without cows or sheep is the stuff of nightmares. It would redefine and impoverish our lives. She breathed the invigorating fresh cold air deeply and contemplated the sounds and sights which as always proved enchanting. Even the slightly disturbing spectacle of a cow lifting its tail before unleashing its torrent of natural fertilisers gratifies the soul. Strangely welcome too is that initially disturbing change of air when passing fields undergoing muckspreading. It all ties us to our country in an organic way that no policy document or algorithm driven media campaign ever could.

Yolanda's favourite Farmer's Market was holding the fort, bringing together produce from several different farms in the area. It certainly isn't a cheap option, but the quality is beyond question. If it is within budget, then the extra outlay is surely worth it. Many are happy to pay a little more, they say the experience itself has intrinsic value.

Yolanda glided gracefully among the farmer's stalls where all manner of wholesome produce, from venison to chocolate could be procured. She spotted Norman Owens, a retired steward of the land of whom she'd grown fond during her many visits. He had often given her good advice, from how to spot a healthy parsnip, to international governmental affairs. She made her way over to him to say hello.

'How lovely to see you again Mr Owens, how are you today?'

'I'm as fit as a butcher's dog thank you Miss Yolanda, which is saying something at my age. I see you're showing off your magnificent hounds again. They are a fine pair, there's no mistaking that. Do you mind if I have a quick feel?'

Farmer Owens crouched down stroking Beau and Captain, prodding at their well-muscled flesh, testing their symmetry and form.

'Yes, splendid creatures indeed,' he said approvingly. 'By the way, there's someone I'd like you to meet Yolanda, a friend of mine is up today. His family have farmed land between Tetbury and Cirencester for generations. He's a regular fountain of knowledge, and he would no doubt benefit from seeing a pretty face on a chilly morning like this. There he is holding counsel by that cheese stall! Noah, there's someone here who enjoys the ramblings of two old codgers like us!'

Farmer Noah Bartlett made his way over, pleased to be of service and more than ready to share a little of his lifetime's harvest of wisdom. His rosy-red face spoke more of fresh air and hard work than blood pressure. He had thick white bristling mutton chops, but not to cliché levels, and was dressed in the classic farmer style, as was his old friend Norman. They could almost have been twins, but separated at birth as Noah had the broadest West Country accent ever heard, that and the fact Noah Bartlett stood around six foot six.

'Noah, this is Yolanda, she's a lovely lady, and revels in tales about life in the country and such like,' said Farmer Owens.

'Good morning Noah, I did hear your name correctly didn't I?'

'That's right Miss, as in the man with the big boat'.

'Are you happy with me using your first name by the way?'

'Yes of course you can call me Noah. We doesn't stand on ceremony where I'm from. And we tries not to stand on celery neither, does we Norman?' Norman laughed politely at his friend's weak agricultural joke.

'Back home they mostly calls me Mr Noah, and my closest friends generally just call me Bartlett. Call me anything you like. I'm sure a lady of your stature wouldn't be calling me anything untoward.'

He offered his hand which Yolanda took nervously as it too was enormous, with thick strong fingers. It was so smooth and leathery, Yolanda thought it resembled a high-quality gardening glove. She needn't have worried, his handshake was firm but surprisingly gentle, and to her surprise, quite pleasant. He knew his own strength as his fingers double as tools and can be as dexterous or vice-like as the task demands. He then went through the same routine as Farmer Owens, assessing the dogs' torsos and hindquarters.

'Two beauties you've got there Miss. They're in fine fettle. They seem unusually sturdy, especially around the collar for Dobermans, or should I say Dobermen?' He was clearly pleased with his ongoing impromptu comedy show. Yolanda briefly halted his momentum:

'Actually, this one's Beau, she's a bitch.'

Visually checking Beau's undercarriage, he said:

'A little bitch are you? Ha ha, I knows one or two of them alright! So she is, so she is, no meat or veg down there! You start behaving yourself better young lady, har har har. I has to laugh at my own jokes Miss Yolanda or no-one will. Now then, let's have a look at them pudding-mashers.' He tugged at Captain's teeth.

'By gumption they're in there all right. He could crack the bones of a rhinoceros with those. He's got jaws like the mother-in-law Godzilla, I mean God bless her. I'm only kidding by the way and don't mean no offence. I always had a soft spot for the wife's mother bless her soul. It was a boggy patch in our lower field and that's where she's buried. I thought burying the old boiler there might dry out the land some but there's no sign of it. I'm being awful aren't I, but that's where all our family are going to be buried one day, me included. I really loved the old girl truth be told but never dreamt we'd get permission to bury owt but dogs or cats. It seems change of use nowadays is a walk in the park, as long as it ain't for food production. Are you local, or is this a day out for you, there seems to be folk here from hither and yonder?'

'I'm just visiting. My fiancée and I live about half an hour away. I love coming here, and lately it seems a touch hit and miss in the shops for fresh produce.' Realising this was a springboard for Noah, Farmer Owens asked if anyone wanted a hot drink. Noah opted for a strong tea, two tea bags and no sugar, or white death as he calls it. Yolanda opted for a skinny latte.

'I'll see you both in about half an hour judging by that queue!'

'Now then Miss Yolanda, as you were saying about food being suddenly scarce in God's own country. A lot of us farmers think there are some dark forces at work. We always used to think it was just that Common Market looking after Frank and Gerry, but things are adding up less and less. Take poultry for example, birds have always been prone to a bout of flu just like us. Now it's talk of new super killer bird-flu strains as if farming only began in our lifetime. Instead of separating them out when they've got a sniffle so to speak, we has to kill the whole blooming flock. What do you think that does to the price of poultry and eggs in the shops?

'I never took to the idea of reducing food crops for rapeseed back in the 1970's neither. They called it set-aside. The only thing it was setting aside was common sense. These 'ere seed oils were only used for oiling your sprockets.' They uses all manner of chemicals and high temperatures to get anything useful out, by which time they've probably turned good to bad. Some say it messes up a bloke's plumbing down below, but it's hard to know and truth is getting harder to come by. Seems to me like they grow summat instead of food, then find a use for it later. Almost a third of all agriculture now is growing seed-oil crops instead of good healthy grains and veggies.

'They've convinced folk animal fats are all bad, yet there are more tubbies keeling over with heart attacks than ever. You only has to watch old films or look at black and white foters to see folks were leaner and fitter back in the day when they were munching dripping butties before bed. Eskimos live on meat and blubber, yet heart issues are virtually unheard of amongst them. I thinks it was smoke either from cigarettes or chimneys be they on house or factory what once shortened our lives; that and the poorest not having the means to buy enough food or keep their houses warm. Mind you I'm still partial to a puff on the old pipe.

'They put the wind up folk over animal by-products and created a market that wasn't there before. Animal products were in everything from make-up to sweeties and we rightly patted ourselves on the back for being like them there Red Indians, what let nothing of the buffalos they killed go to waste. Thanks to the anti-meat crowd, it's wasted and just goes to landfill, what a waste of blooming money! It was natural, biodegradable and organic as it gets. Instead, they uses other methods involving all manner of chemicals and processing and growing crops we didn't need before, all while saying agriculture is bad for the planet. It's all cock-eyed tomfoolery.

'If the last few years has taught us anything, it's that we should be careful about blindly following men in white coats, or politicians who can't even lie straight in bed. We lives in a small country, with a population what's almost doubled in my lifetime. We needs more food, not less, but they're asking us, or telling us more like, to grow less. They're going to starve us all. They're saying stop growing crops, then in the next breath, they says stop eating meat. None of that makes no sense, unless the plan is for us all to eat like birds, that or they plan to thin out the human herds too.

'A lot of folk don't know only a third of our country is any use for growing crops in any case. It's either too hilly, too rocky, too wet or too inhospitable to be viable. Nature, or God if you're a woman of faith, came up with the perfect solution. I'm assuming you're not one of them there vegetarians.'

'No, no, not at all Noah. I like a bit of everything.'

'Good for you Miss, but each to their own. Well as I was saying, animals are hardy creatures, and can thrive in areas we can't grow arable crops on. They's got guts like mongrels they has, and can eat 'most anything. They eats scrub, thistle and weeds and turns it into something we can eat, and that's meat. While they're at it they fertilise the soil with their muck. Cattle, pigs and sheep can easily cope with husks and pods a person can't digest. They eats that, then we eats them, it's the circle of life and as natural as you can get. It's not as though we eats 'em alive, and most have a safer and happier life than if they were in the wild. Some say their lives are shorter but I 'asn't met a cow or sheep what's been planning for retirement. They doesn't know one flipping day from the next, as much as we loves them. Along with some nice fresh vegetables, we gets all the minerals and fats we needs to keep our brains and bodies working like they should. Best of all its blooming delicious.

'We're only doing what animals have done since the beginning of time. Look at me, I'm seventy years old and I eats anything I fancies, in sensible amounts. I uses nothing but butter, lard or dripping to cook it in, and I can still put in a day's work that would see many a youngster off. Fancy being told to start growing wild flowers and trees instead of food, as if we live in blooming fairyland. They'll be asking us to grow magic beans next, or rear geese what lays golden eggs. We only needs a disaster or a war, and hunger will take us before the bombs do.'

As Noah breathed in, Yolanda tentatively interjected,

'I believe there has been incredible upheaval in Holland for that very reason. We have friends there who say they have seen the largest protests ever and led by farmers. Their tractors lined roads for hundreds of miles with an enormous Dutch flag, the biggest flag ever made they say. They tell us the police have acted like thugs and even opened fire with live bullets, yet we've seen nothing on the news here.'

'That's why I says dark forces Miss Yolanda. It's spreading though as more and more people are waking up to what's goin' on. Nothing 'appens by chance, especially when its worldwide and Billy Gates Gruff is involved. He's been buying up farmland in America like there's no tomorrow, and now owns more of it than anyone. He's up to summat and I doubt it's to everyone's benefit.

'We hears constant warnings about floods but they don't dredge rivers no more cos of green policies. It means rivers are only half as deep as they were, so when banks burst it ain't rocket science or any other kind of science for that matter as to why. They builds housing estates with hardstanding upstream causing flooding lower down, then blame it all on the blooming climate. If there's a bonfire in Botswana or Baghdad it's all over the news saying wildfires, but there's no more land burned today than there ever was, and it usually turns out to be arson. It's only as bad as it is because the greenies don't allow clearance of scrub or controlled burning. For years the aborigines were saying the forests were upside down and it would bring disaster. All this information is public, but the TV channels keep it hidden from the masses. Leaving pertinent facts out, is tantamount to, if not outright lying in my book!'

'What on earth did the Aboriginals mean by upside down forests Noah? Is it connected with their Dreamtime creation myths? I love reading about it, it's all so colourful and enigmatic, yet somehow organic and real.'

'No Miss Yolanda, nothing magical or mystical, just understanding basic principles of land management which they've done for centuries. They just meant there was more growth at the bottom of the trees than on the canopy. It creates a veritable tinder box just waiting for a cigarette end or careless barbecuer, or worse. There's enormous protests about these policies all over the world but they covers it up. I'm not one who sees a devil behind every tree, but it seems things are being run by those who don't have our best interests at heart. How often do you hear there's going to be famines thanks to climate change? If only folk would check what they're saying once in a while, they'd see most of it don't add up. If famines are coming then why would they shut a third of farms like in Holland, the world's second biggest producers of food, that sounds like a recipe for famine.

'It ain't just in Holland though neither. We've got exactly the same thing here. They're paying us not to grow or rear food. Our MPs tell us it's out of their hands and is handed down from above government. Above government I ask you! Their hands are tied by so called sustainable development targets agreed at the UN decades ago. I'm sick to the back teeth of folk saying that's conspiracy theory. They told us their intentions and it's happening right now, right before our very eyes!

'World governments agreed to their seventeen sustainable development goals because they spooked 'em somehow. They calls us nutters for saying there's an agenda, even though the UN itself calls it Agenda 21 for the 21st century. Then they has Agenda 30 and Agenda 50 being the actual years they wants to complete items on their checklist, and every item will impoverish us. Everything that's going on is exactly as their documents show, so where's the conspiracy I ask you? I used to clam up too when someone said conspiracy theory then I started actually looking at evidence. It's a trick to say shut up and stop asking awkward questions.

'Too many farmers are committing suicide, it ain't right! Instead of blowing their own brains out, I wish they'd use those cartridges somewhere else, if you takes my meaning. Half our greenhouses are mothballed cos growers can't afford to heat them. Greenhouse food growers use a magic ingredient once known only to them, to scientists and to God. It's called CO2, the invisible miracle, the gas of life, even the breath of God ain't far wrong, assuming that ain't blasphemy. They pumps it in in high concentrations and that's what helps them grow two or three times as much food in a fraction of the time and space. CO2 is the very source of life itself, but there's nutcases want to demonise it, calling it poison and pollution when it's plant food. Any Tom Dick or Harriet can look up international crop yields and see they are up year on year, and at record levels, and left alone they'd continue to break new records. When you get a crop failure which has happened since the dawn of time it's highlighted and blown out of all proportion. Climate change is always the villain, yet even NASA say the planet is greening not browning overall.

'The earth's a complicated place, and if you ain't sure how summat works don't go trying to fix it. And what if it ain't broke? We've only been here five minutes in the grand scheme of things. I remembers when we only had to worry about global warming, then again every farmer knows there were vineyards as far north as Carlisle in centuries past. It seems it ain't just what temperatures you measure, it's also when you start measuring from. Now I ain't got no fancy college degree, but I ain't as green as I'm cabbage looking neither. Farming has been in my family for generations, so I always paid heed to weather and what not, even at school, when I was there that is. We're in what boffins call an interglacial period. Despite the scaremongering we're only one degree above the coldest it's been in 10,000 years. We're two degrees cooler than the warmest it's been in 10,000 years 'n'all!

'Summat else they won't tell youngsters nowadays is in the last interglacial 150,000 years ago, elephants and hippos were roaming the banks of the Thames. Now that'd put London Zoo out of business! Natural history as it used to be called, was once interesting and fun. Now they seem bent on giving children nightmares instead of hopes and dreams. It borders on child abuse by my reckoning. At least two generations have been brainwashed. Now they are rolling stuff out that would have got them tarred and feathered in times past.

'We doesn't want children being afeared of their own shadows like that poor little moppet from Sweden. Poor thing is being used and abused to my mind. They've turned an innocent little green elf into a goblin. That's another thing, if you've got problems affecting the whole world what kind of blithering halfwit would ask a child for advice for crying out loud? They don't tell you she was always a troubled soul as a little girl. She was scared of the dark, scared of spiders, she had eating disorders, selective mutism, asperges, OCD and autism. Twas her grandma gave all that away believe it or no. They even scared her into believing she can see CO2 what's invisible for crying out loud. Her family have always been into theatrics and she's their marionette if you ask me!

'They rarely stops talking about dinosaurs these days, yet they never tell no one CO2 was twixt five and twenty times what it is now, when they say them there monsters were roaming the earth. I says to my dear old wife, it must have been cos them dinosaurs would have needed such outlandish cars and tractors. Seems to me they just spotted that the coldest point in the last 10,000 years coincided with the industrial revolution starting, but correlation ain't causation as the BBC are so fond of saying when it suits. The fact they only tell you half that story makes old cynics like me has my big furry ears pricking up, hence my point about when you start measuring from. They've milked that 1850 date more than us farmers do our dairy herds!'

'So, what do you think it is Noah? I've known for a while, farmers are up in arms, but it seems more and more people are suspicious. My fiancée and I are in unrelated businesses, but amongst our clients, we find an increasing scepticism in the dominant narratives.'

'Well Miss Yolanda, I increasingly thinks it's as much about controlling us as it is anything else. I remembers around the time of Lizzie's Silver Jubilee, they said an Ice Age was almost upon us and our fields would become frozen wastelands. The same solutions were put forward then too: less meat, less energy and less humans. When it stopped cooling for a few decades and warmed up a bit they came up with global warming. The same UN, or unelected nutcases as I calls 'em, eventually came up with a trump card Joseph Goebbels would have been proud of. With a catch all like climate change, anything what goes wrong with the weather can be used to stop your business or raise your tax. It's being used like a slaver's whip and they brook no discussion. It's not just hot weather now, it's rain, snow, floods, drought, and everything in-between. Everything's a threat. Everything's an emergency, yet those doing the warning we'll all be drowned, buys big houses on the sea front and have bigger carbon footprints than one of those brontosauruses in his oversized Hummer.'

'Yes Noah, I've noticed how phrases like "since records began" are used as though it has any real meaning. The same scientists who believe earth is forty billion years old obsessively concentrate on the last century which seems somewhat ludicrous.'

'Now at the risk of making your ears bleed Miss, they talks about average world temperatures, but any fool could work out they didn't have reliable data measuring equipment across most of the world, until the last 'alf century. It's all done with modelling. I thinks their models are like chocolate fire-guards. They almost bankrupted livestock farms with the codswallop from their models during BSE.

I don't know if you know but the twerp who's advice they followed then was Neil Ferguson, or Professor Pantsdown as he'll always be remembered since lockdown. After his covid death prediction fiasco, causing lock downs and almost bankrupting the country you'd think they'd tell 'em to shove their models where the sun don't shine. He seems a reliable so called academic who will always provide them with the fear they need for their programmes. If I hired an electrician who almost burned my farmhouse down I wouldn't keep going back to him, would you? Folks don't seem to learn. It's a blooming great con in my estimation.'

'My occasional neighbour down Tetbury way is a chief culprit too. You may have heard of him. These days he goes by the name of Charles, King Charles III. I wishes Lizzie was still around to keep him in line, even put him over her knee if necessary, king or no. He owns half of Cornwall, a string of castles and his place in Tetbury is a sight for sore eyes. Highgrove would fit me and all my family nicely, yours 'n' all. He's got an estate in Scotland the size of Liverpool, but he tells the likes of us we needs to live more simply. He'll be going the way of his namesake and predecessor if he's not careful. Folks will only stand so much before they crack.

'That might be another reason they're after us farmers, as we're the ones what still has guns. Nothing says not today thank you like a twelve-bore. Has you heard of that there Professor William Happer on the YouTube? He spells it out alright and exposes the con, with heavy duty science and exposes what's behind it. None of 'em dare debate him or his fellow scientists saying stop the nonsense! Oh, hello here comes Norman at last with those drinks. I thought you'd gone to pick some fresh coffee beans Norman. I've just finished a sermon, hasn't I Miss Yolanda?'

'It was quite enlightening actually Mr Bartlett. It's good to get a different perspective now and again, and as you're a farmer I'm getting it straight from the horse's mouth.' Yolanda was becoming like Noah. Her joke aligned well with his regrettable repertoire.

'There's some belting dog food at that stall over there Miss Yolanda, all natural and full of jelly.' said Farmer Owens.

Yolanda blushed a little.

'Oh. I don't know if you've heard about it, but we're using that new Chinese wonder food for our dogs at the moment. I hope you won't shoot me too Noah.'

'No, no Miss Yolanda, I offers my opinions and no more. I've no designs on telling others how or what to think, and my talk of shooting people is only Gloucestershire glouting, I doesn't mean it. It's for each person to make their own minds up, then give their opinion at the ballot box. If we can't discuss things there's no hope for no-one. I did hear on the grapevine there was a trial on for that there dog food somewhere, I just didn't know it was in these parts. From what I can see though, and I have an eye and a nose for these things, these two are looking none the worse for it. I've never seen two finer specimens. How long have they been on it?'

'Oh, about six months give or take.'

'Well, they're looking grand, and no-one can dispute that, but I'd keep a close eye on them. I just hope it's been tested proper like.'

'I hope you don't think we're rude, but we'll have to leave you in peace as we've a bit of business to attend to Miss Yolanda,' said Farmer Owens. 'The chap we're meeting has come an hour earlier than he said and has asked if we can see him now. Would that be alright with you?'

'Yes of course it is, I can drink my latte as I shop, while you gents plan a British uprising, just let me get home before you blockade the roads.'

'Haha you're sharp as a tack Miss Yolanda and no mistake. We won't be doing anything today and we've yet to exhaust meetings with officials and ministers before our muck spreaders and the like take to the streets. I hope to see you and your dogs soon, and I'm sure I will, barring disaster.'

'I hope so too Mr Owens, but who knows what tomorrow brings?'

Yolanda's final words were slightly pessimistic. Had she inadvertently tapped into her "woman's intuition?"

# Chapter 13

## Baked Beans and Brylcream

Across Stockport, using traditional dog food wasn't actually prohibited. Super Doggy wasn't actually mandated, but a campaign of shame was well under way for the Super Doggy stragglers. The stragglers were also called hesitants or undecideds. It was too risky to call them science deniers just yet, over a dog food launch in its early stages. They weren't hesitant however, they were adamant, and completely decided.

Elsewhere, "I use Super Doggy" profiles were adorning Stockport Fakebookers' home pages. As the mysterious, unforeseen supply chain issues had emptied supermarket shelves of all the old dog foods and supplements, rebels had to travel out of town to maintain a deadly tinned meat doggy diet. As usually happens, a few entrepreneurial smaller local shops and petrol station franchisees began to run clandestine under the counter trade. The only problem was that they never knew when a concerned covert council zealot might come calling for a friendly convo. In this case an interesting figure entered a local petrol station store and approached the till. He looked like a wannabe Elliot Ness with a 1930's style tailored baggy suit, trilby and black and white leather brogues.

'Are you just paying for petrol sir?'

'Maybe Mack, but what else might I be paying for, have you got things not on display I should know about, if you catch my drift?'

'Catch your drift? The only drift I'm catching is your Poundshop aftershave, it smells like bloody vinegar! And my name is Riyad, not Mack! Now how are you paying, I'm very busy?'

'Good for you Riyad. The name's Beretta, Jake Beretta, SMBC special investigator.'

'What's SMBC when it's at home?'

'Stockport Metropolitan Borough Council, Mack!'

'I told you my name is Riyad! Are you paying or not?'

'Word on the street says someone is selling contraband in this neighbourhood. Is there something you'd like to tell me?'

'Why would I know anything? I sell fuel and groceries and I don't need you coming in here poking your nose around! Pump Four, twenty-five pounds and eight pence please.'

'Listen wise guy, don't be busting my chops. The shoe-shine boy on Shaw Heath says you seem to be selling a lot of tinned goods lately.'

'I have been, I've had a run on baked beans, they're on offer, 60p a tin, bloody bargain. Do you want some?'

Beretta removed his trilby and carefully groomed his dark, Brylcreemed hair in the reflection in the plastic screen between them.

'Listen Ma...er Riyad. People down at City Hall are getting impatient, it would be in your best interests to come clean. We don't want you to lose your licence to trade now do we? That would be such a shame!'

'Where the hell is City Hall?'

'Stockport Town Hall then.'

'Stockport Town Hall? Is that where you're from?'

'I tend to get moved around. I used to have a small office in Stopford House before the decarbonisation project.'

'Stopford House! That's the ugly concrete pig of a building near the court isn't it! It's in the right place, it looks like a bloody prison! Who designed it, Joseph Stalin?'

'No, as a matter of fact it was designed by Stockport's Director of Development and Town Planning in the 1970's.'

'Bloody hell, say no more. It's a pity it isn't a prison because you lot want locking up with him. Coming round badgering local businessmen. You should be ashamed of yourselves.'

'Listen buddy, selling dog meat isn't illegal yet, but it's antisocial. You're breaking our social contract. Do you get my meaning?'

'I'm not your buddy, and how the hell do you decarbonise a bloody building, and why? Is it because it's full of pencil pushers?'

'They changed the windows, installed air source heat pumps and so on. I think it cost over £17 million with all the other alterations.'

'£17 million and you still have the cheek to come talking to me about tinned dog food. Like I said you all want locking up. Bloody idiots the lot of you. You don't live in the real world!'

'Why did you say dog food? I never said nothing about dog food. Is there something you'd like to tell me Riyad?'

'OK you got me Mr Baretta. I will tell you everything I know. I saw you pull up in your Fiat Panda. I thought why is that idiot wearing that hat in his car when he hasn't the headroom. You've a badge on your charity shop suit that says, "Covert Dog Food Sales Investigator." If brains were dynamite, you couldn't blow that bloody hat off. Why don't you bugger off back to Stopford house and waste another seventeen million?'

'It wasn't a waste. I was told it will pay for itself eventually and much of the money came from grants Mr Smartypants'

'Yes, well that sums you lot up doesn't it? Bloody grants? Who from, the tooth-fairy? It all comes from taxpayers. Where's my grant for all the money I lost through lockdown and now these energy prices thanks to your idiotic sanctions that hurt us more than Russia. As a matter of fact, I don't even want grants because half of the money is wasted with administrators. Let people get on with their lives and businesses and move obstacles out of the way and stop screwing us!'

Agent Baretta leaned forward so his face was right up against the screen.

'Look Mack.'

'Riyad!'

'Ok Riyad, I'm just doing my job. I don't like it no more than you do! It's my job to keep these streets clean.'

'Good idea, I'll get you a brush!'

'Quite a smart Alec aren't you Riyad. You should be on Broadway.'

Agent Baretta had to step back from the screen as he was so close his breath had steamed it up so they couldn't see each other.

'Sorry I steamed up your security screen.'

'It's a covid screen! You idiots made me put it up so I could stay open.'

'That's as maybe bud, but wise up! It might be ideal for deterring microscopic viral particles, but it might not be so good at stopping council sanctions. Capiche?'

'Stopping viral particles? Bloody government and councils are the virus. There's a bloody great hole where you pass me your money or swipe your card you crackpot. Every time that door opens a draught blows round the screen, bringing whatever is in the air with it, like your Hugo Ross aftershave. One big bloody piss take! Speaking of money, twenty-five pounds and eight pence please! Have you got the means to pay?'

'Listen, I'll cut you some slack and look the other way today, but get with the programme, you're on borrowed time. Don't mess with the authorities if you want to stay on Easy Street!'

'I don't even know where bloody Easy Street is Crackpot. Have you got any ID by the way?'

The agent flashed his SMBC badge and offered a generic business card which he'd had printed himself. He replaced his trilby adjusting it in the KN95 super-screen.

'I thought you said your name was Jake Baretta. It says here you're called Graham Barrett.'

'Yeah well, my middle name is trouble.'

'Your middle name is Nutcase more like! I'll give you bloody trouble! Are you paying for your petrol, or shall I call the police?'

'Yes, I've said my piece.'

'Cash or card?'

'Card please. Oh, by the way, can I just grab a bottle of milk too?'

'Yes, it's over there at the bottom of the fridge.'

'Look Riyad, I'm no good at being noble, but it doesn't take much to see that the problems of us little people don't amount to a hill of beans in this crazy world. Someday you'll understand that.'

'I don't know what the bloody hell you are talking about but if you want baked beans there's a stack of them there by the milk.'

'Oh 60p, wow, you're right, that is a good deal, I'll take a couple of those too please after all!'

'Twenty-eight pounds and forty pence please. Do you need a bag?'

'Yes please.'

'OK that's twenty-eight pounds and sixty pence.'

After paying, the agent leaned forward again but getting too near to the screen he knocked his trilby cockeyed.

'One more thing before I go Mack. If you're packing heat....'

'I've told you; name is bloody Riyad and if you don't get out now I'll call my brothers and we'll decarbonise you. Now bugger off!'

The agent straightened his hat and left the premises just as another customer came in.

'Hi Riyad, who was that, one of the Ant Hill Mob?'

'Oh, just some jumped up jobsworth from the council. Did you want some more you know what?'

'Yeah, please Riyad, give us four cans of Pedigree Chum if you've got it.'

'No problem brother, there you go.'

'Nice one mate, I've got a loaf and I'll grab two tins of beans. I've got my own bag, there's a tenner, keep the change.'

'Thank you, see you my friend.'

Riyad the petrol station franchisee is a classic anomaly for some political activists. They are keen for him to be a victim, and therefore a pawn in their political chess game. Like so many he isn't the least bit interested in their rules. He votes Labour but is socially conservative. He disagrees with abortion, homosexuality and trans ideology. He is privately, slightly racist, especially concerning Jews and Sikhs, and isn't wild about what he calls idolatrous Hindus. The unspoken animosity among many, if not most in those groups is mutual. In Stockport, as in most towns, they live and let live, so it stays under the surface, much like remaining or leaving the EU opinions once did. That way, normal life and commerce goes on.

Riyad says the do-gooders do more harm than good when they stir up racial issues, and they should get proper jobs that keep them busier. Riyad is self-employed, highly motivated and independent and always on the lookout for more staff. His family has several diesel-powered private cabs, and they resent excessive government interference. Nonetheless, he is technically a minority and therefore part of their victim club when it suits.

Fortunately for Riyad he faced no further special investigations. Whether this was down to his ethnicity is anyone's guess, but he remains as popular locally as his legendary countryman and adoptive Stopfordian, Mr Ahmed the one-time rug seller. Riyad's bonus profits from his contraband have also softened his attitude towards haram hounds. He would never go beyond owning an outside dog even so.

# Chapter 14

## Dressed Up Like a Dog's Dinner
## Late October 2024

Yolanda's market trip had been a resounding success. She had her light lunch with the legendary Emma Strawbridge who advised of a splendid new venue. They convened another coffee morning, where they could discuss business, market fluctuations and handbags, and this was the day. Timewise, it was only a couple of days after the horrific attack on the young family in Heaviley. The deadly event was on the news, but reporting was strangely muted, with the usual deflection that investigations were ongoing. The main thrust of the reporting suggested it was a tragedy and no more, a one off.

What nobody knew at that stage, was that changes were taking place in the bamboo dogs. Genetic codes were being disrupted like computer programmes surrendering to viruses. Inherent, but latent instincts were awoken and magnified in the Super Doggy population. It was by no means uniform, but when certain things aligned, then trouble was in store. Unlike the issues in the food shops, there would be no interruptions in this particular supply line. The polynucleotide chains were stacking their shelves. An unseen double helix hellscape was unfolding and was a special offer you couldn't miss, and Yolanda most certainly did not miss it.

As we learned earlier, Emma Strawbridge's main expertise was dog behaviour. Although a quiet and unassuming lady, she could control dogs just with her voice. She did this not by whispering, but with sharp, concise commands that even made passers-by stand to attention. As Emma's new venue for the coffee morning was a considerable upgrade from their usual coffee shops, they decided to also upgrade coffee to a gourmet lunch. This new highbrow hotspot was aimed squarely at up-market mamas. The unique angle for this rendezvous point was the compulsory condition they must also bring their up-market dogs. It was situated in a smallholding in the upscale district of Nether Alderley but put all thoughts of farms from your mind. Leaving the main road, its gates were bespoke, and automatic. They bore no signage, and certainly no vulgar dog motifs especially paw print stickers beloved among caravanners. Words were largely unnecessary because luxury was proclaimed from every elegantly designed feature.

Once in the car park a potential patron could quickly assess if they were an appropriate client. It wasn't the Basil Fawlty 'No riff raff allowed' approach. It was the subtle placement of the price list in the glass foyer. There were no prices. The message was clear, if one has to ask, one should not proceed down the red carpet! Once inside, an embossed sign, clearly the work of a skilled calligrapher declared:

*WELCOME TO WAGGER-MAMAS*

*For Canines and Felines of Breeding.*

*No actual cats or sportswear of any kind allowed!*

The rules were strictly enforced. Occasionally, shocked and disappointed David Lloyd Diamond Members scurried home in shame to change. The surrounding environs are overflowing with ladies that lunch, brunch, or sip champagne publicly at any and every opportunity. Wagger-Mamas did not need, nor intend to compromise on their ambience filter. One just knew if one didn't belong there.

Emma had explained to Yolanda that a platinum make-over was advisable before embarking on the Wagger-Mama experience. New hair, new outfit, definitely no Gok Wan inspired designer and Primark combos. Actual diamonds were a pre-requisite, after all they were already taking man's best friend, so a girl's best friend was a given.

Yolanda had even attempted an unsuccessful charm offensive to borrow Simon's Autobiography for the afternoon. Simon said he couldn't risk damage to his optional white ostrich leather seats, even for this extravagant excursion. His staff occasionally asked to borrow the car for special occasions too. He said the ostrich seats didn't mean he could 'bury his head in the sand' for the sake of altruism. He also said people asking to borrow his Autobiography was the 'story of his life.'

Dom Perignon ordered, Yolanda and Emma consulted the menu. No food was offered for the dogs, they were expected to behave and enjoy their water, admittedly served in exquisite silverware. If you can't control your pets, you can't control yourself was the inference. At the next table, a coiffured quintet was enjoying some afternoon exceptionalism. They were what are referred to in Stockport as Bramhall Girls. It is a particular look perfected in the trendy suburban Bramhall Village. As one might expect, Stockport is usually omitted in written correspondence even though Bramhall is in the borough. Cheshire is infinitely preferable as the final locator. Overall they're not a million miles away from Essex girls but without the gobs. A crude limerick is afield from chaps of the rugger fraternity regarding such ladies. Here is offered a sanitized version:

*Their faces are smooth be it nose cheek or jowl,*

*their foundation is deep, tis laid on with a trowel.*

*Through nipping and tucking, and some lipo-sucking,*

*their age has been hid so they look ripe for… plucking.*

*But make-up can crack, as the champagne's knocked back,*

*But mood lighting helps and the end game's the sack.*

*But though their years be concealed, by the dawn they're revealed,*

*So we'll give you fair warning… just be gone before morning!*

Though shallow and dripping with male toxicity, it lacks the more potent venom present in the gossip only ladies themselves can supply; however, Wagger-Mammas was not the place for such bitchery, and all were on their best behaviour. One of the lunching ladies looked over at Emma:

'Excuse me, I hope you don't think I'm rude, but we were wondering if you were Emma Strawbridge by any chance?'

'My word! Am I famous? I had no idea anyone knew who I was.'

'We heard your friend call you Emma and seeing your four dogs and their absolute obedience, we surmised you might be the Emma Strawbridge featured in the Gazette. Your article was priceless, rather like this menu.'

'Your detective skills are impeccable. I am indeed Emma Strawbridge, and it's lovely to meet you ladies. I will be signing autographs after dessert.'

They all laughed politely before exchanging further pleasantries, then continuing with their afternoon affectations. Yolanda and Emma both opted for the braised ox cheek, and being conscious of retaining their winter beach bodies, a shared bowl of olives without bread sufficed for a starter. The main course was a culinary triumph.

'My goodness Emma, this meat is as tender as fillet steak.'

'Isn't it just? This asparagus is exquisite too. Did you notice it said it is sautéed in butter which they hand churn on the premises?'

'No, I didn't see that Emma, but it doesn't surprise me, they seem to have left nothing to chance. How did you find out about this place by the way? I hadn't even heard about it.'

'I heard from a friend at the tennis club. Apparently, part of the exclusivity is that they don't advertise. They work on the assumption that the right people will invite the right people. I hear many ladies have purchased pedigree dogs costing thousands just in order to come here. The no dog, no entry clause could scupper a perfectly delightful afternoon for the dogless.'

'Quite right too. I think they are doing people a favour. I couldn't imagine my life without Beau and Captain now. They are part of the family, even if Simon won't let them in his wretched Range Rover. Apart from that I think he loves them as much as I do.'

The ladies ate the meagre portions synonymous with posh nosh and elegantly sipped their champagne.

'Mmm said Emma, at the risk of repeating myself, that ox cheek was absolutely delectable. I wonder what cut it is exactly.'

'Do you know, I've no idea Emma! I really ought to, as Simon has expansive knowledge about meat, which he loves to share. His grandfather owned a large wholesale meat company and he used to let him visit. I imagine it's a French expression, or a play on words. It could even be more Chinese gobbledegook like Super Doggy. Either way, I think I will buy some next time I'm in Knutsford.'

If Farmers Bartlett or Owens had been present, they could have enlightened them. On the other hand, the ladies may have preferred to have remained ignorant. The farmers would have told them they had effectively just enjoyed a plate of dog food. With cattle or sheep. the more work the muscles do, the tougher the meat. Tender cuts come from the back end and stewing and braising meats the front. The back end of a grazer is basically for ballast. Cattle spend all day leaning forward chewing grass. The front legs and shoulders do the heavy lifting, but the cheek muscles are rarely at rest. In its raw uncooked form ox cheek is almost purple, and hard and springy, like a rubber running track. For centuries, cheek was for dogs and peasants. When Michelin starred chefs started braising it for hours and hours on end, it became a jaw dropping delicacy, ideal fodder for establishments such as Wagger-Mamas. One might say it is fine dining's equivalent of a £40 tin of Winalot but with a five hundred percent mark-up.

As all the dogs present that day were on the bamboo diet, it all passed them by completely. The ladies of the local chattering classes were providing the perpetual jaw movement that afternoon; unaware they soon might be considered a gourmet offering by some present.

All those present in Wagger Mamas that afternoon were largely oblivious to exactly what had happened a day or two earlier in Heaviley. Kevin the long-haired Labrador had become extremely overly affectionate with Ruthie and Ethan, before his lethal transformation. How the children had laughed and giggled at his silly exuberance and frenzied licking as they rolled and tumbled around the floor with him. Jenna smiled to herself as she tidied the kitchen hearing their joy. If Adam had made use of Riyad's contraband and if Jenna had the means, she could have been there with the ladies in Wagger Mamas, if only to see how the other half die.

*Author's note: As the deaths of Ruthie, Ethan and their mummy were somewhat upsetting, further and imminent mortalities will be caricatured.*

'Simba, what are you doing?' Emma said in annoyance. Simba had left the other dogs, Thumper, Hugo, Chestnut and of course Captain and Beau, and was licking her ankles vigorously.

'Sit down!' Emma demanded, 'Sit! I-Said-Sit!'

It was the worst possible scenario she could imagine, her dog acting like a feral mongrel in Wagger-Mamas of all places.

'Stop it, stop it at once! Hugo, do not copy Simba, SIT!'

Simba and Hugo were rottweilers both from the same litter. The new diet caused them to resemble small bison, such were their enhanced neck and shoulder muscles. They were licking Emma with a zeal which became increasingly manic. It was somewhat disturbing for Emma as they were not usually given to such puppylike displays. They weren't barking or growling, just doing what doggies do when expressing their affection. This however was neither the time nor the place. Emma was becoming slightly distressed, as the other ladies and the staff were looking over. Most shocked of all were the ladies Emma had spoken to earlier. Was the Gazette article fake news?

'I am really sorry everybody, I don't know what's come over them. They've never acted like this before. I will take them out right away.'

Emma stood up and pulled Simba's lead sharply,

'Come on Simba, you are in serious trouble young man. Ouch! What are you doing? He's bitten my finger Yolanda, I'm bleeding.'

Simba suddenly growled and barked ominously. It was so loud and threatening, Emma was visibly shocked.

'Stop it! Stop it immediately! Bad dog, bad dog!'

Simba licked her bloodied hand as forcefully as he had licked her ankle, then, as she pushed his face away, he snapped at her, taking two of her well-tanned fingers. He threw his head back as he swallowed them, rings and all, like a pair of bejewelled Pepperami sticks.

Emma's blood sprinkled on Simba and Hugo who licked the specks wherever they fell. The other ladies withdrew, moving as far away as they could in fear. Emma had stopped trying to give commands such was her panic. Yolanda vainly tried to pull Simba away, but he was focused obsessively on Emma and was strong as an ox, even one minus his cheeks.

'Someone get help please' Emma pleaded tearfully. Simba had the rest of her hand in his mouth and was dragging her towards the other dogs. Beau and Captain barked nervously at Simba and Hugo but knew they were no match for those two in a fight.

'No, no! Please boys, stop it!' Hugo now had one of Emma's dainty Kurt Geiger clad feet in his mouth and was pulling in the opposite direction from Simba. To and fro, to and fro they went as they tussled for their tastefully turned out treat. It was like a tug of war at a fete in a village of the damned. Yolanda wondered if she should tie one of the silk serviettes around Emma's slender waist, to mark which dog was winning. She noticed the tableware was by Liberty of London and it would be borderline sacrilege.

By now Emma was just screaming in pain and the dogs shook her like a rag doll, they bounced her up and down as if trying to split her in two like a morbid Christmas cracker. Thumper and Chestnut, a collie, and a retriever respectively, began walking towards Emma and Simba. They gave no indication of how they might act, and the other ladies, and their dogs, hoped they would join in on Emma's side.

At that moment the head chef came running in heroically from the kitchen, brandishing his largest knife. Although he slipped on some blood, and hilariously went parson's nose-over-breast, he still managed to plunge his knife deep into Simba's side. Before anyone could give Chef Andy the acclaim he deserved, Simba wheeled round and took his knife hand off at the wrist with one savage bite.

Thumper and Chestnut, smelling and tasting the blood, which was by then spraying around like fake champagne on a Formula One podium, joined the carnage. They attacked the hapless chef, biting at his throat and neck as he too was reduced to begging for help. All too soon his terrified screams were no more than gurgling death throes, as Chestnut was almost head deep in his neck and chest, snarling and biting, pulling out his innards. Never was Chestnut's name more appropriate. For a moment it looked like one of those old comical sea-side postcards, where a dog makes off down the street with a string of sausages it had stolen from the butchers. In this case, a poor brave man tragically died whilst heroically trying to save a life, so there was nothing to laugh about.

Some of the ladies, now almost blind with fear, made a rush for the door, but shoes by Christian Louboutin and Jimmy Choo are not designed for absconding at speed. Thumper and Chestnut intercepted them with embarrassing ease. The ladies had the wind knocked out of them, but it was nothing compared to their next and imminent dining experience in which they were on the menu.

Yolanda was still trying to pull Emma to safety, but slowly and surely, the dogs were taking her limbs off one by one. It was a shocking turn of events. These creatures were supposed to be impeccably bred for life in polite society. Here they were, tearing off new body parts before they'd even finished eating the last.

Emma's blood was flowing so freely by now it formed what resembled a huge liquid carpet covering the polished floor. One of the still unscathed lunching ladies, whose own speciality was interior design, remarked:

'I know this might be poor taste under the circumstances, but suffering and horror aside, Emma's blood does tie the red carpeted entrance and the restaurant together quite stylishly.'

The other still alive ladies nodded in approval at her astute aesthetic observation. Moments later however, they were making their own contributions to the flowing crimson floor covering.

Emma, her eyes filled with tears and regret said to her friend:

'Goodbye Yolanda, I'm sorry I brought you here only to watch me die. Why didn't we just go to Costa or Lakeland? At least in Lakeland they sell cloths and mops they could use to clean up this awful mess!'

No sooner had she uttered the words, a lethal bite finally ended her suffering. She would have been appalled that one of her dogs had interrupted before her friend could reply. The dogs, meanwhile, maintained their sickening bad manners, as four of them tore her limp and lifeless body apart.

Sadly, for Emma, just like the young policeman, she knew she wasn't in a movie; certainly nothing Julie Andrews would have appeared in. These particular dog bites were not helped by her remembering her favourite things either. It goes to show we should never trust Hollywood for advice on matters of life and death.

The staff meanwhile, had barricaded themselves in the kitchen where they were crying and being sick, screaming for help through the windows. They were too afraid to venture outside in case any of the dogs were on the loose out there. Yolanda was still largely unscathed at this point. Beau and Captain were standing guard nervously which seemed so far to have deterred the other dogs. Like the USA joining a war when it's almost over, the farmer and two lads from the farm next door charged into the restaurant. The farmer's nephew shouted Uncle Sam, what shall I do? Unlike actual Americans they only had two guns between three of them. The nephew was unarmed apart from an oak shafted Spear & Jackson number three shovel with a reinforced brass handle and steel scoop. As much as he would have preferred a gun it was virtually impossible to get a clean shot anyway. Farmer Sam said just be ready with my great uncle Howard's shovel, but let the guns do their work first.

The ladies were all attached to their dogs at their jaws, and shotgun blast is notoriously indiscriminate. Chestnut paused his meal, the chef special, and looked menacingly at the farmer. Being a mere dog with no concept of munitions or vintage British shovel craftsmanship he fancied his chances. With bloodstained teeth bared he raced towards him before falling lifeless to the floor as the farmer discharged the weapon. The lad with the other gun managed to get side on and blast shot at several dogs at once. It was a chance he had to take. It seemed apparent that those ladies were already dead or dying and had become nothing more than beautifully presented sport or lunch for their pets.

They killed Thumper and Hugo, who were still devouring Emma's remains with the zeal of Eric Donnelly's mother at the Chinese buffet. Using rifle butts dining chairs and the shovel, they bludgeoned most of the other hounds to timely deaths. Simba had all but succumbed to his knife wound, but as the initiator of the carnage, he apparently felt obliged to make one last stand. He stood unsteadily but resolutely, eyeing the farmer's boys. He was a fearsome sight. His huge hulking shoulder muscles struck fear into his foes, like a canine version of freshly female swimming superstar Lia Thomas. The farmer's boys left nothing to chance, quickly putting Simba out of his misery with their sturdy boots. The farmer reloaded and pointed his gun at Beau and Captain who were trembling with fear.

'No, no, stop!' Yolanda shrieked, 'Don't shoot! They don't seem to be affected with the blood lust, look they are terrified.'

With doubt in his eyes the farmer relented and lowered the barrel.

'Hopefully there'll be some help here soon Miss.'

Yolanda was crying uncontrollably, and not knowing what to do she went out to her car, pulling her petrified pets behind her. She opened the gullwing doors on the Tesla with its enviable voice command feature and ordered Beau and Captain inside. Onlookers would have been mightily impressed at the obedience of both car and dogs. In truth the animals needed no second invitation, they were so scared.

Yolanda slumped into her driver's seat and tried to ring Simon, but her trembling hands were unable to follow the instructions from her brain. After a few minutes her hands steadied, and she managed to make her call to Simon, still not remembering she could have just asked the car to make the call. In time they say an electric car will not just make phone calls or give directions. They will be able to monitor blood pressure or tiredness and have all manner of helpful features to keep us safe. Time and distance travelled, who we've spoken to, and about what, will all be helpfully recorded and stored and monitored by our benevolent masters.

Simon was quickly distraught when he heard the terror in Yolanda's panic-stricken voice:

'Simon, it's Emma. She's, she's, oh Simon it's terrible, she's, and Simba and, and oh Simon, please come and get me! Please come and get me!'

The more she tried to explain, the less it made sense.

'Yolanda, Yolanda, where are you now darling?'

'I'm, I'm in the car with the dogs. They're frightened but they are safe. You aren't near Lakeland are you Simon? No ignore that I'm rambling. I'm at that new venue I told you about. It isn't listed but it's on the right-hand side, right before the bend on Congleton Road where that sneaky policeman caught you with his speed camera.'

'Okay, listen to me Yolanda. Lock the doors and only open them for me, or anyone from the services, from the authorities, or anyone who- look, I'm leaving now darling, I'm leaving right now! I'll be ten minutes, fifteen at the most, twenty at the absolute outside!'

A dazed and shaken Yolanda gradually became aware of her surroundings. She could see the farmer and his lads stalking around with their weapons and talking loudly to the staff at Wagger-Mamas. She heard Captain and Beau panting nervously in the back seat.

'It's ok my babies. It's ok now. Daddy's coming. Daddy's coming.'

She turned around as fully as she could and reached out to Beau.

'You're not a bitch are you! You're a good girl and mummy should have apologised before now. Mummy's sorry.'

It was as though Beau understood. She looked at Yolanda with eyes full of sorrow and longing. Captain was still shivering and leaned forward like a frightened lamb seeking refuge by its mother's side. More accurately given his bulk, Captain was like one of those big kids with odd and unorthodox mothers who breastfeed well beyond normal time limits. He licked her hand affectionately

'It's ok Captain. My big brave boy.'

She offered both her hands to them, and they licked her hands and fingers letting out little timid yelps.

'Ooh be careful children. Mummy's hand is cut, how did that happen? Ooh it stings. Aah, did you want to kiss mummy better. There you go then.'

It still isn't clear why Captain and Beau didn't attack along with the other dogs. Maybe they were still hoping for a ride on the ostrich leather seats in Simon's car. That never happened. Simon arrived in not much more than fifteen minutes as he promised. He was quite exhilarated by his journey as he'd put the Autobiography through its paces. He'd reasoned the emergency would mitigate any serious punishment for dangerous driving charges, so he gave his right foot free rein. He revelled in the agility of his Range Rover, thinking it hard to believe they were once essentially glorified farm vehicles. He pursed his lips as the thrust from the big supercharged V8 pinned him back in his seat like a rollercoaster as he stamped on the accelerator. He oohed and aahed, as the sure-footed British icon slalomed through the twisting bends, the car gripping the road as if on rails, also like a roller coaster. His dynamic suspension fought with the inevitable body roll but won hands down.

He shaved minutes off the journey time, thanks to the late braking enabled by up rated brakes which gripped the huge, flawlessly engineered brake discs like Sweep's teeth on a bone. He completed his mercy dash with a sumptuous, perfectly controlled raking drift, leaving him parallel parked with the gates. I hope my dashcam does that justice he thought to himself.

He leapt from the car like Starsky and Hutch, or one of them at least, probably the darker one, then athletically over the gate, almost landing on it as it had begun to open. That would have been embarrassing! He sprinted over to Tess the Tesla to be a hero for his stricken damsel but wondered at the strange shadows on her windows. As he got closer, he realised it wasn't shadow, it was blood, lots of it! Licking the blood on Yolanda's hand and wrist had awoken the devils in Beau and Captain. After licking her neck Beau had taken Yolanda by the throat, killing her almost instantly. Neither the farmer, nor his lads, nor the Wagger-Mama's staff, had even heard anything. It was quick and mercifully painless, compared to Emma's prolonged, uncomfortable and embarrassing ordeal.

Yolanda rescued the dogs from the gun of the farmer, but they were treacherously ungrateful. Simon was beside himself with grief, and he pounded on the glass of the Tesla in anguish. Thanks to the smooth curves of the gullwing door glass, Tess now resembled a blender, sadly though it looked like a blender someone had used to make a beetroot smoothie. Enraged and distraught, Simon marched grim faced over to the farmer.

'I need to borrow this my friend; don't worry I will return it.'

Probably because of the fire raging in Simon's eyes, the farmer gave up the shotgun without hesitation or protestations about the strict rules around firearms. Simon walked back to the Tesla and unleashed both barrels, shattering the windows and annihilating Captain and Beau. Tess/Nelson Mandela was damaged but still had the last word. The blasts from the gun caused the huge battery to ignite. It took two fire engines and many hours to extinguish the fire and the firefighters had to wear breathing equipment due to the noxious fumes. Thank heaven this wasn't a multi-storey or underground car park Simon mused. To add insult to injury, the Tesla was under seven years old, so wasn't even approaching achieving carbon neutral, even with the deceptive creative accounting.

Yolanda's death and cremation took place that day on Wagger-Mama's car park, but a memorial service was held some weeks later. Simon wept uncontrollably at the loss of his beautiful and beloved fiancé. He wept also for his own callous attitude on what he thought was a rescue mission. His friends comforted him explaining he couldn't have possibly known the seriousness of the situation. They also said they'd like a copy of his dashcam footage when he felt ready.

As Emma Strawbridge tragically had no living family, Simon graciously decided upon a joint funeral for her and Yolanda, although obviously, they were in separate coffins. Technically, they could have forgone the coffin for Yolanda, and gone straight to the urn, as burning electric vehicles reach 5000 degrees Celsius. No solution was ideal because there was no telling what was what or who, from Yolanda, the car or the dogs. As a final tribute to Emma, his choice of music for the closing of the ceremony seemed obvious to Simon. He opted for The Von Trapp children singing: "So long, goodbye, auf wiedersehen, farewell!" He realised too late it was far too chirpy and up tempo for such a solemn occasion, but everyone forgave him.

It should surprise no-one that Wagger-Mamas closed down, out of respect for the many bereaved. The farmer's boys thoughtfully gathered up and removed any dog muck from the venue. This they later secretly combed through, somewhat sickeningly, hoping to find diamonds or gold devoured along with the wearers. Although their search was somewhat deservedly unsuccessful, they were grateful there was no gross stench, thanks to the dogs' Super Doggy bamboo diet; every cloud has a silver lining!

The lads' appalling behaviour was out of character but ultimately got what it deserved. A spectacular ring they found had them dreaming of noisy exhausts and ludicrous bass upgrades for their hot hatchbacks. Upon valuation, it was found to be a Diamonique specimen from QVC, leaving them downcast and disillusioned. It is difficult to say whether they, or the tricksy deceased lunching lady, were the more treacherous. To some extent she had partially been punished as she purchased the ring the same day she secured her own George Foreman kitchen clutterer, which was completely at odds with her minimalist kitchen styling.

Ultimately, Wagger Mamas won the treachery title. They re-opened two weeks later, after a thorough deep clean, and having taken on a new chef, Michelin starred no less. They opened under the name Wagger-Mamas. You see, those who knew, only told those who needed to know.

# Chapter 15

## The Slippery Slidey Stone

Adam, Jenna, Ruthie and Ethan August 2024

Saturday morning dawned, and the Woodhouse clan rejoiced. It was overcast, but with the weather app giving only a twenty per cent chance of rain, which in Greater Manchester equates to a severe drought warning, adventures were in the offing. They could head to one of their favourite places, or two places to be precise. There were two adjoining parks no more than a mile or so from their home. Adam asked with a tone that betrayed total confidence he was getting a resounding yes,

'Who's for Woodbank Park?'

In Woodbank they could let the children and their beloved Labrador Kevin run free. Adam and Jenna's little eight-year-old angel Ruthie, hopefully enquired:

'Can we go in the posh park too daddy, and slide down the slippery slidey stone?'

'I don't see why not, has mummy told you to ask me that, so she can go in the posh park's coffee shop for her cappuccino and cake?'

'No daddy,' she fibbed sweetly with a smile.

Their route to the park took in the long and steep, and curiously named, New Zealand Road. Every time he traversed that road Adam remembered his grandma's funny if confusing explanations:

'Grandma, why's it called New Zealand Road?'

'Well sweetheart, I think it's because you are going from so high up, to so low down. They say if you went down any further, you would end up in Australia with the kangaroos.'

He remembered his grandad smiling and saying, 'Don't ask son! Bloody Australia for crying out loud!'

Adam was still smiling as the young family entered the car park at its lowest point. Here it is only a few feet above the lively River Goyt running alongside. They could hear the rushing water splashing and crashing over the weir. This was Ruthie's posh park and home to her slippery slidey stone. The park was commissioned and donated to the people of Stockport by prosperous Joseph Vernon in the mid-19$^{th}$ century. He was a wealthy businessman and owner of Stockport's Vernon Mill, which still stands a brisk short walk away from the park, and clearly visible beyond the trees.

The family passed by the rather unchallenging shrubbery maze, pausing as they always did at the large ornamental pond. The children wanted to watch the ducks which were semi camouflaged as they lazed among the long grasses in the centre. The ornate, cherub adorned central fountain looked dry and uninspiring. Ethan asked quizzically 'What's that red thing daddy?' Adam sighed

'It's an old plastic toy car Ethan. Maybe it belonged to one of the ducks, and they dumped it when it failed its MoT.'

'What does that mean?' said the confused little boy.

'It doesn't matter Ethan. Some twit must have thought it was funny or clever to throw it in there.'

'It was someone very naughty wasn't it daddy!' his little lad proclaimed disapprovingly. The water level in the pond was low, which was a shame, as it is a grand pond, about the size of the centre circle on a junior football pitch. As if other twits thought the pond needed a theme, there were two semi submerged traffic cones which had finished their temporary stints as hats or loudspeakers for drunken revellers. It was a sad sight in many ways. Adam had seen photographs of his grandma holding his dad as a baby, standing by the then pristine and glittering fountain. On the pictures, the park was filled with smiling people, and everyone looked so smart. They were more than likely in their Sunday best. The photographs were black and white, yet they seemed more colourful than the pond did that day. The pond of yesteryear looked deep and clean and well kept, and the plumes of water were inviting and splendid in the sunshine.

'Ah well,' said Adam with another deep sigh.

'Are you okay babe?'

'Yes, I'm fine Jen, I just wish people weren't such scrubbers.'

The children had begun a game of hide and seek among the tallest holly trees you could hope to see. For decades, park topiarists had created beautiful, darkest green works of art. They had shaped the trees like something between a bell, a cone and a gherkin if there is such a shape. They are most impressive in half-light, as they stand like brooding sentinels on the lookout for deadlegs. The effect is greatest when a ground mist at dawn shrouds their bases and polishes their leaves, though that vision nowadays is more likely to be seen by recovering drunks than poets or artists. Brave and careful children, unafraid of the odd prickling from the harsh foliage, can even crawl beneath their low spikey canopies.

It would normally be the perfect place for spying or hide-and-seek. With Kevin present that was hopeless as he constantly gave away the hiding places as he tried to join in. Ruthie's deafeningly loud whispers pleaded with Kevin to clear off, but they were to no avail. Realising this game wasn't going to work, she skipped over to Adam and Jenna who were stealing a romantic embrace while the kids were preoccupied.

'Can we go to the slippery-slidey stone now please, pretty please?'

Ethan ran up saying: 'Yes, can we, can we, can we?' In his deepest voice Adam said:

'Of course we can! But are we ready to climb the troll's steps?'

'Yes, yes!' the children answered with their sweet little musical voices. Kevin barked in agreement with no idea what was happening, but sensing something enjoyable was about to occur.

The slippery-slidey stone is a dark grey standing stone which sits (or stands) just beyond the summit of a precipitously steep stone staircase. The steps spring their challengers a full fifty feet from the lower park, with one almost unbroken thigh burning ascent. To be expected, with any Victorian construct, ornamental cast iron urns sit majestically upon the robust stone balustrades and bannisters. The staircase rises to the middle section of the park whose rake follows the contour of the road to New Zealand or Australia, depending on the grandparent. The walker may then choose, as they regain their breath, to enjoy the steep mature tree and rhododendron laden embankment falling away to the left. It slopes away steeply down to the glistening river, now far below. It is long and steep but careless ambulators have plenty of vegetation to catch hold of in the event of a tumble. Alternatively, look to the right and enjoy the winding paths, lawns and the Welsh-slate roofed bandstand. The masochist might even gaze further afield beyond the bandstand and boundary trees to the depressing but functional commercial buildings on the edge of town. That is a view guaranteed to quell any romantic musings, unless of course you share the imagination of a certain Laurence Stephen Lowry.

The Woodhouse children always wanted to climb the steps to the slippery slidey stone. They rarely climbed beyond halfway before calling on their occasional sherpa daddy. It is no trifling matter for adult or child to climb the huge foot deep, wide and black steps. Well-worn middle sections bear witness to countless feet of all sizes, completing the kneecap clicking challenge either up or down.

Like many thousands before them, the children loved the old stone. Adam had fond memories of both parents and grandparents holding his little hand on excited descents when he was Ethan's age. He often recounted those days, adding with a cheeky grin that they were far too old to be doing that, and should have let him have a go.

Whilst visions of Stonehenge or the Giant's Causeway may be developing in the minds of readers, the visible stone actually rises only to two or three feet and is not much wider in any direction. For all we know however, it could actually be vast, and the base of the stone be in New Zealand. It may even house deep and dark concealed caves, inhabited by sightless subterranean societies, or even provide a nightly refuge for fairies or elves. There is no telling what enchantments may be being woven neath is unyielding and inscrutable surface, but cursed is the meddlesome knave who would entertain any egregious excavation.

Countless exuberant children have made the fleeting descent on its little sloping face. Innumerable tiny bottoms have polished it to a finish a stonemason or jeweller would be proud of. All who return as adults expecting a huge stone, marvel at the contrast between their memory and the reality. Such are the wonders of a child's precious and innocent imagination; innocence which parents and grandparents should guard with their very lives.

Jenna and Kevin, the honey blonde Labrador, took a more gentle route than Adam and the children. They were on the path which winds beside one of the sweeping lawns and meanders around the ornamental garden in between. In contrast Adam's troop took the route of champions, or Trolls if it's after dark. When Jenna and Kevin rounded the bend which passes by the top of the steps, Kevin went mad with delight, yelping with joy at seeing the children and Adam again. He sprinted towards them veering away at the last second, then repeated the crazed movements several times. The staircase reunion was always a surprise to him, and every time he celebrated it like the first.

There was still some serious ascending to be done to Woodbank Park or to the park café. The challenge is incline rather than distance but regaining your breath in the café or within the large circular rose garden with its high hedge, makes recovery most pleasurable. As they walked up one of the many intersecting paths, Adam recognised one of his workmates approaching. He turned to Jenna and discreetly slipped a twenty-pound note into her petite hand.

'Do you want to take the kids to the café now babe, and get them an ice cream or something? The guy up ahead is Johno from work, and he hasn't got any filters. There's no telling what he might say in front of the tiddlers. I won't be long. You can leave Kevin with me.'

Jenna was quite happy and secretly plotted a double helping of cake.

'Oi, is that you Johno? I haven't seen you here before!'

'Ay up Woody. I've not been here before that's why. I dropped me mam off at that big fuck off mill with shops in down there. She said this park was mint, so I've come here while she wastes her money, buying shite and talking bollocks.'

'You really love you mum don't you mate?'

'Yeah, she's safe to be fair, when she's not talking!'

It was all bravado of course. Johno, or David Johnstone to give him his real name, ferried his mum everywhere. Her kitchen vase was never without flowers thanks to "Our David." Johno wasn't referring to Vernon Mill. He meant another prodigious construction, that of Pear Mill, yet another beautiful and imposing edifice nearby, dating from around 1900. It is famous for its towering brick chimney but much more so, a huge, intriguing pear, perched on top of its tower. Once upon a time the pear was green but was now weathered white.

'What's that big white thing on top of the mill Woody?'

'It's a pear Johnno.'

'Nice one! Is that why they call it Pear Mill?'

'You're on the right lines mate. It was a factory in Edwardian and Victorian times, my great grandma worked there. They wove cloth like lots of the mills round here. It was ideal for textiles because they needed it to be damp, and in Stocky it's always pissing down, and of course it helped being next to a river or two. I think it's recorded on the building somewhere, "The Pear Spinning Company."

'Our kid goes to a spinning class. I wouldn't have thought the Victorians were into all that fitness shite though. I'd have thought they were too busy, making iron and wearing daft clothes on the beach.'

As the men chatted, their dogs went through the customary canine greetings of gross butt sniffing.

'So, this is the famous Kevin is it? I can see why you called him that now. He's a ginger twat like his namesake. Anyway, what kind of bell end names his dog after a footballer?'

'Remind me what yours is called again Dave.'

'Keano, cos he's a pit bull like Roy! Having said that, since he's been on that new dog food he's become a little pussy.'

'Literally?' Adam asked mischievously.

'Yes, literally mate. He won't even go after squirrels anymore, even when I chase the little bastards towards him.'

'I think you should try some of it yourself then Johno. Are you still getting into fights?'

'One or two. I think I'm calming down a bit since I did that anger management thing.'

'Was it good then?'

'Yeah, it was sound to be fair. The trouble was a new guy took over. He was a bit of a dick. I challenged him on summat and he started going on with himself, and I ended up chinning him. I tried to make it up and offered to take him for a pint, but he wasn't having it the fanny. I don't know what's wrong with some people, he was meant to be there to help me, not stress me out!'

'Did he not report you for hitting him?'

'Nah mate. I said I'd leather him if he did, so we just agreed to disagree. I could have sued the muppet but that's not my style.'

'I doubt you'd have won pal, you weren't paying were you?'

'No, it was a judge that made me do it, instead of doing time.'

'Hey, look Jonno, it was good to see you mate, but I've got to jog on. There's a coffee up there with my name on it going cold. Then I've promised to take the little-uns down to the river. No offence.'

'I might come and have a look, I've never seen a coffee with knobhead written on it. Is there a dog biscuit with ginger twat on it too? Look No worries Woody, I'll leave you to it. I'll have to pick me mam up soon so I can't go where I can't get back from. Take care lad, I'll see you next week if I don't see you first. Come on Keano, it's about time you had a shit!'

Several happy hours later, Adam, Jenna and the children had completed yet another long bonding walk. They'd left the formal beauty of Vernon Park with its fern and flowering shrub flanked walkways. They'd run up the "easier steps" passing through the laburnum arch, which only a few weeks earlier had transformed the staircase into an enchanting golden corridor, punctuated by the occasional empty cider bottle.

They passed the manicured lawns of the bowling greens, along with the enormous stone urns which tower ten or twelve feet high. Adam paused again deep in thought, as he remembered how his grandad would play bowls on those living carpets. He remembered his fascination with his grandad's strange cylindrical leather bowling ball case and his own struggle to lift it, because they were so heavy. His grandad joked when Adam flexed his biceps and said they were like knots in cotton. It was many years later Adam realised why his grandad had burst out laughing, after Adam, before seeing or handling a bowling ball, asked him why his ball bag was so heavy.

He also said he should have taken his bowls back because none of them ever went in a straight line. He said they're like your Uncle Bill next door, after a skinful on a Sunday afternoon session. Speaking of beer, in those good old days, in summer, draught ales were served in dimpled beer glasses from the old Accrington brick pavilion, days which were long gone too, thanks to the dramatic increase in thieving scratters.

The children pretended to pick the weathered noses on the stone faces decorating ornate urns in front of the old museum building, lacking its museum. From there they entered the adjoining wilder and sprawling twenty acres of Woodbank Park. Occasionally their haphazard route veered from the upper park, back down to the river, where Kevin ran among the wild garlic plants blanketing the embankment. His rummaging released their heady aroma, and the children spoke excitedly of garlic bread and pizza, and which movie they would watch next. Ruthie and Ethan laughed and played, skipping carefully along the almost perpetually muddy paths. They shouted to Kevin as he zig-zagged among the tall trees and countless evergreen shrubs, which had also only a couple of months earlier given up the last of their pink and purple spring blossoms; blossoms which now lay strewn on the woodland floor like grubby scrunched up dishcloths.

This was a young and hopeful family enjoying their lives in an uncomplicated and wholesome, time-honoured way, like many millions before them. They were looking forward to all that the future could offer. The Disneyland fund was growing steadily. They anticipated that 2025 at the latest would see that particular dream fulfilled. Ruthie and Ethan cried at first when they learned that Kevin couldn't go too. Adam reassured them he would be happier at home with their grandparents and would be scared by the rollercoasters and fireworks anyway. Kevin would be waiting excitedly for them when they got home like he always did. The children accepted this, wiped away the tears from their bright and trusting eyes and stroked and hugged their best friend affectionately.

R.I.P. Jenna, Ruthie, Ethan and Adam.

After the funerals, Adam took his own life. Without his reasons for living, he chose to follow them. Curiously his body was found lying in the very spot where they had died. His family and friends were devastated anew, but none of them laid any blame, only flowers.

# Chapter 16

# Heroes and Villains

Johno made a new friend as his mother tarried. He'd supervised Keano's toilet trip and dutifully picked up the doings in a poop bag. As he looked for a dog waste bin and could see no bin or other park visitors in the immediate vicinity, he chose to launch the packaged package into the bushes instead. As he made his way down towards Pear Mill, another dog ran over, making acquaintance with Keano, shortly followed by an elderly gentleman in a long grey gaberdine coat and a flat cap.

'Come here Flash you little rascal! I'm sorry son, is he being a nuisance?'

'No, he's sound chief, don't you worry. Is he a whippet or a little greyhound? I'm never sure of the difference.'

'He's a whippet. He goes with the cap.'

'Haha nice one. Are you having tripe for tea n'all?'

'No son, I can't stand the stuff. I'm having kippers and boiled potatoes with a quarter pound of butter.'

'Half a pot of salt too I bet.'

'In one lad. In one!'

They both had time to kill so sat down together on a park bench.

'I love whippets. They go like shit off a shovel don't they?'

'They do that, although this fella's getting on a bit, like me. I have to keep an eye on him because he carries quite a nip, although he's much more placid of late. I'm careful with him and its good folk don't just let their dogs wander around on their own like they used to.'

'Too right, there's always some shithouse trying to nick 'em.'

'Aye that's true, but I meant people don't leave them roaming the streets like they once did. I remember a time when you walked round corners carefully, in case there was a stray Alsatian waiting to have you for dinner. I remember when I was still quite a young lad. I turned a corner and there was a ruddy great creature stood there. I think it was one of those German Wolfhounds, a big grey thing as big as a donkey. It started snarling and baring its teeth and walking towards me. I was petrified. I was only a skinny little runt and you see more meat on a butcher's pencil. My dad used to say I had to run around in the shower to get wet. To make matters worse, in those days we were all still in short trousers until secondary school, so it made me feel even more exposed. Not that a bit of cloth would make much difference with teeth like I was looking at. Luckily, another dog came past and it lost interest in me. I remember sprinting home, scared out of my wits. My dad said I was trembling like a Frenchman on the front line. I still feel that fear when I think about it, even though it was over seventy year ago. There were dogs everywhere in those days, and dog dirt all over the ruddy pavements, and it would stay there until it turned white in fine weather like this.'

'What the fuc... sorry, what the heck is white dog muck all about?'

'You saw it everywhere! It was because dogs all ate mainly just meat and bonemeal. When their muck dried out it turned white, because it was mostly just calcium that was left. We used to chuck it at each other when we were kids. If you were unlucky, you'd get a lump that still had a soft brown centre. Backwards Bounties they called them in the sixties, after the chocolate bars. It's a pity it didn't smell of coconut though lad. You'd smell it on your fingers weeks later cos the stench got inside your head. Looking back it was crackers, as many a kid went blind back then from touching dog muck because the dog had worms.'

'Sounds minging mate, but if it's true calcium is good for you Keano would've been laughing.'

'How do you mean son?'

'The dirty little get likes eating dog shite, even his own. He's a knob, it's no wonder his breath stinks. What's your name by the way, I'm Dave.'

'My name's John, but people call me Jack. I've never understood how or why it happened. A nickname with the same number of letters and syllables never made much sense, but I've been Jack for half a century or more now.'

'Nice to meet you Jack!' said Dave offering his hand, which Jack shook willingly.

'You too David, you too!'

'He looks like he could be a handful' said Jack, squeezing Keano's sturdy muscular back and back end.

'He used to be, but since he's been on this new Chinky food, he's a right mard arse. He can't even handle the neighbour's cat lately the tart!'

'Aye it's funny is that. Flash is much softer than he was, and he looks two or three years younger than he used to.'

'Get your missus on it Jack, it might put a spring in her step, or yours more like.'

'Haha I might if I still had her. I lost her five years back, but life goes on. That's why I'm so glad I've got old Flash here for company. She chose him so it's nice to think of that.'

'I'm sorry Jack, you must think I'm a right plonker.'

'Not at all son, we can't tiptoe around for fear of upsetting someone. Folk seem to look for reasons to be offended nowadays. You wouldn't have said it if you'd known, and none of us are mind readers!'

'Do you know it's funny what you were saying about stray dogs Jack. I remember our kid telling me stories about when he'd go on the playing fields. I was never sure if he was taking the piss. He's nearly fifteen years older than me, I think I was an accident. He reckons they'd play footy for hours on end, eleven or twelve a side sometimes, because they all used to troop round knocking on for each other.'

'Aye it was the same in my day. You'd get all your mates together and your mum were glad to see the back of you for a few hours. We'd walk down't street with our arms round each other's shoulders chanting *All join on for a game of togger!* We only had three sets of clothes in those days: school uniform, Sunday best and playing out. We looked like ruddy war orphans. Of course, there wasn't much to do in the house with no tv or owt. When you got to the playing fields, there'd be another gang who'd done the same. We'd pick sides and play until we could hardly walk, or it was too dark to see the ball.'

'Yeah, that's what our Ray said. He says in summer when they got knackered, they'd all pile round to the corner shop. Some would buy sweets and what not and while the shopkeeper was distracted the others would nick stuff. He says they'd go back to the field and lie on the grass eating the sweets, and whatever they'd nicked, then here's where it gets a bit weird. Do you reckon this is true? He said all the lads would be pissing themselves laughing, because there were always about twenty dogs of all shapes and sizes. He reckons they'd all be trotting round in a giant circle with their noses up each other's arses.'

'Did he mean him and his mates or the dogs? Haha, I'm only kidding. He wasn't lying son. It was exactly like that. There was always at least one vicious one though, so you left well alone. We always kept good big sticks, or even catapults, or an air gun to hand in case they turned nasty. Can you imagine that now?'

'Yeah, imagine telling Dibble now that you're only mooching around with an air rifle in case a big dog attacks you.'

'Aye it was so different, some of it was good and in fairness some of it was bloody awful. Still, back in the day, if you were a kid up to no good, at least a Bobby was more likely to give you a clip round the ear and take you home than lock you up. They knew us and we knew them. They knew our parents too, so we had to be careful because they'd give us a whack too if neighbours saw police at the door. Bobbies were like another set of parents and helped us not get into worse trouble due to a lack of painful consequences. I'd bring back the cane and all, everything's gone soft, and the softer things are, the worse everything gets.'

'If you don't mind me asking Jack, would you turn the clock back if you could? It's just that I often hear people of your generation saying things were better in the old days?'

'In some ways but not in others Dave. Obviously, I'd go back to be with Mary. I still expect her to be next to me when I wake up. Many's the time I've hugged my pillow pretending she's still here for a few moments like. When you lose someone you love, they take a part of you with them. I've never been the same since, it's like I'm hollow, if you get my meaning, but you have to crack on. Would I turn the clock back? It's a tough question, because when you look back you tend to remember the good stuff. I wouldn't want to go back to opening the curtains but not being able to look out of the bedroom windows because they were iced up. Shivering your cobblers off first thing in the morning trying to light the fire was no fun, even though the memories have become fond. We had nowt like the choice of food and drink we've got today neither. Everything was much more expensive relative to us wages. I think we can thank the unions for changing things. Having said that, they seem to have lost their way nowadays, one or two aside.'

'I can't be arsed with politics Jack. I don't trust any of them. My dad never had time for them neither.'

'It's sad to hear that David, tragic in fact. There was a time when men of good standing with moral fibre were in politics and public service. I'm sure there must still be some, but they hide it well.'

As Dave Johnstone usually gets agitated about politicians, he was quick to change the subject, however clumsily.

'It's a nice park this isn't it Jack, do you come here a lot? You could definitely keep fit with all these hills and steps.'

'I do in summer, I like a game of bowls up top, then I go for a pint. I just go in the Park Inn nowadays, that hostelry over there, since the Rifle Volunteer shut down and halved my choices.'

'I don't live round here Jack, so I don't know the boozers. I'm a 'spoons man myself. I can get rat-arsed and still afford a kebab.'

'I can understand that. We went as much for the company as the ale. We'd put the world to rights, and of course a generation ago, you'd usually be in the company of lads who'd seen things no-one would want to see, given a choice. I used to talk to a lovely old chap by the name of Alf Horrocks. He lived round the corner from the Volunteer, and it was his home from home. He's long gone now himself, but he told me how his little brother lied about his age to join up for the Great War, the first world war that is.'

'And was his a good story?'

'He was little more than a kid Dave. He fought in Gallipoli in Turkey, and like so many poor buggers, young Harold got dysentery. He was evacuated to Malta and that's where he died, two weeks after his 18th birthday. They just wasted away until they were too weak even to breathe. Brave young lads full of life and filled with hopes and dreams, cut down before they'd had a chance to live or even find a sweetheart. He's buried out there, as there was no money to bring bodies home. Tears your heart out, doesn't it?'

Dave, clearly moved by the tale, was silent for a good few minutes. He breathed deeply and blinked repeatedly. He cleared his throat,

'So was the pub named after him Jack?'

'No Dave, his kind of death were quite normal in those days. Even leaving wars and tragedies aside, life expectancy was a good twenty years less than what it is today. When working men retired, they were generally gone soon after. That's the upside of the modern world. I suppose us working lads didn't help ourselves, smoking Woodbines, Park Drive and Capstan Full Strength fags, with no filters. Amongst working lads, filters were for women and pansies. Then again, the tobacco companies had governments in their pockets, and told a pack of lies, much like the big food and drugs companies of today.'

'I know Jack. I'm still using roll ups though so I'm not helping myself. I was wondering about your friend's brother, because I've heard The Wilfred Wood, the Wetherspoons in Hazel Grove, is named after a dead soldier.'

'Can I ask you a question Dave?'

'Anything you want Jack, fire away.'

'What do you think the average twenty-one-year-old is up to of a weekend nowadays?'

'Oh, I dunno, probably go out for a few bevvies, then have a fight or a kebab, or even better, both!'

'Have you never thought of taking up boxing Dave? I did that myself and never had another fight outside of the ring.'

'I did for a bit Jack as it happens. The trouble is, most of my fights are when I'm bladdered. After five or six pints I turn into a knob and want to fight everyone. I get battered half the time. Our kid says I've been down more times than a pit head lift. It's all good fun though.'

'You're a rum lad you are David. Well, in answer to your question, Wilfred Wood, who the Wetherspoons is named after was a Stockport lad. Aged just 21 he was crawling along with a Lewis gun in the face of enemy fire. He managed to get round the side of a machine gun nest and got 140 of the buggers from the other side to surrender.'

'No way Jack, balls of steel or what? Sounds like John Wick.'

'He didn't stop there Dave. He carried on, and another hidden machine gun nest opened fire. He charged that too with his Lewis gun, firing from the hip, which he'd have to because they're bloody heavy! They used to mount them on fighter planes. He killed their gunners and another 160 soldiers surrendered when they saw he was in their trench with a mincer, or meat grinder as the yanks call 'em.' Those Lewis guns were brutal all right. If someone opened up on you with one, they could use you to strain lettuce afterwards. He won the Victoria Cross did young Wood.'

'And he was only 21?'

'Unbelievable isn't it? What some of those lads went through for this country must have 'em turning in their graves with the nonsense going on today. Wilf Wood would have seen a lot of it too, he batted on into his 80s. He was a railway man before and after the war. They even named a train after him. Salt of the bloody earth men like him.'

'Same goes for that other kid too Jack. No less brave in his own way. Oh, hang on, my old queen's ringing. All right mam? Do you want picking up? No, I'm talking to a gentleman I met in the park. I'd introduce you to him, but you'd do his nut in. OK no worries, just give me a shout when you've done.'

'Is everything all right Dave?'

'Yeah, safe Jack mate. She said she's in a big vintage shop in the mill. She's found a café in there, so she's having a brew and some cake the dobber. She'll be as happy as a pig in sh… in a pigsty. Anyroad, did you say the pub has closed down now Jack?'

'Oh aye, years ago. It's apartments now because it's on the river.'

'The same river as that one over there?'

'No Dave, that's technically the River Goyt but it joins with the River Tame and becomes the Mersey. You see that wall over there, the River Mersey is under that, flowing right under the road.'

'Hang on Jack, I thought them Scouse bastards owned the Mersey, they're always singing about it.'

'Aye well, it's a bit more impressive by the time it reaches Liverpool to be fair, but its source is right here in Stockport. You're not the first to be confused about that, nor will you be the last. It's a crying shame the Volunteer shut down though because it's another link to our past. The Rifle Volunteers were what it sounds like. They were young lads who volunteered outside of the regular army, thousands of them, and lots were in the Manchester Corps. They were actually formed around the time these 'ere mills were being built. Those young lads would put a week's work in that would kill a lot of youngsters today, never mind wars. A week's graft for a pittance then they'd get on a tram to go to Ardwick and learn some warfare. Call of duty 'n' that.'

'So, was that during the first world war or the second Jack? I'm not the sharpest knife in the toolbox as you've probably guessed. My dad always said I was dead from the neck up.'

'Don't put yourself down lad. I'm glad I'm not a young fella in this day and age. There just don't seem to be any straight lines anymore. A lot of things that young fellas like you used to strive for, are put down. It's not right. Our young men aren't dying on the battlefield so much as topping themselves at home, through depression and what have you. Which world war you asked. It was actually before either. It was around the time of the Crimean War. You've probably heard of the Charge of the Light Brigade.'

'Yeah, my dad used to say it every time he got his lekky bill.'

'Haha, I think we all did that Dave. Have you lost your dad, only you seem to speak of him in the past tense?'

'Lost him? No he just fuc…. buggered off when I was eleven. I don't blame him in a way, cos me mam would do anybody's head in. He used to bounce me on his knee and call me his little soldier. He always bought me toy guns or bows and arrows and I'd be dressed up like either a little soldier or cowboy or Indian most days. Since he left the bastard has never sent me so much as a birthday card though, which I think is what makes me get into so many scraps. I don't even know where he lives. Anyway, bollocks to him! What were we doing in Crimea and who were we fighting? I keep hearing them going on about Crimea on the news headlines.'

'Like everything Dave, it's bloody complicated. Russia is frozen up half the year and needs warm water ports to move goods in and out. Crimea is important to the Ruskies for their own security too, like we say the Falklands is for us, except Crimea is right on their doorstep. They'd taken back some territory from the Ottoman Turks, and it made us and other world powers nervous, thinking they were eyeing up the Middle East. It all sounds familiar doesn't it. There's always a giant game of territorial chess going on we don't get told about.'

'Who or what are Ottomans Jack? I'm guessing they were like Navy Seals or summat.'

'Haha, no David. They were Turkish Moslems as it happens. I told you it was complicated. They once had a massive empire that stretched down to the Baltic and the Black Sea. They ruled North Africa, operating out of what was called the Barbary Coast.'

'Ah right, nice one. Is that why we've got all these Turkish barbers everywhere? I have my hair cut by one. He's called Boran but I call him Borat. He's sound as a pound. When I go in, I say Yakshemesh. He says: I am king in the castle. I have a chair. When he's finished my barnet, I say wowawooah and he says: You like? High five!'

'I've no idea what all that meant Dave but Barbary was an Arabic word, meaning North African, nowt to do with barbers. I checked that because the same thought crossed my mind. They invaded Israel, half of Spain and were in France and the Baltic, but by the time of the Crimean War their empire was on its last legs, a bit like me and Flash. Empires always fail. It's usually corruption, debauchery amongst the rulers or the expense of controlling vast areas and populations.'

Bloody hell Jack, you're frying my brain. So, who owns Crimea?'

'Well, technically Ukraine, but as I understand it the people there now count themselves Russian, but I think of Crimea as a ping pong ball. It's a peninsula, a bit of land that sticks out and is almost an island. It's joined to modern day Ukraine like the Wirral is to England, so you might say it's Ukrainian. Having said that it's almost joined to Russia too! In fact, it is connected, by a bridge, that's how close it is, and it's been part of either on and off for centuries. As I said, it's mainly populated by ethnic Russians, just like the Falklands and Gibraltar have British populations. You'd never guess that watching the news, would you?'

'I don't really watch the news Jack, I just listen to the headlines.'

'Probably true of most Dave, but boundaries have changed right through history if you look at old atlases. Like I said it's complicated.'

'Did you say before that the Muzzahs were in Eastern Europe Jack?'

'Oh aye lad, that was the problem between Serbia and Bosnia. A lot of Bosnians converted to Islam but the Serbs, stayed Orthodox Christian. When it kicked off over there in the nineties they split down those lines. Lifelong friends and neighbours were suddenly on opposite sides and started slaughtering each other. The same thing happened between Hindus and Moslems when they split India to create Pakistan for the Moslems to have their own homeland. Over two million died as they hacked each other to pieces in the fields and streets. It was at the same time Israel was given back to the Jews. It was a time of bloody upheaval alright.

'Anyway, the Ottomans enslaved the Slavic people which was normal with ancient Empires. They were pretty ruthless 'n' all. In fact, Slav is where the word slave comes from. This idea that we invented slavery is cobblers. Slavery was the rule, not the exception, in terms of world history just as empires were. The Barbary Pirates as they were known, enslaved multitudes and they were ruthless despite the whitewashing being done nowadays. We joined in for maybe two centuries out of all of human history then we abolished it, when we came to our senses. About twenty thousand of our sailors died policing the slave ships across the world and it nearly bankrupted the country. It was a horrible trade, and being a Christian country, we should have known better, but youngsters are being kidded nowadays.

'There's summat going on, and they are using emotions to get youngsters onside for some other scheme they're plotting. They seem hell bent on causing divisions while spouting on about unity. One thing you can be sure of, they don't really care about slavery, or they'd do something about the modern version. There's more slaves today than any time in history. Worse still there are kids in sex slavery but they do bugger all about that either. It makes my blood boil!'

'…kin ell Jack, it's all a shit show innit?'

'Just a bit Dave. That's why we should be careful before we jump into other people's fights. We don't always know why a fight started and what and who caused it? Sometimes the truth doesn't come out for decades, and sometimes never!'

'I know what you mean Jack. A bloke I once worked with saw a geezer giving his wife a good hiding and he jumped in and nutted him. It turned out she'd battered their four-year-old kid and broken his arm and some ribs. I've got into the odd scrap too and found out later some knob had just been shit-stirring and I should have been on the other side. I do quite like history though. I watch loads of stuff on the History Channel. Ancient Aliens and that.'

'I'd stick to the earthly stuff if I was you Dave. We've enough to sort out between ourselves without worrying about little green men.'

'It's well weird though Jack. Thinking these lads were working in these mills, volunteering for wars, supping in the boozers with all kinds of shit going off all round the world they knew sod all about. First time they learned about it was when some bastard stuck a gun in their hands and said Front Line for you son. Time to serve your country. Working class cannon fodder that's all they were.'

'It's the way it's always been Dave. I'd think twice about joining up for anything now, if I was still fit to carry a gun. I love my military history as you can probably tell. I've got hundreds of books and you can see long understood facts getting changed and twisted the more modern they get. It's like they don't just want information anymore, or to let you make your own mind up about who was good, bad or in between. For want of a better phrase, nothing is ever black and white. They want to just use the stories for summat else which is exactly what they accuse old historians of. At least that's how it seems to me.'

'You can probably tell I don't read much Jack. I do the odd audio book but I'm usually gaming. I'm more likely to be playing Call of Duty, than being on duty fighting on any front lines. I'd drink with them volunteer lads, but I wouldn't be going with 'em at weekends.'

'You won't believe what happened to the Volunteer after it closed down by the way David.'

'I thought you said it was apartments now.'

'It is now, but it turned into a place for them sex perverts for a time.'

'What, kiddy-fiddlers?'

'No, no lad, nothing like that. It was one of those ruddy bondage clubs with whips and chains and what have you?'

'Did you never try it Jack?'

'Did I thump! I'd lock the dirty buggers up in their own chains if I had my way. They should think themselves lucky there were no rifle volunteers left. They'd have shot the bloody lot of 'em, or at least chased 'em back where they'd come from!'

'Haha, old school are you Jack?'

'I suppose I am. To be honest lad I'm half joking. Folk can do what they want as long as they keep kids out of it. I wish they'd keep all this sexual stuff indoors though. There's no telling where it's all going to end up.'

'I'll tell you where kiddy-fiddlers will end up if I catch 'em Jack. In that river, with their bollocks stuffed in their mouths.'

'Not many would disagree with your sentiment son. By the way, if you like local history, you'll see old brick buildings on your left behind the glass shop and garages just up the road on the way to the motorway. It used to be Needham's Iron Foundry. They made grids and manhole covers and what have you, before all our heavy industry got shipped off to China and elsewhere. You'll find them all over the country with Needhams of Stockport still crystal clear, some like they'd been made a week ago. I even found one when I was way down on the Dorset Coast. I always take a picture whenever I find one. I've got hundreds by now. Their name was imprinted in the moulds like. They've had people and horses walking over them. They've had cars and lorries driving over them for a century or more, yet you can still read most of them they were so well made. I think a lot of lads struggle nowadays, because they never get their tensions out with a hard day's graft, then seeing the fruit of their labour. Life was tough back then, so it was good for them to feel like they'd done their bit, and had a stake in society, even if the pound wasn't shared out fair.'

'You might have something there Jack? I'll be looking out for them grids and what not now, no mistake. Oh, hang on I think my old queen is messaging me. Yes, she is, she says she's finished. I'll have to go and pick her up, or it will be whips and chains for me too! Talking of grids, she moans like a bloody drain too!'

'Haha, okay Dave, it was lovely to meet you and Keano. I'll keep an eye out for you in the future and look after your mam son.'

'Yes, you too Jack, and to be honest my old queen's alright. She never shuts up and complains for England but I remember when my dad left how it affected her. They were always arguing and giving each other grief, but when he pissed off, I heard her crying herself to sleep for months on end. I'd often see her knelt by her bed praying for him to come back, and that I'd be alright without a dad. I think it's stopped me from seriously trying to meet someone and settle down, but you have to follow what your heart's telling you don't you?'

'You're a good lad Dave. I'm sure she'd be fine if you got yourself a nice lass. We often complain about things but when push comes to shove, most folk have our best interests at heart, especially parents. She might be afraid of being abandoned, like you feel, and you know how that affects you. You wouldn't have to disappear, would you?'

'You're right Jack. You've given me a lot to think about today, not least where I'm going with my life. Anyway, good luck with the bowling, and look after yourself. I might even re-join the library and sort me head out! I'll be giving Borat some grief too about his pirate relatives next time I'm getting my ears lowered.'

After the impromptu social and military history discussion, Dave and Keano, Jack and Flash, went their separate ways. Though not by choice, their paths never crossed again.

# Chapter 17

## Becoming History

A few weeks later, Jack had been reclining in his favourite ox-blood-red leather armchair. He'd triumphed at bowls and toasted his victory with a pint or three of Old Speckled Hen. The beer and the warmth of the fire eased Jack into a welcome mid-afternoon snooze. As he dozed he recalled many an old crown green bowling victory, each one cheered on by Mary his adoring wife.

As Jack drifted into a deeper slumber, old Flash who'd been curled up in his lap, licked his beloved master and friend affectionately. If Jack stirred, Flash raised his lithe little body with his paws on Jacks chest twitching, as if wishing to gatecrash Jack's contented dreams. Before long however, the ox blood red chair became Jack's-blood-red, as Flash succumbed to the DNA disruption and took the kindly old gentleman's windpipe out as he slept. There wasn't much meat on Jack, but Flash ate what there was, and after all, as a whippet, he had no room to talk.

When the poor old chap was found, he was no more than a skeleton, still sitting upright in his armchair. The alarm was only raised, ironically thanks to the smell of Flash's decaying body. He'd eventually died of starvation, due to the lack of visitors. Flash had cleaned old Jack's bones so well, there wasn't much to generate enough niff to notify even the nosiest of neighbours.

Before long, Dave too went the way of all flesh, when Keano enjoyed a late-night buffet consisting of Dave and Mrs Johnstone. Dave was by far the tastier treat as he was marinaded in Jack Daniels and Boddingtons Bitter and stuffed with kebab. Keano was actually a little tipsy after eating Dave and was a bit wobbly when he made his way upstairs to tuck into Mrs Johnstone. She'd heard nothing of his first course due to her prolific snoring.

This was all after Dave on his travels, had found two of the Needham's manhole covers and one grid, still doing what they were made for as if produced yesterday. He shot them on his phone along with another photo for clues to their location. His picture collection never had time to rival Jack's decades old portfolio, thanks to Keano.

Dave and his mum's meagre remains were cremated. Courtesy of a note Dave had written one night whilst drunk, his memorial stone included glowing tributes to his beloved mum, Keano, and Eric and Robbo, Keano's predecessors.

# Chapter 18

## From Barnsley to Paradise

As the harrowing and inconvenient deaths mounted up, it was increasingly difficult for local and mass media to invent new cover stories, though valiantly they tried. A Facebook group known as Stockport County's Mad Hatters, had been conducting discussions on its dismembered members, and questioned the dominant narrative. They were quickly re-labelled Stockport County's "Tin Hatters." and accused of being anti vaxers even though most were jabbed and boosted. Soon after the group was closed down by the California based android Suckerberk.

The initial go-to argument for the unprecedented carnage was of course, climate change. The almost one-degree Celsius temperature increase over the past century and a half was clearly the tipping point. It apparently Africanised the dog population to act like their distant cousins of the "dark continent." Even some of the thousands who have sweltered on holidays in Southern Turkey, and seen the docile street dogs wandering in and out of shops and cafes, still believed the heat induced horror tripe. Many a death certificate even gave climate change as the primary cause of death, with "torn to pieces and eaten by dogs" as secondary or only contributory factors. It couldn't be the new dog food, as it was well established it made dogs softer, not more aggressive. It was reported 97% of scientists agreed and so was no longer up for discussion.

An anecdotal story claims that when advised a hundred esteemed scientists and mathematicians disagreed with his Theory of Relativity, Einstein replied: "One hundred? It only needs one if they are correct." Facts must be proven, not voted on. Ignoring such obvious truth they pressed on. Super Doggy's reputation had to be protected because countless other reputations and dividends depended upon it.

Sadly, governments and technocrats long since learned their population can be manipulated and adjusted if mass media are part of the illusion. To illustrate, stage illusionists and mind manipulators like Derren Brown explain and describe their techniques in detail. After the explanation they are still able to make people do what they want them to. At the end of performances, Brown has shown audiences videos of things from the show they just watched but hadn't noticed; crazy things like groups of dancing monkeys they didn't see because he'd used multiple cunning techniques which distracted them.

Anyone going to these kinds of shows are usually aware of what they are going to. They pay their money and are entertained, and the deception is fun, and innocent. The notion these techniques might be used to push any government policy, especially regarding health or pharmaceutical response, should chill a population to the bone. It is a show which must not go on!

Totalitarian governments have routinely used such techniques against their own people, and we are rightly appalled, being grateful it doesn't happen here. Meanwhile Government, the BBC, Sky etc are unashamed in speaking about nudging and creating behavioural change. These techniques also operate below the level of consciousness; therefore, it is mind manipulation. The UK military developed a model used to control and manipulate British minds called Mindspace, and they are proud of it.

They are brazenly bypassing the ballot box, not only changing behaviours, but actually producing them. Across all media and official government sources, damning information is in plain view. Most people never see it, relying on their favourite experts to do analysis, usually without cross checking carefully to see whose side they're on.

It was concluded, what is good for the BBC is good for SMBC. Just as psychologists were being drafted in, like self-confessed-communist behavioural change experts to a Pandemic response team (another true story), an unexpected door opened.

It was early October 2024, and that door came in the form of Chamali Hussein Ali. Chamali neither came from, nor lived in Stockport, neither did he own a dog. He was a short-to-medium stocky fellow, of Bangladeshi descent and always claimed he was still growing. He offered doubters the brown balding crown of his head protruding above his thick black hair as evidence. Chamali also had a hero chin of Desperate Dan proportions and like Dan he enjoyed a few cow pies in truck stops but washed down with some dark brown Yorkshire tea. He was tough, funny and cheerful and worked most daylight hours and then some.

Chamali frequented truck stops because his family owned and ran a small hazardous waste disposal company out of Barnsley in South Yorkshire. Like many transport and haulage companies, they sometimes struggled to find drivers to cover their busy operation, and this was one of those days. All the family were capable and resourceful and could all do the book-keeping and drive the small tankers and other company vehicles. That is, apart from his mother and his elderly grandparents. They maintained an active interest in the business even so.

One murky morning there was a need to transport some relatively low-hazard chemical waste to South Manchester. Chamali said he'd do this one as the weather forecast wasn't looking great. His route took him through the rugged, breath-taking terrain of the Peak District National Park via the legendary road known as the Woodhead Pass. Whilst it is an inspiring journey even in average weather, Woodhead can equally be a brutal expedition when it freezes, which is often.

'Is that right you are taking that waste over today love?'

'Yes our mam. I'll do it today cos the weather looks proper dodgy tomorrow. Even today it's in the balance ovver the tops.'

'Okay son, make sure you take a flask and a blanket just in case. You know what Woodhead can be like'.

'If bad becomes worse I'll stay ovver someweer but don't worry I'll be reet.'

Chamali had a curious combination of South Asia and South Yorkshire accents. As people were not always sure whether to pronounce his name with a Ch or a K he was usually quite happy to go by his trade nickname of Chemical Ali. Blanket and flask dutifully stored Chamali set out. Tuning into Radio Sangam, hoping for some banging Bangladeshi choons, he went on his merry way.

Anyone familiar with that route knows getting a signal for anything is well-nigh impossible along many stretches. Soon he was driving in silence, apart from the reassuring rumble of the tanker's big powerful Gardner's diesel engine. It had no acceleration, but even after half a million miles it could still pull a wall down. After a while he opted for some entertainment from the tunes downloaded to his phone, oblivious to the fact he'd left his battery pack behind. Halfway through his journey, as expected, he had neither music nor means of communication. He wasn't overly concerned and drove on cheerfully in the weak and waning sunshine.

The scenery on the Woodhead Road, begins with leafy canopies above, and to the side myriad streams and rivulets, babbling and racing along beyond the narrow pavements. As the climb begins, the trees become increasingly sparse until many miles of sweeping greensward is mirrored on either side of the winding thoroughfare. It eventually gives way to dramatic heather covered fells, windswept and forbidding as the road climbs relentlessly over the brown and purple moor. In places there are green fields on one side and wild barren moorland on the other, betraying the direction of the weather. Looking ahead, the road snakes off into the distance. Slow-moving trucks and lorries resemble Wild West waggon trains, as they toil up the inclines, and negotiate the sharp dips and bends.

Chamali had long since passed the postcard pretty miles, along with the bleakness of the moors. Even so, as can happen on Woodhead, and just as Chamali and his mother had feared, the weather turned. It began to rain lightly, quickly turning to sleet. The failing sunlight was overwhelmed as an ever-deepening mantle of gloom began filling the horizon. The sleet turned to snow, and the flakes increased in size by the minute, swirling and billowing in the bitter wind as the temperature plummeted.

'What the bloody 'eckers like?' Chamali sighed in resignation.

The snow began to drift on his left-hand side as it blew down from the hill to his right. Good job I'm in this beast he said to himself by way of consolation, as he turned the blowers and wipers to full power. He glanced at his phone, it was dead and useless. Even though he'd slowed right down, and the big truck tyres were ideal for this scenario, his tanker skidded a couple of feet to the side.

'Abey Chamali, steady on son this could be a Yorker. Eyes on't road and mind on't job lad. Tha's too work much on to be troubling Paradise today.'

He couldn't even see the reservoir which is always a welcome sight whatever the weather. In sun or moonlight, it glistens and sparkles like a mesmerising vale laden with ever shifting sapphires, diamonds and jet. One made up tale says it is not really water at all but the treasure hoard of a vast ancient monster which stole the gleaming stones from the nearby Blue John Mines in Castleton. Either way, it lifts the spirits of travellers, especially intrepid cyclists who take on the hills and often ferocious Arctic side-winds in their optimistic insanity.

Sunlight may have been a forlorn hope for Chamali, but he wasn't expecting it to be so bad, especially at this part of the journey. He was nearing civilisation, or at least civilisation as the people of Glossop and Hadfield understand it. An old saying about Hadfield went thusly:

*"Dear Deidrie, I'm very worried, I'm nearly fifteen years old and I've never been pregnant. Do you think my brothers might be gay?"*

Of course, all that was merely a slanderous Stockport perspective and is adapted for use on any small village. A visit to the picturesque town would enable readers to draw their own conclusions.

Unfortunately for Chamali, eternity rather than Hadfield or Glossop was calling him. Despite his careful and skilled driving, a sheet of invisible black ice rendered the tanker uncontrollable. He fought valiantly to regain mastery, turning into the skid like a pro, but it was futile. He careered off the road and over the drifted snow, fallen in such volume it had created ramps over the stone walls that protect the drop down to the reservoir.

His initial exit from the road took him straight through one of the many sections of wall demolished in earlier collisions. Visibility was so poor it's unlikely anyone would have seen the calamity, even if they were nearby. As it was, the road was unusually quiet at that moment, so unseen by human eyes, he hurtled helplessly into the water where he would pray his final prayer, and swear his final swear.

There was no great panic back at the yard because his mother had seen his forgotten battery pack. She knew well the signal problems on the route, and of course his promise to find lodgings in an emergency. That conversation resulted in delaying a search and rescue operation for more than a day. In reality there was no way of finding him quickly anyway. Snow had covered all evidence of the accident. There was no tell-tale sign even of a newly flattened dry-stone wall.

As he prepared for his final au revoir in the reservoir Chamali pondered the old saying his mother had drilled into him:

"Always put clean underwear on in case you have an accident son." He had done, but the saying clearly never took the actual accidents into account. There were several skid marks, very real ones, unlike in the Pete Wallace borrowed gruds incident. Sadly, none of them were on the road where they might have been of some use to accident investigators. When the snow melted, all was serenity and beauty once more. The traffic resumed its steady flow, oblivious to the poor soul lying entombed in his rig within a stone's throw of the road. Chamali was taken prematurely and tragically. It was a couple of weeks of unusually dry weather which eventually revealed the whereabouts of his tanker. He was just below the waterline, but nothing could have saved him as he lay trapped and helpless.

The good news however, was that he was an oven ready excuse for the dog horror. The reservoir only supplies a fraction of the domestic water supply to greater Manchester, but there was a generational truth drought. The incident was seized upon and embellished to explain the still unfolding dog-ostrophe. Chemical pollution from fossil fuel and industrial waste, was a godsend for the spin doctors, nurses and support staff. The moment was seized, and the climate argument was gradually dialled down, and placed on the very low burn back burner. The story of a lethal cocktail being unleashed into the water supply, quietly supplanted the previous piffle.

It was music to the ears of those who supervised the Super Doggy debacle. With renewed vigour they took up the baton to conduct the orchestra in a symphony of insincerity and deceit. The orchestra was unusual, as it consisted entirely of dog whistles. Unperceived, the picture of a careless Asian man from a negligent, environmentally unfriendly business was painted in people's minds. The picture was framed by his irresponsible nickname. As often happens, sections of the 'kinder' political persuasion, quietly allowed the racially charged undercurrent to gently circulate. Chamali and his nickname clearly made light of the demon who was reputedly one of Saddam's enforcers. Like Chemical Ali, Chamali-Hussein Ali could not have been a good man. The truth about the hard working, jovial and good-natured Barnsley lad was submerged as quickly as his tanker on his final fateful foray.

The waste from Chamali's tanker wasn't even especially lethal, unless you were taking it neat, or with a dash of tonic water. Diluted by an entire reservoir, it was barely measurable. However, in these days of flexible facts and mutable truth, this proved to be no obstacle to the story makers. The horror attacks saw a modicum of mainstream news exposure; the caveat was always these rare, inexplicable episodes were now very likely due to Chemical Ali and his toxic tanker. With even the most superficial scrutiny, any reporter or government official with integrity, would know this was a red herring.

Dangerous conspiracy theorists pointed out the similarities with the Wuhan Wet Market decoy story. Two possibilities had been advanced during the "pandemic," a lab leak or zoonotic transmission. The latter occurs when multiple strains of diseases multiply and mutate in what scientists call a zoonotic reservoir. These reservoirs, however, consist not of water but of livestock or wild animals, and unhygienic environments. Viruses can mutate and make their infectious leaps from species to species, possibly even animals to humans.

Big tech and legacy media love the phrase 'lacking context'. Its purpose is to tell us a claim or article is not the truth, the whole truth and nothing but the truth. Legal statements are carefully framed not to leave loopholes or opportunities for vague generalities or double speak. Rarely are these principles evident in media or major government announcements, almost never by big tech. With similarities in the actual and fictional stories, a brief detour seems justified. A quick comparison with context supplied.

**Suspect 1.**

There was, and is, a wet market in Wuhan. For context, there are tens of thousands of them across China, selling all kinds of bewildering and unlikely hors d'oeuvres and aberrations, as they have for millennia. We were invited to revile and ridicule the Chinese people for their dangerous dietary deviations, just as the likes of Chamali are occasional scapegoats, as the narrative demands. The pangolin and bat eating baloney served the same purpose as videos of people falling over in the street, and bodies floating in streams. None of these things happened anywhere else in the world for an identical infection but they were only the warm-up act for the main event. Context complaints from the authorities or media were absent, as was any confirmation. The fear was allowed to permeate and percolate the populace with disturbing disinterest from press or officialdom.

**Suspect 2.**

The Wuhan Institute of Virology overseen by the fluffy and cuddly Chinese Military. Like all institutions in China, it reports directly to the Chinese Communist Party. It is quite literally a Chinese military bio-weapon facility. Research programmes included the work of Zhenglie Shi, also known as the "Bat Lady." She visited bat caves and collected their guano (bat droppings), which contain genomes of new (ie novel) corona viruses. She was just bat-shit crazy. Despite highly dangerous efforts, her team was unable to culture them in the lab.

Enter Ralph Baric, American virologist, and expert in corona viruses. Baric had developed reverse genetics, enabling him to bring viruses to life from their genetic codes. Jurassic Baric mixed multiple viruses seeking to take the "spike" gene from SHC014 and move it into a genetic copy of the SARS virus already prepared in his lab. It was a kind of Blue Peter for the criminally insane or at least the criminally negligent. The spike is the key used by the corona virus, to open and invade living cells.

From here, Baric et al could develop lifesaving vaccine$ just in case the viruses arose naturally or were accidentally or intentionally leaked. It was an accident or opportunity waiting to happen.

Is it conceivable a politician worth his or her salt, or concerned for the people, would not wish to learn everything about the Wuhan Institute of Virology from the start? Much like the IPCC, the clue is in the name. It would be preferable had the virus arisen in a wet market as it would more likely be a multidecadal event, even once a century.

The Lab explanation is infinitely more chilling, as only a toddler in a shitty nappy would believe only one deadly, world threatening pathogen was being developed. Far more likely is multiple vials filling shelves and refrigerators of labs and not just in Wuhan. This would also better explain the "experts" confidently predicting the certainty and imminence of another probably even more deadly plandemic.

Wuhan research contracts and experiments with western involvement are a matter of record. Leaders and media cheerfully conceal it, telling half-truth, untruth and nothing-like-the truth. When MP Michael Gove attempted to raise the Lab Leak Theory during the Covid Inquiry he was immediately shut down and in no uncertain terms told it was not in the remit of the inquiry. THE most important question was under no circumstances to be asked, let alone answered. Right there and then, in the full glare of the media, another conspiracy all but ceased to be a theory and once again the vast majority of the population missed it.

It has quietly been revealed the first three recorded cases of Covid 19 were scientists employed in the Wuhan Laboratories. Patient 1 ironically was called Ben Hu. His should be the most famous name on the planet at this point. Instead, governments and mass media will say, Ben Who?

Just like Wagger-Mamas, the Wuhan Institute of Virology didn't close down. Brass necked beneficiaries have no fear of judge nor guillotine (for now). It is still fully operational and still part funded by American money and linked to top US Universities. Everything is easily verified. Cowardice, mind numbing stupidity, or deliberate wickedness, seem the only explanations for suppressing these truths.

As this is a fictional short story about dogs in Stockport eating their owners, readers are directed to the work of Dr David E Martin. He is an international patents expert and financial analyst also previously employed by the US government to identify possible international bio-weapons programmes. Giving chapter and verse, he has delineated the multi decadal corruption and the patents that guarantee unimaginable wealth for the holders in all things Covid.

Dr Martin is labelled a conspiracy theorist. However, he just turned stones over, that anyone can if they choose to. Silic*nt Valley are trying to hide him but his work can still be viewed on Rumble and Gettr.

Some people hearing this for the first time, instead of being angry they were duped by the wet market lies, will not get angry with themselves, politicians or media, but will instead turn on those sounding the alarm. The old decrepit dogs in Turkey are astonished at the naivety of the western humans, thinking: What a pilava!

As for Chamali, the tried and trusted blurring of timelines was implemented. People struggled between Chamali's calamity and Climate Change. In the meantime, interest rates, energy prices, drowning women, missing submarines, international arson and soaring inflation ensured public distraction. Folk were advised not to mix Super Doggy with local tap water and use only bottled water instead. Chemical Ali polluted the reservoir, so the war on plastic had a ceasefire for the duration of the latest emergency as a million extra bottles were required. Ironically a branch of the fossil fuel-based plastics industry had seen a sales boom during Covid, with war time scale production of plastic screens and keep two metres apart stickers.

Land and sea life is now choking on the trillions of discarded masks laden with their microplastics but just like with BLM protests, if the cause is approved, destroy or pollute what you want. Sales of bottled Buxton Spring Water created waves. Trust and confidence were restored. Rare and isolated instances of people being eaten by their own, or other people's dogs, was now just an epidemic of the unbottled.

Meanwhile, Chamali became nothing more than a statistic, despite his innocence and his family's grief. Not a newspaper nor major tv channel spent even a moment to clear his name in the interests of equity, diversity or inclusion. They were all-in, and Chamali Hussein Ali was a scapegoat to be remembered only in crude and unfortunate rhymes involving his vehicle. May he rest in peace.

# Chapter 19

# Dust to Dust

Another unprecedented practice arose during this new abnormal normal. Newspaper editors turned their expertise to the obituary columns. No longer would even a eulogy be exempt from intense editorial scrutiny. Content must be monitored and manipulated:

*'Eric and Brenda Donnelly of Edgeley in Stockport have sadly and suddenly away, along with their faithful friend, Oscar the Jack Russell.*

*This terrible accident has brought grief to their devoted children,*

*other family members and friends. Funerals to be held at St Matthews Church Edgeley and the Rowan Chapel in Stockport."*

*Dates and times to be confirmed."*

It was a tragedy but was no accident! Oscar had killed Brenda, and Eric had killed Oscar. As she often did Brenda was unnecessarily cleaning the house for the third time that day. She had donned her headscarf and scrubbed the doorstep, even though every other housewife had abandoned that practice half a century ago. She'd put the ancient but still functional Ewbank round, with Oscar hitching a free ride as he always did, as such antiques don't carry the menace of a noisy modern vacuum cleaner. To be on the safe side, out came the Pledge for yet another bout of dusting.

Oscar was still giddy from his ride and Brenda experienced the furious, over affectionate ankle licking. She asked Eric if Oscar had been over effeminate with him too. As soon as she leaned forward to pet him it was all over, as the old girl's dangling turkey neck made it easy for Oscar to gain a lethal purchase with his sharp teeth. Oscar had seized the moment but had barely begun his meal before Eric's huge fingers entered his eye sockets from behind dislodging his eyeballs. Even as altered Oscar snarled and growled Eric snapped his neck and stuffed his still writhing body into their little log burner, or as it was later christened by his family, his little dog burner. It was not the most tasteful joke but Oscar was after all a bona fide granny killer.

Soon after, eye socket and neck apart, Eric went the same way in the Crematorium. As the local press were busy attempting to bury the story along with the deceased, they messed up the timeline. Eric did not die on the same day as Brenda and Oscar, but over two weeks later. The loss of the love of his life had broken Eric's big heart. It seems he'd just given up at the prospect of living without his malapropic, mammoth mammaried mermaid.

He died quietly in his sleep, marking his exit from this world with another long, rasping brassy old man fart. Such was the force of the ghastly, ghostly gust, it arrived at the Pearly Gates shortly before Eric's actual spirit, but not a moment too soon for either. St Peter had despatched an army of angels, to search heaven for one who could interpret the strange speech of a lady called Brenda from Edgeley, who had arrived a fortnight earlier. They had tried to hear her confession, but St Peter and even Michael the Archangel were in bewilderment. St Michael knew well all tongues and dialects ever uttered amongst men or angels. To him all enigmas or tortuous puzzlements, however subtle or labyrinthine, are as but a trifle or childish riddle, but even so he still had no idea what Brenda was on about. Fortunately, they accepted the testimony of Noble Eric the

Interpreter and Landlord's Friend, and she was admitted. Eric wisely told Brenda to keep schtum until they were in. This was in case she repeated her encyclopaedia paedophile confusion and buggered things up for both of them.

# Chapter 20

## Grave Warnings

Unfortunately for officialdom, excess death counts in Stockport continued to spiral, though only those directly affected seemed aware. The government, media and big tech lockstep was just about holding, but even a pinhole in a dam will cause it to burst eventually. Drastic action was called for, so the council convened special meetings to formulate a response. As the meetings were of a sensitive nature, it was agreed non legacy media and public be excluded due to the emergency. Phones and electronic devices were to be left outside the chamber and minutes were not taken, to avoid future liability.

The dastardly dogs were devastating the bamboo Nirvana narrative. Draconian measures, however unpalatable were called for as they had fully entered a dog-eat-dog or dog eat human reality. Nobody wanted their career to be curtailed by something as avoidable as public accountability. They hatched a near foolproof plan to stop the dogs from killing their owners. It was genius in its simplicity, magnificent in its malevolence. They planned to secretly kill all the dogs to eradicate the evidence! The only complication was carrying it out without it becoming public knowledge. Reputations and pensions were already on the line.

Experts were called for. They considered consulting the Gill and Lucinda Bates Foundation for advice but knew it would involve shameless profiteering. As it happened, Gill Bates, founder of MicroAgression.com had heavily invested in the technology and publicly funded its promotion. When the attacks and deaths mounted, he quietly divested himself of all his shares and said he knew all along it didn't really work properly and rejoiced over his billion-dollar dividends.

The main fly in the ointment was the green contingent who argued that dog's rights were equal to humans and the plan was a non-starter. They were adamant their consciences could never allow such barbarity. When reminded of the potential consequences of their earlier negligence and nefariousness they agreed to hold vigils and grieve privately instead. To enact the mercy killings, an army of likely lads, and the odd lass, were drafted in from local abattoirs on a pay-as-you-slay basis. The majority came from a secret arrangement with Manchester's Smithfield Market.

Attired in the finest close fitting body armour for PPE, their weapons were stun guns and specialist slaughter tools called pithing rods. In the hands of a master slaughterman, the pithing rods resemble the sabres used by duelling French Noblemen. They were used historically to hasten death by maximising damage to the brain and severing the spinal cord. The initial stunning from the bolt guns created a hole for the rod to be inserted and wiggled. It is quick and painless, even if it isn't Saturday morning family viewing. This unlikely band of butcher boys and the odd lass, eventually became known as "The Abattoirians."

Special holsters were fashioned for stun guns and scabbards for the pithing rods that had been mothballed during the BSE bullshine. They didn't want the hounds thrashing around after dispatch, drawing unwanted attention. The older Abattoirians lived up to their title well. Their muscle memory kicked in, and they resembled dashing musketeers with their nimble pithing swordplay. Few of them though would have been at home in any Royal House of the Ancien Regime, unless of course there was free beer and curry.

An initial suggestion of actual guns was dropped due to fears of loud bangs and stray bullets. Lethal injections too were rejected due to the ongoing sensitivities of recent times. A show of hands was taken and coincidentally, 97% of them agreed so it was irrefutable. The nays would have been higher, but two of their number could not attend the vote as they been unexpectedly eaten earlier that week.

Operation Arse Cover was launched without fanfare. The early stages of the operation were conducted after daylight hours. As soon as a dog was away from its owner, the Abattoirians, smeared in Super Doggy, lured the unsuspecting creatures to a swift and painless death. Meanwhile their colleagues distracted owners with blood curdling tales of rampant and ruthless rabies strains, and how the weather is much hotter since the time it was much hotter.

It was not a cheap endeavour, as slaughtermen are creatures of the dawn, and are usually pissed up just after lunch. Working in the evening required double time, but if you want the best you have to pay a premium. The butcher brigade was so skilled and successful, some officials wept that they finally had a policy that worked perfectly, but they could not go public. In complete contrast, some among them were wracked with guilt, and privately vowed to accept responsibility and seek catharsis by confession. Whatever the personal cost, the people must be told. This they accomplished by anonymous leaks on social media. Using ghost accounts, they courageously exposed Stockport's dog's-blood-stained office holders.

As these leaks spread, the council were quickly discovering that lies rarely live alone. Their game of Whack-a-Dog had become more like Whack-a-Mole, as the two narratives clashed irreconcilably. They couldn't secretly kill every dog in Britain, neither could they admit only dogs in Stockport were deadly. The only common denominator of Super Doggy was now the elephant in the room. Unable to think clearly, some of them were panicking, and harbouring irrational fears. With the talk of dogs, elephants and moles they feared they were creating a new reservoir of zoonotic horror. Such is the fruit of deceit, it destabilises all it touches.

A new desperate measure was agreed upon. The culling contracts were watertight with non-disclosure clauses being a pre-requisite for payment. Even so, to slow the effects of the leaks they needed a public show of confidence. They wanted to convince the people Super Doggy was safe, whilst in the meantime, the butcher boys and the odd girl carried out their clandestine culling. At such a chilly and damp time of year, they knew climate claptrap could never fly. They decided instead that the whole council would present themselves to the public, each with their own dog or dogs. It would show solidarity and restore confidence. It would reassure everyone that everything in the town was under control. That is possibly the title for another story.

It was the eve of the Christmas shopping season. Those who found it difficult to get to Manchester's Trafford Centre with its free parking, would instead be thronging the walkways of Merseyway. All Stockport officialdom would address the people from the heart of Mersey Square. For potential visitors yet to embark on their first ever Stockport pilgrimage, mental preparedness is advised. Mersey Square has the magnificent Plaza Theatre, but no actual plaza. Continentals might picture shrub laden lawns and shimmering fountains; paved walkways with piazzas and coffee shops overlooking the river. However, it is a rendezvous point for clattering buses rather than the chattering classes. The 1970s concrete façade of the shopping centre remains an eyesore half a century later. Almost unseen, the River Mersey makes its secretive, subterranean journey under the town thanks to an earlier catastrophic planning decision.

Opposite the shopping centre entrance, the A6 trunk road sweeps down into the town, then up and out again in either direction. Pedestrians heading north on the Merseyway side, can look down into the square with an unbroken view, until the pavement flattens out, passing the former Debenham's poo-brown building.

In the evenings the Plaza Theatre lifts spirits with its dazzling green and red neon lights, accentuating its beautiful art deco architecture. Alongside it and opposite are grand red brick buildings with Victorian facades. Tucked round the corner is the handsome, former Co-op department store, now inhabited by Mr Ahmed's imitators.

Buses were temporarily re-routed, to enable a goodly crowd to gather and be educated by the enlightened. The finest Christmas tree in the land was ordered and erected, with three times as many lights as ever before, and all either blue or yellow. When the mayors switched the lights on, it was to be a symbol of Stockport as a light to the nations again. A sign was added, stating they were all low voltage LEDs, and environmentally responsible. Another sign declared:

*Stockport Council wishes all its residents a*

*Merry Christmas and a Happy New Normal.*

A few of the least nervous deer were borrowed from the Lyme Park Country Estate. A male and female Santa shared the grotto with a Drag Santa who was over-representing the trans community. Fairey's Brass Band was re-hired to play neutral Christmas tunes, and complimentary mulled wine was available to all officials.

There was sudden panic when one of the deer was spooked by a balaclava clad scally as he wheelied around the bus lanes on his unregistered scrambler. On-duty officers briefly thought of accepting his challenge and giving chase. They couldn't do so because his posse were also present and would cause mayhem by scattering in all directions on their knocked off electric bikes and scooters. The main reason, however, was the local officials requested the police stayed nearby, in case of another type of trouble, and they duly obliged.

Shortly afterwards, two officers did suddenly break rank with the councillors' blessing. Tasers in hand and batons drawn, they raced toward the glass bus shelter separating Mersey Square from the main A6 trunk road. Determination and fearless devotion to duty was written all over their faces. This was their Omaha Beach moment, the people must be kept safe and this was their calling. Some feared a terror stabbing, but their dread was allayed when the police heroically put paid to the imminent and unfolding danger. They apprehended and escorted two ne'er-do-wells from the scene. The villains were irresponsibly distributing free copies of the Light Newspaper and playing an episode of UK Column News through an amplifier.

As Fairey's Band went through their new repertoire of Shaking Stevens, Wizard and Slade, everyone was happy as they anticipated the great switch on. The Super Doggy distribution company generously sponsored some entertainment for the masses. Diagonally opposite the main shopping centre entrance, is an understated, underused and under maintained open-air amphitheatre. It does not rival Rome or Athens but for Stockport it ain't bad. For this auspicious occasion the weeds had finally been cleared from the curved steps and it looked altogether tidy. At the top of the steps were a couple of barrels of barely lukewarm water, and baskets of sponge balls. At the bottom was a fairground style stall mimicking medieval stocks. The victims were tied on to it with arms and legs splayed. There were two of them, both short and chubby chaps, dressed identically with brightly coloured breeches fastened halfway up their bulbous stomachs, accentuating their rotundity. Their faces had been powdered to appear even whiter than normal and each wore jester's hats, the branches of which were red, white and blue. They also had stupidly oversized clown shoes to complete the fool costume. In the middle of each of their stomachs had been sewn a single letter. One bore an M, the other a D. The people were invited to throw the soaked sponge balls at them, symbolising public shame, surely due to such pathetic and blameworthy specimens.

As some of you may have already guessed they of course represented our old friends Misinformation and Disinformation. Only using the initials emphasised the essential vagueness of the propaganda. Many people unquestioningly joined in the symbolic suppression of the very truth that might liberate them. Some water bomb throwers with brightly coloured hair, procured their own rotten fruit which they hurled with extreme, but inclusive aggression. Fortunately, they were rubbish shots. They were also oblivious their protests against the billionaires they say they want to "eat" are at odds with logic. Many of those billionaires are the prime movers and beneficiaries of the causes they defend and support.

The seasonal excitement of the crowd was contrasted by the pensiveness and unease felt by the town officials before they began their latest public deception. At least half of them knew they faced no peril from their own dogs. They had never been close to Super Doggy and its potential benefits or harm, apart from during the promotions. They told themselves someone would be needed to look after the people if disaster struck so it was sensible to be cautious.

All manner of uncloaked activists have explained that individual action is not as important as systemic change. Their own diesel-powered cars, continental holidays and hosts of consumer goods are just not as problematic as yours. Systemic change is change brought about by obedience of the oiks, not their moral superiors.

As if to rub the noses of oiks in their own subservient stupidity, our beloved king had not long since put on a show worthy of the Stockport Plaza's opening night. Along with his queen he travelled to France in sumptuous luxury for a previously postponed state visit. As a climate zealot he could have given his climate catastrophe speech via Zoom from one of his hundreds of sprawling potting sheds. Instead, the venue was the Palace of Versailles, the very symbol of profligacy itself. To magnify the contempt for the masses, the banquet had separate celebrated chefs for each course and it was fittingly served in the Hall of Mirrors.

It is reported Charles insisted no asparagus be on the menu as it was out of season in France and should not be flown in, unlike him and his vast entourage. He later attended a parade on the Champs Elysees, with a spectacular fly over by nine asparagus free French fighter jets. No bugs were on the menu, nor was it vegetarian, but he did outlaw the serving of fois gras. Force feeding ducks to swell their livers is unacceptable, unlike force feeding the masses the global elite plan to impoverish them. The banquet had to be extravagant and filling as it was no time to be playing hunger games. Charles the Green King might in the end be nothing more than a buffoon, but it must be borne in mind his own father said, as reported in the Guardian:

*"In the event that I am reincarnated, I would like to return as a deadly virus, to contribute something to solving overpopulation."*

If an elite takeover with fifteen-minute cities and denial of anything but grinding austerity or mass death for the hoi poloi succeeds, those same elites will be able to say: We told you so!

Back in Mersey Square, police vans were kept nearby should the officials need refuge in any unforeseen "dog related incidents." Observant individuals might have noticed however, that one and all were giving a wide berth to the police dog unit van on hand. In contrast to the celebrations of that warm and hopeful spring day in April, the Mayor duo on this occasion were nervous and timid. Their faces were pale and drawn, puffy eye bags suggested a lack of sleep. Neither wanted the honour of making the address and preferred it all to be low key and more about the town than themselves.

The mayors agreed that they would say a couple of lines each, alternating until they had finished their address or clammed up. As they stepped forward, the band played a rousing fanfare which briefly stiffened their resolve. But the time was still not quite right, and their mood was not helped by many good Stockport folk rudely chatting loudly amongst themselves. How they yearned for those heady, almost forgotten days of Covid. Emergency powers enable tuppeny tyrants to teach the disobedient lessons they won't forget. In those halcyon days they could deploy drones to target lonely walkers in the remote Derbyshire countryside. Sweet old ladies sitting alone on park benches enjoying the unexpected sunshine could be terrorized, ordered home or be arrested. After such still unatoned for despotism, Thomas Jefferson's words should be displayed on every billboard and be compulsory on all campaign leaflets:

*"When governments fear the people, there is liberty.*

*When the people fear the government, there is tyranny."*

Better still it could be written on flags flown outside all public buildings or tattooed on politicians arms with a total ban on Savlon.

Still somewhat twitchy and irritated that their benevolent presence was not sufficiently respected, the mayors requested a second fanfare. The band struck up again, but just as they were about to reach their crescendo, the music died mid note. A deep sense of unease and foreboding filled the dank Stockport air. Shadows entered the minds of all who were gathered and they looked around aghast and afraid. Some of the musicians dropped their instruments and their arms hung limply by their sides. Children began to cry but didn't know why, and the hundred of dogs present barked feebly and without conviction. People looked at each other with dread and uncertainty, suddenly aware of the steaming plumes from their breathing which was now almost turned to panting. The air was still, and no breeze troubled it. Anyone looking down from a passing 192 would behold the whole square filled with statuesque figures shrouded in the mist from their own mouths, the only recognisable sign of life.

In the stillness and confused paralysis, some forced their eyes toward an eerie and discomfiting sound of what seemed to be many hundreds of booted feet marching. The feet beat out a rhythm with metronomic precision. Many quailed at the sight of shadowy soldiers in their hundreds, steadily making their way down the main road from the direction of the War Memorial on Greek Street. They were clothed in ill-fitting, stained and worn uniforms. Many bore grievous battle wounds and some winced with pain as they continued their journey in a foreboding silence, other than the steady tempo of their footsteps.

Some people recognised uniforms from the two great wars and other conflicts. Some even fancied they saw departed loved ones long ago lost in battle. Despite the unsettling apparition, the startled shoppers did not sense malice. There was a wholesome air about the ghostly soldiers despite their initially troubling sight. The soldiers continued their march, looking neither left nor right until they filled the visible section of the road and pavement. Gasps came from the crowd when without discernible signal nor audible command, the soldiers suddenly, as one, stopped their marching. They stood as still and as silent as stone, still facing northwards towards Manchester. All at once, and again without signal or command, in unison they quickly turned their heads, and fixed their piercing stares on the officials in the square. Although the shoppers and onlookers felt no actual fear, the officials experienced something quite different. They sensed their thoughts and deeds were being weighed and measured. Their legs became like jelly, their eyes watered and not a few shoppers coughed as their leaders expelled foul gusts from oscillating anuses.

Although most of those gathered were too distant to clearly physically see into the eyes of the soldiers, their pale, fearsome faces were not only visible, but somehow magnified in their minds. The townsfolk saw only pain and sorrow and felt the burden of the fallen warriors' hearts as they lamented the indifference to their sacrifice. The officials saw both sorrow and anger, yet sorrow was still the overriding emotion.

As both groups wrestled in their minds with the scene, even stranger things took them. They all began to see terrible visions which left them disoriented and disconcerted. They saw fast moving and quickly changing scenes. Young men were waving to family, friends and neighbours who cheered them off as they set out on what they thought would be great adventures of war with hope and courage in their eyes. These were quickly followed by images of them being cut down by the cruel bullets of the enemy or blown apart in front of their horrified comrades by deafening artillery. All around them swirled smoke and gas. A stench of trenches and disease-ridden makeshift hospitals arose, and their hearts were pierced by the sound of the wounded and dying crying out in fear and agony, uncertain whether they would ever go home or see their loved ones again.

Next, they saw letters being delivered, or sombre personal visits being made, followed by shrieks of horror, then sobbing and cries of despair, as wives, mothers and fathers received the terrible news they hoped would never come. All at once the images, sounds and smells stopped, and a brooding silence fell once more. After a few moments the perturbing platoon, again as one, turned on their heels without a word and marched back up the hill in the direction from whence they came. Nobody moved, as sinew and muscle froze in place. The shoppers and onlookers were transfixed, the town officials stood with hands and buttocks clenched.

As they processed what they had just seen heard and felt and just as the people began to relax, another apparent apparition began to manifest. All those gathered shifted uneasily as their ears were penetrated by strange and faint haunting voices. No-one could tell whether they emanated from above or below, or even from within their own imaginations. As the sound increased it became clear one voice in particular came from the direction of the railway viaduct. The viaduct seemed to grow, increasing in size until it filled the horizon, looming menacingly in the gathering darkness. The voice was clearly that of a young man. It was enjoined by other thin baleful voices, frightful yet almost musical, gaining in strength and intensity as they continued, now apparently gathered together. Suddenly they spoke as one:

'Do not listen! Heed not their lies! They weave webs of deceit which neither they, nor you will escape from, if you do not hearken! They too are moved around the chessboard, most of them oblivious to either the game or the board. The treacherous chess masters are unseen or trusted and unsuspected. Save yourselves or you will be bound, then devoured once the digital revolution has captured all.'

In the frozen minds of the people began to form the indistinct shapes of the messengers. The figures gradually solidified until could be seen a young man and woman and two young children. They could see a little girl and a younger boy, though it was not clear whether they were seeing with waking eyes. The young man seemed to be whole, whilst the young woman and the children seemed in one moment to be whole, then ragged and frayed like rotten corpses blowing and rippling in a foul wind of death and ruin. Whenever the figures embraced one another, each became whole again. The warnings continued:

'Trust the evidence of your own eyes. Follow the impulses of your own hearts, or you will be fatally deceived, and all freedom be taken from you. You will stand as cattle before your herders who will sneer, oblivious to your belated braying as you bemoan the catastrophe you sleepwalked into! Many have questions but are afraid to ask. A spell lies upon the land and deceit is everywhere. Do not seek comfort in the crowd for they are enchanted by a lie. Listen to your own heart. You will find the truth there as your eyes are opened! But you must then follow it!'

Again, deep silence fell. The shapes became blurred and indistinct, until they blew away like smoke from a candle despite the stillness. The very air was heavy and oppressive. The people realised the crying of children and barking of dogs had stopped. Unfortunately for the officials, the quietness made their terrified toots all the more obvious.

As if summoned by some heavenly entity, every eye was now drawn to a disturbance in the darkness of the night sky. Another shape was forming, swirling around in tormented circles, as yet too far away to be properly discerned. At first some thought it might be some kind of Christmas laser light show, even a holographic Santa on his sleigh. Straining their eyes, they gazed entranced, becoming increasingly dismayed as the circular movements became wider and faster and more frenzied. Icy chills traversed their bodies and their minds sought to block out the horror quickly enveloping them. Those with companions held on to one another tightly.

The menacing shape came now speeding towards them, like a dragon from an old terrifying tale a snidey dad might tell his boys at bedtime. Swooping then rising above their heads it came. But though resembling a flaming demon, this was no ancient serpent, it was in fact the spectre of a dog, a dog devoid of purpose other than to suffer. It wailed out sounds of loss and remorse. It seemed to spit out blood and fragments of flesh and bone from its tormented jaws, with harrowing cries that pierced mind, body and soul.

Discerning dog lovers in the crowd gradually recognized it was in fact a ghostly Labrador. It was not ablaze after all, rather its flaxen coat was golden and red, a thing of both beauty and dread. It was a creature doomed to an eternity of misery and suffering. It bears in its flesh undeserved wounds, born of the greed and deceit that fuelled its unwitting crime of devouring those it loved, and who loved him.

Whatever it was, it screeched the hopeless lament of a being utterly lost, before flying at last high into the empty void of the night sky which swallowed up its cries. The doleful wailing was heard no more, nor was he seen again, except in perpetual, sweaty, troubled dreams of the officials. From then on, none of them would have peace, other than those whose consciences were seared and felt no responsibility or shame. They were all hoping their crimes and negligence could be covered until the central bank digital currency could be introduced. At that time, official culpability could be ended once and for all.

For the desperate creature so tormented and bereft of either peace or hope, doomed to traverse the emptiness of nothingness for all eternity, the name of Kevin the Labrador simply lacks gravity, but in life that was his name. Eventually a welcome if chilly breeze began to blow, and the shadow lifted. As people awoke from their stupor, the lead scally briefly took off his balaclava and said to his mate:

'What the fuck was that? Poo, have you shit your pants?'

His friend didn't answer but instead gathered his wits then made a silent, if stinky get-away on his electric bike.

By now the town officials were almost unable to function as it seemed forces both seen and unseen were arrayed against them, making accountability almost inevitable. Their knees knocked, and their teeth chattered uncontrollably resembling the racket of primary-school-band percussion sections. The lady mayor's hands trembled so violently she could barely grip her microphone, although the three complimentary mulled wines helped a little. Despite the wine, her mouth was so dry she feared her tongue would simply cleave to the roof of her mouth. She stepped forward to the makeshift podium but before she could speak, another harsh and raking voice filled the air.

'These people are evil' the voice cried, 'Believe nothing they say!'

Everyone turned towards the new voice, expecting to see yet another eerie phantom robbed of the peace of its eternal slumber. Some in the crowd murmured that surely four apparitions would be overkill, and that Charles Dickens had set the standard. Those particular fears were unfounded as it was just a leader of some animal rights protesters with a loud hailer, and not even an electronic one. They came to expose the secret slaughter leaked by the council dissidents. Their somewhat dishevelled leader, unmissable thanks to his hi-vis jacket and loud obviously non-local voice, addressed the crowd confidently:

'They're killing your dogs without your knowledge. How dare they say dogs must die to protect humans! They have as much right to life and protection as any of us. If for any reason our dogs attack and kill us or our children, they are only following their natural instinct. They shouldn't be judged or condemned for it. If we must die then so be it, the planet will be better off without us anyway. Humans are a blight and a stain on the planet, and Gaia, Goddess Mother Earth is angry with us.'

'Oi Dick Head!' said a voice from the crowd, 'I've got a dog myself and I love it to bits, but if any devil dog comes near me or mine, it will be having it. If you try and get in the way, you'll be having it too, you scruffy stuck-up twat!'

At this point the police decided to wade in and remove the protestors with the blessing of the local officials. This suited them because the guy protesting the protestors was from the sprawling Brinnington Council Estate. An escalation with the Brinny Boys would be a certainty and not a challenge the police were in a position to take at that time. It almost seemed in poor taste the police officers used the dog unit to chaperone the animal rights protesters away from the scene. One of them ill-advisedly tried to dog whisper to a big police Alsatian. This fearful beast was surely the progeny of the beast who confronted Jack when he was still a nine-year-old John. Sadly, for the protestor it bit part of his nostril and top lip off and continued to follow orders.

Some bloodthirsty readers may be anticipating another Wagger-Mamas bloodbath at this point, but the police dogs were unchanged as they had been on their regular meat and supplement diet throughout the experiment, but all in good time.

# Chapter 21

## The Mayoral Banquet

Eventually, after the multiple unearthly and earthly interruptions, the official speeches could begin. With quivering hands and a little slurring of speech, the Mayoress picked up her own beloved Cockapoo and greeted the crowd, going to her mental safe spaces:

'My dear friends, may I, on behalf of Stockport Borough Council welcome you all this evening. This is my own little doggy Emmeline. I named her after Emmeline Pankhurst the suffragette and my inspiration, as she made it possible for women like me first to vote, and eventually be elected to be your leader, I mean representative.'

Another strident voice arose from the crowd:

'So, when did women achieve suffrage then Mrs Mayor?'

'Not until 1928, an appalling state of affairs, I'm sure you'll agree! Women were put down and oppressed by patriarchal tyranny and toxic masculinity for centuries, but Emmeline Pankhurst gave her life to help us achieve basic freedoms like voting. 1928 marked the year of suffrage for women, which for the uninitiated meant the right of women to vote!'

'And when did all men achieve suffrage Mrs Mayor?'

'I I I really couldn't tell you that!'

'I thought not! I'll tell you when Your Ladyship, 1918, only ten years earlier!'

'Yes, but previously only men could vote, that's my point!'

'Only some men missus. And then mainly only the wealthy for centuries. Not us working class types. I just don't like the way it's downplayed when it was more about class, money and power, than all men being woman oppressing tyrants. And did you know Emiline Pankhurst also sold her body in the back alleys of Soho and sold black puddings using rat's blood instead of pig's?'

'Look sir, I just want us to…….what, really?'

'No, not really your ladyship I made that bit up because I know I'm up against it with this one. All I'm trying to say is that throughout history men and women have been partners not enemies. They faced travails together, to put food on the table for their little ones and dependents, battling nature and hardship for the most part. Even today that is the case for the vast majority of the population. Ordinary men and women are not at war with each other, and those who promote that lie want only to divide us or appear enlightened.'

'Well, we can all be pleased that we can all vote today sir!'

'Absolutely we can, but tell it how it really was, rather than what you want people to think to suit your own agenda. At that time the residency laws would have meant lads who'd been fighting abroad for years couldn't vote. We all just saw those ghost soldiers so it should sink in more easily. Those lads had been off risking their lives for their country but wouldn't even be able to elect their own representatives. It was easier, and safer for government to extend the franchise to all men. It might not have been such a good idea to carry on denying them the vote seeing as there were suddenly a few million warriors to deal with. It was working class blokes that did most of the dying, and a battle-hardened population might be less easy to order around. If you want to make a point about suffrage, you should be concentrating on our vote having less and less meaning, with crooked international treaties and unelected international policy groups calling the shots! You're chucking all those hard-won rights in the bin anyway; how many more biological males have to win woman of the year accolades before you wake up?'

'Well let's not get bogged down in the minutia sir. As a woman I just think it was a great day when women were finally recognised.'

'Recognised for what though?'

'For being women. Giving us a voice! How is that wrong?'

'I never said it was wrong. My issue is that you lump every bloke into some kind of tyrant class. Educated people like yourself do it even though you know full well most working-class lads lived and died like serfs, working themselves to death to provide for the women and children they loved. The picture was never the way you paint it!'

'Okay okay, I'll accept your point. Can we at least agree that Emmeline was a great champion of women's rights?'

'That we can your ladyship, then again, what is a woman to you?'

At this point the drag Santa popped his or her head out of the grotto, intrigued as to what her reply might be. The lady mayor, realising she had opened enough cans of worms to feed a new normal family, quickly changed tack back onto Super Doggy. After all, being face to face with the electorate, is no place to be discussing policies, especially if they are intended to change their entire way of life.

'Erm, as I was saying, Emmeline here, has been on Super Doggy since our launch on April 1st and is healthier and happier than ever.'

She paused, expecting some applause which didn't come. Stockport people are not easily impressed. She continued nervously:

'Well, anyway, we wanted to celebrate the success of Super Doggy here with you all, and switching on the lights will mark the beginning of a new era for our town. There will be some free gifts distributed around the retail units and a free to enter lottery is also available.'

This was met with warm applause, it was an approach the people of Stockport were impressed by, although at the time they didn't know first prize in the lottery was only fifteen quid and a box of Twiglets.

What the lady mayor hadn't realised, was that Emmeline, her little princess, had been for a wee walk a few minutes earlier, during all the excitement. A couple of the more misogynistic police dogs had helped themselves to a little sniff of Emmeline's nether regions, with a view to making her one of their bitches. She in turn acted little better than a ho and lifted her tail, then nuzzled the handsome Alsatian that had earlier bitten the protestor. She had since been licking tiny specks of blood which now fizzed on her tongue and in her brain like a shedload of sherbert fountains.

As she was caressed and cuddled before the crowd, Emmeline showed her own overt appreciation and affection, until the inevitable happened. The lady mayor's gold chain framed her neck perfectly and Emmeline obliged with a good old throat bite. Since the outbreak of Sudden Adult Death Syndrome, hundreds of thousands of people have quietly found themselves being prescribed blood thinners. This was also the case for the lady mayor, and was a nightmare for the event, as it made her watery blood spray around like atomised Vimto. It squirted all over the man mayor's back. He was still mulling over his own speech, being too preoccupied to notice her plight. As happened in Wagger-Mamas, any nearby dogs on the Super Doggy diet transformed at the sweet taste and aroma of plasma. At first the carnage was fairly well contained in the vicinity of the officials, and members of the public planning on photo-bombing, but not for long.

The lady mayor was fortunate to survive, partly because Cockapoos are not natural killers, but also because one of the policemen on duty was PC Craig Brown from chapter six. He reacted once again with admirable speed, pulling Emmeline off the now dishevelled dignitary. He drop-kicked Emmeline into the River Mersey more than twenty feet away, with a single bounce off the stone arch. He knew his charity crossbar challenge skills would come in handy one day. The impressed crowd applauded warmly.

The man mayor however, was not so lucky, as he went the way of poor Emma Strawbridge. He had slipped on the lady mayor's blood on the podium, landing in an undignified heap on the ground. There he came face to face with a big Staffordshire Bull Terrier with a temper and appetite to match. It wasn't clear whether this particular Bull-Terrier was a bamboo eater or just a regular dangerous dog. Either way he tucked into the mayor's eyes, nose and mouth with relish. He wretched and spat out the mayor's nose because its bushy nostril hairs were tickling his throat. He then became embroiled in a fight with another dog he didn't like the look of. A St John's Ambulance volunteer rushed over to tend to the stricken man mayor, but quickly realised it was hopeless, seeing only his chin and forehead remained of what was once his face. She turned to one of the onlookers and said:

'From the gold chain I'm guessing this poor soul was the mayor.'

The sharp witted and politically disillusioned shopper quipped:

'I don't think so. He just looks like another faceless bureaucrat to me. Ta-daa!' A drummer and percussionist from the band momentarily put aside their fear and supplied the ba-dum-tsh!

In the confusion, the mounted scally king swept by and seized the mayor's gold chain. Assuming it was real gold and holding it aloft triumphantly, he rode off before anyone could move, shouting as he left:

'This fucker will be in Cash Converters on Monday!'

Some muttered that he'd get more if he went to Cash for Gold or Stockport Bullion, but their words were drowned out by his noisy baffle-less exhaust. Unbeknown to him, as he was waving the chain around in triumph, he was splashing mayor's blood everywhere. It triggered dozens of dogs brought along for the announcements and celebrations. Two of them were pit bulls owned by his neighbours as chance would have it. They not only recognised him, they also knew the blood they had tasted came from the trophy he was parading. They quietly made their way to him through the crowd like prowling lions. When they reached him, he was sitting astride his bike, mayoral chain around his neck, lighting up a joint.

He cut quite an impressive figure, being illuminated by the red and green neon lights of the Plaza Theatre behind him. His hunters approached him at first unseen, one from the left and one from the right. Finally spotting the beast approaching from the left he fired up his bike and tried to spin around. Seeing the other coming from the other side, he had no alternative but to try and make his escape up the Plaza steps situated at the side of the theatre. These steps are yet another throwback to the days when the lean limbed people of the town laughed at lifts and escalators, and a 50ft climb was of no consequence, even with several bags of shopping. Even pensioners regularly took the many steep steps and brews rather than the longer, slightly less onerous routes up the zig zagging hills.

Some of those shopping bags would have contained items which would not have looked out of place on this gruesome day. The long-gone United Cattle Products shop, better known as UCP on nearby

Princes Street, sold heads, hearts, tails and cow heels amongst other horrors. A modern child might well be traumatized if instead of coming home hoping for the enticing aroma of pizza, they were met instead with a sheep's head in a pan. Times were hard, and a tasty bit of sheep's head broth or brains on toast filled a gap. Most of what they sold would today be given to dogs (in other towns obviously).

When the boss wasn't in, the more mischievous UCP lads would put a sheep's lung on the counter and hide below. Curious children would stare at them wondering what they were. Then the lads would blow into the still attached windpipe inflating, then deflating them making them appear to breathe, looking like some gross alien invader. They would also ask shoppers if they wanted something to see them through the week then offer a handful of eyeballs. The gruesome visual punchline to their heads or tails question answers itself.

If only the scally king had such a bag of goodies he could toss to distract the pair of pit bulls from their pursuit. It was not to be. The dogs took off like greyhounds, their speed and agility belying their heavy muscular frames. He negotiated the steps with impressive twists and turns, using the landings to gain momentum for his next sprint. The dogs were just laser focused on a hearty meal and headed straight for him. He was so frightened he didn't even notice the urine smell so typical in the once pristine corners of the landings.

Down below, people wondered if he would make it. He was almost at the top and would soon be able to escape to his fiefdom on the Adswood Council Estate. Alternatively, he might just join up with some homies and cause trouble in the McDonalds on station approach. Unfortunately for him, but to the macabre joy of many of the onlookers, right at the very top his escape was blocked by another small group of scroats on scramblers. Their barrier was unintentional as they were only trying to get an idea of where the police were from the elevated vantage point. The dogs weren't bothered either way and gleefully leapt on their prey. His balaclava was no protection from the strong jaws that crushed his thin head. He put up a much better fight than the mayor, but a scrawny, nine-stone twenty-year old against two hungry and highly motivated pit bulls was a miss-match. Each punch or kick he landed cost him a finger or toe or two, until his blows caused him more pain than his attackers. Behind them his throttle had jammed, and his bike was spinning around like Sam Smith caught between two donut stalls. His bike was now in little better condition than he was. It was hard to tell where the blood and snot ended, and the oil and petrol began.

Thus, the scally king was dethroned. In the greater scheme of things, he was really just a wayward and naughty boy, betrayed by his own ego and too much weed. Far more malevolent people have walked and still walk the earth with no fear of retribution. Even so, the pensioners he'd terrorised for years on pavements and parks weren't entirely sympathetic. Some said his was a tragic and sorry tale and he probably had a troubled childhood which drove him against his will to such shenanigans. Others said he was a total pain in the arse and deserved all he got. They all agreed they would always think of him and the two pit bulls when their meals on wheels arrived.

# Chapter 22

## A Great Awakening

The murderous mayhem was multiplying en masse. The gene genie was out of the bottle and wreaking havoc in once lovable family pets. Their ribonucleic acid was carrying messages of destruction to their brains like millions of tiny psychotic nano-postmen. In and around Merseyway, crazed dogs had begun attacking anyone and everyone. The police were a credit to their now blood-spattered uniforms. They remembered their first calling, to serve and protect, tasering and baton-striking the often cute but ferocious animals which were attacking man woman and child. Strictly speaking:

To Serve and Protect is the American motto but you get the picture.

Thanks to the fruit of the countless gyms all around Stockport, the police were aided and abetted by a small army of well-toned meat heads and gym bunnies. Their skin tight but flexible clothing enabled smooth and unrestricted movement and they were up for the battle. The dogs were about to encounter some high protein Stockport roid rage. A few of the lads had seen the "gains" made by their pets and secretly sampled Super Doggy themselves. Fortunately for them it was species specific and carefully engineered so they were safe.

A few calls were made and some lads with white vans commandeered knives, hammers and tools from Wickes and B&Q which became makeshift armouries. In military terms, it was less modern warfare and more mediaeval peasant's revolt: this collaboration of plod and public, embodied the original dream of Sir Robert Peel, the founder of the Metropolitan Police. The police and the public were supposed to be a combined force, working together against the criminals. It was meant to be a mutual arrangement in both parties' interests. Back then of course, Peel could never have envisaged crimes might be "mean words" any more than 90% of the population do now. Recent years have seen the police increasingly become the enforcers of policies hostile to the people, but on this cold and bloody day in Stockport, the old spirit was born anew.

Entire families had been mauled to death whilst MP's, councillors and acolytes sheltered in the safety of police vehicles. Word spread and eventually PC Craig Brown had seen enough. He told his fellow officers to order the officials out, to stand shoulder to shoulder with them, and help defend their public for once. They pleaded to be left in their makeshift bunkers but were told time was up.

The police stood proud and tall (or at least as tall as modern height requirements demand) gaining strength from their new-found sense of purpose. PC Brown, embodying all that is good and true in his venerable profession, bellowed above the din, causing all, even the dogs to listen to his proclamation:

'My brethren in blue, we are meant to be a force set apart from government and council! We are called to enforce the law, and then only laws that are just and fair. We are not mere pawns or playthings of western oligarchs and their minions in public office; they who would strip away centuries old rights and freedoms. We are a thin blue line separating the people from tyranny and thraldom! Magna Carta must prevail! Only laws made by accountable ministers should stand! Habeus corpus, the right to a fair trial prior to conviction or sentence must endure forever in these isles! All emergency powers be damned! 'There may come a day when we bow and scrape before corrupt rulers, fecklessly doing their bidding, as even our own flesh and blood are downtrodden and mocked.

"I see in your eyes the same fear that would take the heart of me. A day may come when the courage of men fails. When we forsake our friends and break all bonds of fellowship. But it is not this day!"

Realising he had drifted into Aragorn's speech before the Black Gate, PC Brown smiled at his grinning Tolkien fan colleague who had recognised it.

'Sorry I couldn't help myself!'

Then he shouted in an impassioned voice that echoed around the Square and kindled courage within even the faintest of heart:

'Come on lads! Dog's flesh is on the menu! Have at you, you mangey mongrels!'

Some of the councillors, so stirred by his words, cast aside their virtue infusing rainbow-coloured lanyards and special privilege passes and showed solidarity with ordinary people. They fought alongside Dibble, meat heads and gym bunnies and all who believed in what is pure and good, disdaining their many wounds and teeth-marks.

Another enchanting figure moved effortlessly through the chaos with the grace of a ballet dancer and focus and destructive penetration of a Patriot Missile. Stockport's Iniesta, Phil Foden himself was in town as he often is, having his latest fade. He'd missed some of the earlier madness due to the whine of his barber's clippers drowning out the din. He fought fearlessly alongside musicians Joe Donovan and Tom Ogden of Blossoms who number among his greatest admirers, and who had been secretly stalking him, as is their wont.

Despite young Foden being the very epitome of attack, on this day he was the people's defender. Many awestruck but reckless youngsters clamoured for his autograph, and he was forced to defend them from vicious jaws signing and slaying seamlessly. It was a masterclass as he despatched many a mutt with no look thunderbolts from his Phantom GX's. At one point it seemed English football's greatest hope would perish right there in his hometown. A monstrously oversized Dalmation, with muscles, crown and jaws swollen by months of Super Doggy had made a prodigious leap of easily twenty feet towards him. In its vast horrifying head, the fires of hell were ablaze in its eyes. Its fearsome fangs were bared and about to end the young man's life and career.

Fortunately, Joe Donovan had spotted the Dalmatian danger, he quickly joined the dots and decided on his course of action. He reached over his shoulder like a Samurai warrior into the backpack he was wearing and pulled out one of his spare cymbals. For a moment, possibly due to a lifetime of traversing Greek Street, Joe appeared to be a living embodiment of Hercules himself. He launched the cymbal like a deadly discus. The Christmas tree lights played on its surface as it sped in a spectacular arc like a blurry blue and yellow rainbow towards Phil's airborne foe. It hit the deadly assailant with such force there was a blinding flash like lightning, as it separated the Dalmatian's huge head from its body mid-leap.

Foden spotted the big, severed bonce in the corner of his eye, thanks to his near 360 degree vision. Due to it being white with black spots, it resembled the footballs he had grown up kicking around the playing fields of Adswood and Edgeley. He instinctively controlled and volleyed the head high into the night sky in one sublime movement. It landed foursquare on top of the Christmas Tree where it remained throughout the holiday season. People cheered at the sight, unfazed by the blood that spattered them as the head spun towards its final resting place atop the mighty Nordmann Spruce.

Meanwhile, Stockport superstar, Tom Ogden, swung his guitar like a war hammer and fired flaming arrows from its strings with honey sweet precision. Like his bandmate Joe, he was well aware the Burnage Boys Noel and Liam Gallagher would be crying their hearts out missing the chance to be Phil's co-combatants. They knew however, they shared a common bond, and that little by little they would roll with it, then get over it. After all they were both on tour with their bands half a world away.

In saint like humility, young Phil Foden graciously stole away from the mayhem for a moment to kneel in reflection on the Scally King. He knew his haunts well and recognised in other circumstances it could have been him on the wrong side of the tracks, but for the magic in his feet.

Meanwhile, in one of the police vans on the other side of the square, a councillor had earlier pulled his terrified pet Boxer from the battle scene. They were sitting huddled together, whining, whimpering and pooping. The other fourteen councillors and one MP were less than thrilled he had brought his dog into their overcrowded hidey hole. Before they could propose a motion to have it removed, let alone have it seconded, the bamboo binging Boxer took off his proverbial gloves. As the officials scrambled to escape, one grossly overweight chap sadly died suddenly and unexpectedly and lay blocking the latch and freedom. The Boxer dog or Tyson, as his owner had humorously named him, unleashed his fury. He bobbed and weaved and ducked and dived like a champ. None of the councillors laid a glove on him, as he worked on their bodies, opening up their chins for the big finish.

At the final bell, or at least when the van door was eventually opened, there slithered out a heaving mass of flesh, vomit and excrement. Tyson was so stuffed he was too fat to move and no threat for the moment. A passing kid on a skateboard looked inside before saying:

'So that's why they call them meat wagons.'

His joke only received the ba-dum as the cymbal player had lost both his arms to a pair of grisly guide dogs. No one saw that coming! The battle ebbed and flowed, and it was impossible to tell whether man or dog would prevail.

Moving almost unseen amidst the mayhem, were the Abattoirians. They had woken up, sobered up, and were now racking up, well-earned bonuses. Only the councillors and officials knew who they were, swiftly moving in their strange garb among the baying hounds. Due to their mysterious appearances, the abbatoirians in later times featured in tales, which told of an army of angels who helped in Stockport's deliverance; much like the legendary ghostly knights whom it was said rode amongst the Crusaders ousting the Ottomans in centuries past. On some Fakebook and Insta-sham posts where grammar and spelling are of little or no concern, the stories spoke of an army of angles, which suggested the battle had been more protractored than originally reported.

Another eerie but welcome sporting sight gripped the crowd. The ghost of Fred Perry, Britain's only ever tennis grand slam winner fired ghostly tennis balls down at the most fearless and vicious of the hounds from the horrible car park roof. Fred was born at 33 Carrington Road, Portwood, the precise neighbourhood of the Needham's Foundry, the Rifle Volunteer and the slippery slidey-stone. His unearthly tennis balls could not pierce flesh, but they did rob many a fearless mutt of their confidence as the ethereal orbs crashed around them. It may be Perry's decorated derriere once added its own contribution to the sheen of the grey standing stone whilst his dad span cotton. He would certainly, like Ethan and Ruthie, have gazed at ducks around the fountain and climbed the

Troll's steps. Fred ended his days in Australia, some believe exhausted from his Australasian adventure in an unsuccessful quest to find the base of the slippery slidey stone.

Even with such unbridled heroism and valour seldom seen in modern times from both living and dead, a terrible scene was unfolding. Around the town centre, thousands of dogs which had previously escaped their houses, along with one or two old fashioned dogs who escaped their kennels, gathered together in a vast murderous pack. They had devoured their owners but were still hungry for blood and intended to be satisfied. In other words, they were not in town to just trot around in great circles with their noses up each other's arses. Every one of them was 'the vicious dog' and they had no fear of catapults or air rifles. When people beheld this deadly dog gathering, all hope left them. The dogs were no longer the gentle and friendly pets once beloved of their owners. There was no redemption for them. Their DNA had been dislocated and disrupted, they were a new breed of creature never seen before, possessing neither mercy nor fear. They smelt the terror of the humans whom once they served in submissive servitude. They weren't there for revenge as they were still essentially dogs and not burdened by human emotions. They lifted their heads and howled like werewolves, filling the air with soul crushing threats of death and ruination, turning courage to dread and hope to despair.

Only PC Brown was unbowed. He threw off a pair of particularly aggressive Highland Terriers leaving them alive but unconscious on the pavement. They weren't dogs, just two members of the Scottish National Party down to check out the latest token wokery opening. PC Brown had given strength to so many, but at last all hope seemed forlorn as many thousands of blood-soaked and bloodthirsty dogs were making their way down into the town from every direction. It would have been millions but this was real life and not CGI, but it was no less terrifying. Though all were oversized for their breeds due to their feasts from the east, some of the little yappy breeds would be easy meat for the equally bulked up bodybuilders. The problem was the sheer numbers, razor sharp gnashers and their will to kill. Relentlessly they came, and before them they cast a deathly glare as the streetlights reflected in their eyes and teeth made white and radiant after six months of Super Doggy. Such ruinous radiance cause doubt to flash briefly even across PC Brown's mind.

Just when the day appeared to be lost, a strange and unhoped for miracle occurred. The deranged dogs suddenly and inexplicably stopped attacking the people and turned their wrath upon each other. The exhausted humans sank to their knees and looked on in wonder, many scrambling for their phones to get it on camera for social media likes. Some wept with relief, others wept because they didn't have enough charge in their phones or had damaged them in the battle and couldn't get decent footage. As the dogs fought each other to the death, many were helped on their way by the brave volunteers.

The bloodshed had been horrific but wasn't confined to Merseyway and its environs. The apparitions had played their part. The calcifying cries of Kevin's calamity pierced the lugholes of every Super Doggy muncher in the borough. In their beleaguered brains, Kevin's tortuous, tormented travail was reverberating like a thousand bonfire nights come at once. It was an SK escalation, a postcode lottery with no winners. The fear of the dogs which had not yet been transformed knew no bounds. Gripped by unbridled terror they sought comfort from their owners, most of whom were still unaware or in denial of the alarm in the town. They loved their dogs and wanted to comfort them; apparently still oblivious to the fact it could be their final act. The affection given to the dogs in their unbalanced state brought on overzealous displays of gratitude. The animated animals and their abnormal affections led inevitably to many deadly attacks upon the comforters as Super Doggy did its final damage.

More penetrating or even simply professional investigations from the media might have alerted people to the signals of impending attacks, but once again this was buried like the poor souls left exposed by the cover ups. Tragic scenes were played out with some misguided family members siding with the dogs when they saw them coming off second best. Many a naïve numpty failed to recognise the dog was the main threat and rescued it only to become its main course. Some folk began fighting with each other, gradually realising the bites they were experiencing came from the pooches they were protecting and not from some Mike Tyson style ear attacks. At least the deranged dogs could point to the destruction of their DNA.

As had happened in Mersey Square, eventually the destabilised dogs turned on each other. They resembled Stella fuelled mates knocking seven bells out of each other over a well fit bird they both fancy. The Abattoirians were devastated that they were suddenly redundant. They'd booked fully inclusive all-you-can drink trips to Benidorm on the back of previously undreamt-of bonus expectations.

As if the canine cannibalism wasn't enough, the bamboo brain bombs had one more startling surprise. Single dog households saw their pooches turn on themselves. Just as with most of the previous attacks it began with excess affection. It was pleasure and pain for them, as typically they licked their genitals, after the manner of their species. This of course made their attack far more painful when the biting began. They howled in pain but redoubled their irrational onslaught, eventually eating themselves alive. These were no microaggressions, it was suicidal savagery.  In less genteel households, popcorn was munched as they watched, intrigued to see how much of itself their dog could eat before expiring.

Thus, in the most unexpected fashion, the horror ended less than a year after it began. In the battle memorial book, a few verses about the final triumph were penned by PC Craig Brown and his Tolkien fan colleague and fellow infringer of copyright:

*"And then all the hosts of Stockport burst into song, and they sang as they slew, for the joy of battle was on them, and the sound of their singing that was fair and terrible came even to the city" (of Manchester).*

*This day in Stockport hope was born, that set our hearts a blazing.*

*A grotty town that got us down, was suddenly amazing.*

*A local plod was sent by God, in hearts a fire he lit,*

*We cried as one let fear be gone, for Stockport isn't shit!*

*This PC Brown from our hometown, has joined these flames together,*

*A lamp to light the pilgrims' paths, it's just a shame about the weather.*

*But let thy feet be lithe and fleet, to miss this would be folly,*

*Let Stockport be thy journey's end, just don't forget your brolly.*

For many weeks the funerals were conducted in a seemingly endless conveyor belt of grief and sorrow. Barely a family was left untouched. Businesses had to bring in agency staff from miles around to fill the vacancies, but they could never fill the void of lost friendships. Children wept at their desks as they returned to school to discover who had and hadn't survived this horrific lesson in avarice and stupidity.

Fortunately, Stockport people are gritty and resilient, so the local economy and sense of community did not completely collapse. Nonetheless, inconsolable cries went up all around at various and unexpected times, as people fought to come to terms with the tragedy. Stranger comforted stranger and new friendships were forged, as the shared experience of loss enabled a slow and painful recovery.

Along with the community feeling, fights also broke out, as the pain of loss drove some to anger and a desire to lash out at anyone for little or no reason. In all honesty, before the town's nightclubs were closed down due to the drug problem, that was normal on a Friday or Saturday night. Whether the town will ever be the same again is hard to tell. For a short while Stockport was unarguably, utterly and absolutely shit. Still, at least now it had the world's sympathy.

**Aftermaths**

Readers may or may not be wondering what the upshot of all the horror was for Stockport and beyond. Was there a customary cover up or did integrity break out? Therefore, this story has two optional endings. To maintain interest, assuming this book isn't in the bin or on the banned list despite the disclaimer, readers can rate the most likely outcome.

The options are entitled as follows:

**Chapter 23 Cover Up and Carry On**

**Chapter 24 Remorse and Restitution**

# Chapter23

## Cover Up and Carry On

After the emergency, and when the catalogue of funerals was almost completed, much soul searching was taking place. Despite the endless list of contradictions, unasked and unanswered questions, an official line emerged. The authoritative statement was released and repeated ad infinitum on every news and current affairs programme until almost everybody could quote it verbatim:

*"It is both immoral and insensitive to suggest negligence or malpractice, especially as many "public servants" were injured or lost their lives.*

*Many officials also lost loved ones, including their own pets,*

*therefore we ask the public to let sleeping dogs lie."*

A detailed and urgent inquiry was already underway, with findings to be published sometime. It was likely this would occur during another disaster when people weren't paying attention. The terms of reference for the inquiry were set by the same establishment figures running the experiment. It didn't really matter since the inquiry outcome was predetermined well before the start of the experiment. During its planning all possibilities were war gamed.

The lady mayor, meanwhile, had been left with heavy scarring to her neck and chest from Emmeline the Cockapoo. For this reason and despite her discomfort, it was decided she should do as much of the public relations, especially speaking on camera, as possible. Whilst this seems counter-intuitive, the weight of public sympathy generated would be priceless. She had suffered terrible damage to her vocal cords and underwent laryngeal framework surgery. It was essentially a voice-box implant, though much more intricate and sophisticated than Sweep's simple saxophone reed. Due to swingeing funding cuts resulting from the Super Doggy emergency, a saxophone reed was considered initially. It was shelved as comedy value was considered neither appropriate nor beneficial to the authorities at this time.

The burning and obvious question amongst the public was:

"Which specific safety data on Super Doggy had been studied."

The burning and obvious question amongst officialdom was:

"How do we avoid answering that question?"

As the media were in the tank as usual, there was no chance of them asking. With the official inquiry ongoing, it was deemed inappropriate for the public to ask, in other words, a model political solution.

Over time it became clear people were dividing into two distinct groups. One group wanted clear unequivocal answers about safety data, trial data, financial liability, financial beneficiaries and specifically detailed documentation showing who owned which parts of the process? They also wanted to know how, when and where the product was developed, along with the underlying scientific basis and if and when any relevant patents were filed and by whom? Finally, they wanted detail on what was known about the possibilities of DNA modification and when?

This group mainly consisted of people who didn't own dogs and those who did but had used the likes of Riyad for their contraband carnivore comestibles. They were a majority on one side, yet oddly, not the majority overall. They also wanted these answers to be provided under oath and with supporting documented evidence and to be subject to cross examination. Anything less invited a whitewash and an invitation to do it all again. If any of that information was absent or unclear, how could the media have supported Super Doggy to the exclusion of any dissenting or concerned voices, including prominent doctors, scientists and vets?

Despite another economy wrecking mass death event, there was a strange unquestioning acceptance among those who had trusted their leaders. They apparently gave them the benefit of the doubt. The powerbrokers on the other side took this Stockholm Syndrome silence as a form of consent, as devious councils and ministers are increasingly doing in many situations. Vague notifications on little visited government web pages wrapped in gobbledygook, ensure smooth passage of Bills the public would be appalled at, if they knew the detail and implications. Therefore, they simply ignored all the reasonable and surely desirable requests for clarity. They assumed the moral high ground, claiming it was small minded and immoral to be obsessing over safety trials or deceitful profiteering when the planet was dying.

Recently, the compromised head of the Unelected Nutcases coined another bizarre and grossly inaccurate phrase. UN Secretary General, Antagonistic Guttersnipe, said the period of global warming is over, and we have entered a time of global boiling. Global power brokers have clearly concluded they are now beyond criticism even for patently nonsensical statements. National, and increasingly local governments and major city mayors are following the lead lecturing and talking down to their electorate.

Many people who theoretically want to make a difference to the environment are beguiled into thinking they should begin with healing an entire planet. Like misinformation and disinformation or even the new twist, malinformation, it is reassuringly imprecise and undemanding. As pretentious as the idea is, it is much easier to deal with than old fashioned notions like getting off your backside and picking up litter on beaches or riverbanks.

The problem is, once the quasi-religious first-principle is embraced, any amount of green self-flagellation can be preached on the back of it. Technocrats and billionaires meanwhile, in their Vaticanesque Palaces, beachfront mansions and on their private islands, produce edicts, rites and rituals for the masses. They have embraced the idea they are like Popes speaking ex cathedra, that their pronouncements are infallible. To challenge them means excommunication from polite society. It can range from losing a Fakebook or Insta-scam account to losing a career or bank account. They don't need inquisitor priests though as they control both the levers of power, and the digital money presses.

The naive people of Stockport were victims of their own good and trusting natures. The hymn sheets in praise of Super Doggy were so inspiring, promising reward and virtue to the obedient and damnation and shame to the naysayers. It caused them to suspend their reason and rush headlong into death sentences for themselves or their pets.

The new religion has been well planned, but the technology to implement it wasn't ready until now. Even so, things have been painstakingly put into place. The trans movement receiving support and funding from oligarchy should alert people it has nothing to do with trans rights. They don't care that hundreds of children die every day for lack of clean water so why would they obsess over gender dysphoria and its effects. It is yet another means to cause societal division, to fracture and weaken unity and set the people at each other's throats to distract them. Increasingly, rebel scholars are speaking out and believe it is also a nefarious scheme to demolish all accepted understandings of what it means to be human. We are being programmed to see ourselves as irrelevant clusters of atoms in an infinite purpose free universe. It paves the way for the stated aim of Satan Klaus and his elites' not transgenderism but trans-humanism, the fusing of man and machine. We are now just hackable animals according to Yuval Harai a darling of Davos and humanity is to be regarded as mere machinery to be tweaked and tuned like Eric Donnelly's beloved Cortina.

You as an individual will be no more than a commodity and may be decommissioned, even scrapped, even if you were running on locusts. The fact these people readily embrace the idea the spirit and soul are redundant concepts, or that life is not in any sense sacred, should terrify everyone. Every mindless compliance emboldens new experiments and encroachments by these opaque overlords.

The same narrow group of technocrats are found on the boards of all powerful corporations and think tanks with political influence. They are all funded by another homogeneous group who control the money supply. The names and faces are painfully repetitive. The main leaders are financial behemoths yet are relatively unknown as they hide amongst the undergrowth where journalists fear to tread. Many claim the greatest amongst them is the devourer of the wealth of nations: a dead eyed beast with a moral vacuum which could swallow the universe, the mighty Clepto-Soros.

Whilst the people of Stockport grieved and many fought suicidal urges to end their personal pain, these magnates said you can't make an omelette without breaking a few eggs. They were quite comfortable the broken eggs were only some expendable eaters from Stockport. The class of people running the world claim to want "equity". They literally ran the show through the pandemic where small businesses suffered most under restrictions and lockdowns.

Cafes, pubs and small independent shops were closed. In contrast big business thrived and faced few restrictions. It produced the largest transfer of wealth in history, from the poorest to the richest. As George W Bush almost said:

'Fool me once, shame on you. Fool me twice, shame on me!'

As an example, any buffoon could have easily verified for themselves that the Chemical Ali story was drivel, yet it still floated in the backs of the minds of the unengaged. People were reminded there had been a couple of very hot days during the summer which may have contributed. This blatant baloney was even entertained by many who routinely head to baking hot countries at every opportunity, or who sweat breathlessly in their leisure club saunas or steam rooms.

In the end, the second group, made up from the most wicked, the most innocent and trusting and the disengaged won the day. The media and fact checkers were relentless with the message that the events were inexplicable. There was no conclusive evidence of a link between Super Doggy and excess deaths. Postmortems were unable to be carried out as it was a state of emergency, and in the panic all the dogs' bodies were burned. Some green officials objected to emissions from such a burning, given the climate emergency. They eventually accepted the need to destroy evidence was also an emergency, a pressing and potentially jail-saving one.

In time the lady mayor courageously began a comedy impression career, making use of a new multimedia voice-box developed for her by a Chinese conglomerate. Her show included special guest appearances from Sweep, until she discovered her voice box could be tuned to produce an exact replica of his squeaks. On learning this she unceremoniously dumped him from her act. The broken and disillusioned mischievous entertainer sank back into obscurity, where he now battles depression and alcoholism. Meanwhile his soulless clone draws acclaim that should be his.

The good people of Stockport were heralded for faith in their leaders. To mark their steadfastness in the face of suffering, they had the honour of bearing the cost of the tragedy in increased council tax.

The various patent holders, advertising agencies and deep government operatives retained their profits and reputations and calmly planned their next venture. The world joined with Stockport in its suffering giving generously. In contrast the government agreed that if death or 60% disability resulting from a dog attack could be proven, a one off, derisory maximum compensation payment of £120,000 could be claimed, payable by the British taxpayer.

President Joe Biden sent a carefully considered and heartfelt email:

*"We the people of America send our condolences to*

*President Sanouk and the people of Southport.*

*No, I, I, I really mean it, it's not hyperbole! Come on man!"*

President Biden obviously doesn't stammer while typing but it was dictated. In another of his extreme senior moments he'd begun to type out some names from Epstein's client list in a crowded White House. He regained semi-consciousness in time to Tippex them out, sadly ruining his computer monitor in the process. Reporters who happened to be present, saw some of the names. They decided Russel Brands' shenanigans are a far bigger story than paedophilic politicians, depraved heads of international corporations or celebrity perverts and so maintained their customary disinterest. As with the shameful near media silence around the underaged and underprivileged victims of the British grooming gangs, it is clear only certain girls matter.

Stockport disaster fund donations were spent variously including:

The commissioning of a beautiful posthumous portrait in honour of the man mayor. It was the least they could do to compensate his family after his public loss of face.

A vast sculpture of nobody-quite-knows-what, which now blocks from view yet another section of the viaduct.

A huge baroque style painting was commissioned depicting MPs, councillors, and other officials' heroic exploits in the battle of Mersey Square. It is to be displayed centrally in the main body of the Greek Street War Memorial in front of the dead soldiers' names.

Another commemoration was erected in Mersey Square itself. Encased in Perspex to protect it from the rain, it describes the tragic van incident:

*"May we never forget the tragedy of our councillors and MP*

*who valiantly lost their lives in the Battle of Mersey Square.*

*Desperate to assist in the fight they were unfortunately*

*trapped in a police van whilst rescuing and protecting a*

*frightened and vulnerable Boxer dog name Tyson.*

*A postmortem report showed they all heartbreakingly suffocated.".*

The moving memorial was officially unveiled by the Gypsy King himself, Tyson Fury, to highlight the passing of Tyson the dog, the gentle creature that died quietly in his master's arms. Tyson Fury also demanded to be told where that big dosser Eric Donnelly lived, so he could spark him out for the yellow brick story. Hearing of Eric's tragic death he accepted it was only a joke, eventually seeing the funny side but maintaining Eric was a sausage (pronunciation: sossij).

A row of towering conifers was planted in front of the war memorial blocking out the view from the town hall. No official reason was given!

Finally, PC Brown was assigned desk duty and given an enhanced pension plan in return for media silence. His desk was beside PC Danny Andrews who had still not fully returned to active service. Danny's arm was not yet completely healed from the attack by Kevin the Labrador, the ginger twat who started it all.

**Almost The End**

# Chapter 24

## Alternative Ending - Remorse and Restitution

The people of Stockport gradually realised they had been used as guinea-pigs. Many had lost family, pets and futures, some had even lost guinea pigs. When the dogs were in the grip of their murderous malady, the most deranged were attacking anything and everything, however un-nutritious. The relief of the reprieve was now turning to anger. People wanted answers. There had been so much bloodshed normal rules of democracy were not deemed inappropriate. People had died by the thousand, and waiting months for the next local or national elections left too much opportunity for more malfeasance.

In panic, the most well-heeled among the officials had fled to their holiday homes to recuperate or hide. Unfortunately for them, they were hunted down by steadfast Spartans who sought them whether they were at home or abroad to be brought to account. They had to pay for their crimes of negligence, brainless compliance or worse.

Councillors and officials were summoned and paraded through Merseyway Shopping Precinct. The little-used upper tier was an ideal vantage point, as it always had been, to throw soft missiles from, or to flob greenies on unsuspecting ground level shoppers. Many wanted to publicly beat the officials with bamboo canes or redundant dog leads, but opted to wait on their responses, and hear their pleadings. It was testimony to the good nature of Britons, that even those who had suffered multiple bereavements showed admirable restraint.

The townsfolk present on the night of the battle were torn. They had seen many officials have epiphanies when PC Brown rose above the clamour to unite the true of heart. They had seen them eventually gallantly fighting alongside the meatheads, gym bunnies and Abattoirians where several of them fell. But they also remembered their own dead and injured friends, relatives and loved ones, not to mention their lost dogs and guinea pigs. The people decided to reserve judgment recognising their own humanity was now being weighed in the balances.

The gathered townsfolk, growing in number by the minute, looked among themselves hoping for a champion to step forth. They needed someone to articulate the instinctive emotions and impulses they all felt inside. It needed to happen quickly before any malevolent minister or conniving councillor could beguile them again with sugar coated deceptions. A young rapscallion in the crowd noticed a certain young policeman standing quietly amongst them, clearly deep in thought, but holding his counsel.

'Oi mate! Aren't you that pig, I mean policeman that made that top speech the other night? Can't you say summat?'

PC Brown was reticent. He wasn't sure how things might pan out for him if he went against his bosses again. He'd read Cover up and Carry On, the earlier alternative ending, so was naturally nervous. Beside him was off duty PC Danny Andrews in his civvies. Nudging PC Brown with his good arm he said:

'Go on Browny son. This is your moment. That English Lit degree you said was a waste of time might just come in handy again.'

A sharp-eyed young lad with a cheeky freckled face and tousled brown hair spotted the discarded loud hailer from the night of the battle. It was bent and bloodstained, but he spat on it and wiped it on the coat of an unwitting lady who was gazing admiringly at PC Brown. He said:

'Me dad was right. He reckons goz is like WD40, you can clean owt with it. There you go Dibble. Your mate says this is your time. Show us what you're made of. And don't slip in it!'

'You little scamp!' said PC Brown ruffling the lad's hair.

He planted his highly polished Doc Martens firmly on the pavement in a wide but comfortable stance and put the loud hailer to his lips:

'People of Stockport, we've all witnessed terrible things these last few years, and more so the last few months weeks and days. It's time now to come together and weigh soberly the actions taken by all. Our belief in overarching good has been abused and manipulated. These officials waiting on your judgement are also beside themselves with fear.'

'Shitting their knickers you mean!' the freckled boy shouted.

'Maybe so, maybe so. But at times like this we show our own mettle. There are few, if any among us, who haven't believed and followed things our minds were telling us couldn't be true. Conflicting information has left us uncertain about who or what to believe. I think that was exactly what it was supposed to do. Politicians and journalists told us not to believe all we read on the internet and be careful who we listen to. Then they shamelessly mobilised their own army of empty-headed social media influencers and pop stars, whose stock in trade is usually unbridled narcissism!'

'What's narcissism Dibble?' asked another ragamuffin in the crowd.

'Essentially it means self-love!'

'Oh you mean they're a bunch of wan……'

'Let's keep it clean,' PC Brown said, 'but you're not far wrong. The clues were there; we were being propagandised. We exchanged logic and common sense for blind obedience. This nation has always prided itself on having common sense, but we proved it isn't so common after all! I will repeat the warning that if you put a frog in cold water and heat it very slowly, it will boil to death before it thinks to jump out and save itself. Friends, I believe even now we are still in our pans and the heat is still being turned up!'

Another angry voice spoke, that of a man recently made a widower:

'Why don't we just throw this treasonous shower in the Mersey. At least hardly anyone in Stockport will ever see them.'

Appreciation rippled through the crowd for his clever and amusing irony in the face of his suffering. PC Brown continued:

'Look, for those who don't know me, my name is Craig Brown, PC Craig Brown. I'm a copper but under this uniform I'm just like you. I'm one of you. I've been fooled like everyone else. I've followed orders of which I'm now ashamed. I believe, and I don't say this lightly, I think the last hope of this, and of many countries, is in the police force and the military. Over decades us Bobbies have been moved further and further away from the people. We don't mingle and become part of the community like we used to. Our ranks are full of officers who are more interested in career progression than nobbling nonces and villains. They are re-writing everything we ever stood for! I believe it's been long in the planning. We are just becoming enforcers for a ruling class. We've got body armour and weapons and increasingly guns, and we need to make our minds up whose side we are on. I've got friends who are soldiers and veterans and there is disquiet among them because they feel the same way as I do.

'Thousands of people have witnessed their own children being eaten, yet to this day believe the assurances of the experts. Some of those same people even applauded when those trying to warn them Super Doggy was the killer, were shut down or sacked from their jobs. One courageous MP stood tall in Parliament and said he had seen proof of the danger to Stockport and wanted to present and debate the evidence in the People's House. However, when he addressed the House, he was virtually alone as gutless cowards avoided hearing what they either didn't want to, were afraid to hear, or were too weak to stand up to the party whips. Not one MP from Greater Manchester was present, not one! It proved the moral bankruptcy of the weasels in what was once the mother of Parliaments.

People of Stockport, that one brave MP has now been ostracised by his former colleagues, simply for asking for a debate about unforeseen and unsuspected deaths amongst often young and healthy people. He has since been called a Russian asset and Putin sympathiser, probably because he likes cabbages and potatoes. He was eventually perfidiously kicked out of his party on false pretences with blatant lies about antisemitism. I ask one and all to stand with him!

'Having said all that, we cannot allow ourselves to be portrayed as anything approaching a mediaeval baying mob, as that will surely play into the hands of those behind what has been happening. States of emergencies are the foundations of tyranny, so we mustn't give them an excuse, but at the same time we must no longer be complacent.

'Turning to the gathered officials, PC Brown asked if they had a spokesperson. A councillor came forward by the name of Marcia Hunter, an official most inspired by PC Brown on the night of the battle. She had talked long into the night with him and spent many hours in reflection. She looked at the loud hailer doubtfully but knew using it was a sacrifice she had to make under the circumstances.

'Thank you, PC Brown. You have opened many eyes this week, not least my own. I know many of you here think we are all wicked and corrupt, but that is not the case. We have only been seeing the same information as you. We are not party to the detail of everything that comes down to us. Our own party leaders advise us what our experts say, most of us are not qualified to question complicated science.'

Another voice boomed out, a big gas fitter from the nearby locality of Heaton Norris, a part of an area called The Four Heatons:

'It's not good enough sweetheart! We are taxpayers and British citizens, not bloody serfs and peasants. Much of the time we know more than you buggers because we aren't bound by party rules or conventions. You don't have to be a scientist to read how many people were dying before Super Doggy was released and how many are dead now. It's a matter of being able to add and subtract just like with the pandemic! This time you haven't got the smokescreen of excuses gifted by the lockdowns.

'I was listening to podcasts whilst mending or fitting boilers. I listened to highly decorated and even Nobel Prize winning scientists who have been cited and published in major scientific journals for decades. They were speaking out, deeply disturbed at what was, and is going on, saying medicine and science has been bought, including long established and esteemed medical journals.

'Big pharmaceutical companies effectively regulate themselves. The typical response from your shower is to demonise those doctors and scientists and belittle the likes of me saying we think we're experts because we heard something on the internet. Where else can we hear alternative voices if the mainstream media is also bought and paid for and controlled? I wouldn't mind if any of you had ever read any of the science yourselves. Now, instead of answering or debating the critics you are trying to shut down alternative media hiding behind misinformation bullshit.

'Some of us have followed the money and seen how scientific opinion tracks funding almost exactly. The truth is that 97% of scientists agree with whoever is funding them and the remainder are cancelled. I've got a long memory. I'll never forget those bloody pandemic death counters or picking up the paper and seeing how many had tested positive in Heaton Mersey, and how many in Heaton flaming Moor. Nobody died from flu for two years, my arse, and only one treatment was given to every patient, for something they were supposed to know nothing about. Every respiratory disease in history has responded well to Vitamin C and D, yet you locked us in our homes away from sunlight and fresh air, and buried the information that would have helped us! Now we've seen it again with this bloody dog food. You've taken us for fools.'

'I know, I know sir. But like I said we have all been taken for fools. Maybe pride or hubris stopped us from listening to certain voices, or even fear of being sidelined or being victims of name-calling. Anyone who was seen as anything approaching a conspiracy theorist could say goodbye to their reputation or career. The bar for being a conspiracy theorist is now so low it is applied to anyone questioning any official line, so we self-censor for self-preservation. Doctors, scientists and academics can lose their grants, tenures or even be struck off. On the other hand, I had residents telling me if we didn't mandate Super Doggy, I was evil. It was just easier to run with the crowd.'

'I just hope you've learned your lesson love. There was twenty-five years of research involving millions of people in dozens of countries proving masks do more harm than good, but it all suddenly got scrubbed off the internet. Now they want to ban gas, well I'll tell you something, we're getting sick to the back teeth with it all! I'm in the gas trade and I drive a white van like a lot of the lads here. Pardon my French, but if you really want to fuck with us, you'd better be ready to face the consequences, and trust me, we won't just be waving placards. It's you lot, not ourselves that we'll be glueing to the road!'

'I hear what you are saying sir, really I do. All I can say to you all is that we all want to put ourselves up for re-election. We all intend to ignore Party orders unless they agree with what the people of this town want. We realise to do anything else is to fly in the face of democracy, another word I agree has been so abused and hollowed out, it now has little left of its original meaning.

'We will look more closely at individuals on the boards of big businesses and NGO's, Non-Governmental Organisations, and begin to follow the money trails. The thing we need most if you put any of us back in office, is your help. We rode roughshod over your opinions because you have been so quiet. You have lost loved ones and livelihoods because you didn't speak up loudly enough. Write to your officials, don't complain amongst yourselves but fight with the same determination as the heroes of the Battle of Mersey Square.

'Everybody knows our consultation documents are curated. They are designed to produce the outcomes we desire, much like many opinion polls. We ask several questions designed to eventually bring you to a point we want, and the answer you really want to give isn't amongst the options. It is a game you can never win. We have in effect despised and belittled you. We've been like the insane officials in Sandford telling ourselves it was for the greater good.'

Another mudlark piped up: 'Do you mean Sandbach missus? My dad went there on cub camp when he was a kid. He said it was shite!'

'No, I meant Sandford. Maybe PC Brown might like to explain.'

PC Brown stepped forward again looking delighted:

'She means the imaginary village of Sandford son. It's from Hot Fuzz, Councillor Hunter knows it's my favourite film. Sandford was a pretty little village down south and won Village of the Year prizes because it was so beautiful. Local councillors and dignitaries, including the police chief, were secretly killing people who they thought were spoiling the look or character of the village, risking its reputation and chances of winning again. It's a parody of what can happen when leaders think they know best. It's a gory but funny movie, but it shows in a daft way how terrible acts can be committed then covered up, if enough bigwigs are on board. They believed what they were doing was for the greater good which they chanted at their creepy meetings.'

Another agitated voice from the crowd rang out:

'Oh, nice one plod. I recorded that the other night and haven't watched it yet. You could have given us a spoiler alert you muppet!'

'Oh yes I should have, I'm very sorry but you'll still enjoy it, I've watched it about ten times. The Greater Good is one of the biggest dangers of our age and a shortcut to tyranny. The wellbeing of the here and now is being compromised for what may be in the future. I was put on standby to go down to London to squash any lockdown protests because they said they were mass spreading events. I was measured up for body armour and had training with kettling, baton striking, pepper spray and gas masks. When the Black Lives Matter marches were going on, a few of us asked why they were not outlawed for the same health and safety reasons. The answer we got was basically the greater good.

'We thought there would be outrage over the obvious idiotic double speak, then heard so called clever people and politicians justify it. A deadly disease that brought the world to a standstill was suddenly not so deadly and less important than social change that is happening anyway. I think that is what made me start to wake up and smell the bullshit!

'We have to always be on guard in case some megalomaniacs or sociopaths are bent on taking over. We may not be there yet, but when it has happened in the past, the things we are seeing today preceded it. Hitler didn't come to power by force or by inheriting tyranny. Germany was a free and liberal society. He swayed many ordinary Germans to embrace unimaginable evil, and I don't just mean putting towels on deckchairs or pushing in queues. Many covered their eyes and ears and pretended not to see or understand and cowered in fear. Others embraced the lies and remember; it wasn't that long ago! Back to you Councillor Hunter.'

'PC Brown is right! As he referenced Hitler and the Germans, permit me to read you a confession by a German Pastor Martin Niemoller regarding the Nazis:

*"First they came for the socialists, and I did not speak out— Because I was not a socialist.*

*Then they came for the trade unionists, and I did not speak out— Because I was not a trade unionist.*

*Then they came for the Jews, and I did not speak out— Because I was not a Jew.*

*Then they came for me—and there was no one left to speak for me."*

'Many of us in authority lost our way. We often attack our critics rather than listen to them. When we do pretend to listen it's often only for show. Now, even the banks are cancelling accounts for wrong think. I confess, as someone who sits just left of centre, I turned a blind eye when those on the right have been targeted for their views. Niemoller's lesson asks, how can I complain should my views be next to be deemed unacceptable or hateful?

'I naturally recoil at the idea of huge corporations who crush the little man and take over everything. I've realised causes I was drawn to, are funded and promoted by those I would naturally fight against. We lost our minds, tricked by what I understand is called mass formation, a psychosis where entire societies follow a manipulated, often self-destructive course. I hated Bogus Johnson, but I followed his advice to the letter, even if he didn't. It is starting to add up now.

'They are not coming for trade unions yet, they are not coming for socialists or even classical liberals like me yet, but I now realise in the end, they will be. Many of us are slowly realising that truth and reality is being inverted. Whether left or right, communism or fascism the ultimate end is total control by government, or more accurately, those who control governments. Big government in bed with big business used to be the definition of fascism. Today they call it public private partnership. It sounds so sweet and innocent but they are just changing the words. A new version of China is being built; state capitalism, top-down government, but an unelected one, a behind-the-scenes exercise of power by the wealthiest. Shutting down bank accounts has followed shutting down social media accounts. If they can do it to anyone, they can do it to everyone!

'I know I'm rabbiting on a bit, and some of you might be dozing off. What I'm trying to say is it is time for all of us to unite and realise we must protect each other, even those holding many views we don't like. None of us have any real power but at least for now we have a modicum of freedom. Warning signs are everywhere, but people are not seeing them or not even looking. I hope people everywhere rise up as you have. Unfortunately, I don't think they will until they find they are in an electronic digital prison, and by then it will be too late.'

Time was moving on and it was getting chilly. The big gas fitter from Heaton Norris interjected again:

'Hearing what you've said tonight gives me some hope missus. Having said that, it's 'kin freezing out here and actions will speak louder than words. Have you finished yet, only that speech was more like a passage from a novel than an actual public address given to folk likely to have fairly short attention spans.'

'Yes, you are right sir, I will end with this. We often hear outrage and outcries about certain nations' actions being against the Geneva Convention. What isn't proclaimed is its central tenet. It was agreed that after the sickness and inhumanity of the Nazi doctors, no medical treatment should be imposed on anyone against their will ever again. That was either by force, manipulation, fear tactics or unusual persuasion. For almost eighty years no one challenged it. It sends shivers down my spine today thinking what I posted on social media about jab mandates and uncaring people. We must all take stock.

'I used to think young politicians like Canadian PM Justin Truedope the blackface fanatic were the future even though he's a relative simpleton. However, in the Pandemic he spoke about people who for whatever reason didn't want to take the shot and said:

*"They do not believe in science, are often misogynists, often racists too; it is a sect, a small group, but who are taking up space, and here we have to make a choice....should we tolerate them?"*

'Taking up space? Should we tolerate them! At the time I was so in the Covid moment, I defended him, despite his words being chilling and sinister. What Truedope and others like him said is literally how tyrannies have been spawned throughout history. Little wonder he is a star pupil of Heir Schwab the Hairless, Penetrator of Cabinets. But he was not alone, and as I have said, many colleagues and I strayed into territory of which now makes our blood run cold. We were wrong about so much it is terrifying, and we now see that science was confused with power, propaganda and coercion. We beg forgiveness for doing it all again with Super Doggy!'

The words of PC Brown and Councillor Marcia Hunter saved the day. No officials were hung, drowned or beaten with canes or dog leads. At worst a few were gozzed on by kids from the upper tier of the shopping precinct. They remembered at last they were public servants. Misinformation and disinformation bludgeons were put aside. Rich or poor, could express their opinions without fear of reproach, whether in public, online or even in hyperbolic satirical literature. People rejoiced at the return to the best arguments winning the day, rather than pile-ons, fines or censorship.

The ripple became a flood as town by town, then city by city felt the refreshing waters of true democracy washing through their courtrooms and council chambers. They admitted dissenters weren't all simpletons going down rabbit holes needing a worthy official to rescue them. They stopped treating people like cattle, like beasts of the field without reason or subtlety. It eventually even reached Westminster. Most importantly of all, the books were opened. Government contracts were made public. Power was taken back from think tanks, so-called charities and social change networks and placed in the hands of accountable elected officials, who must declare all behind the scenes discussion.

Once the influence peddlars had their influence cut, their funding streams quickly dried up. Adam's father was spot on about he who pays the piper. As for the elite social change zealots, their desire to shape society was revealed to be relative to their remuneration.

Any ministerial meetings with billionaires were subject to minuting and a genuine oversight by neutral observers, especially meetings with the bespectacled Kermit soundalike Smurf with man boobs.

All international agreements were put to the people. They were to be revealed in real time, stage by stage, before any narrative was developed, vote taken, or contract signed. All agreed our liberty is not a plaything of the powerful.

The Abattoirians, heroes for a season, resumed relative anonymity, though they recounted their deeds in taverns by firesides in return for a free pie or a pint. Many wore chains with symbols and tokens recording their kill counts. The Billy Big Balls wore dog scalps on belts around their waists and formed their own sub-group called "The Abattoir Apaches." The odd girls wore charm bracelets made up entirely of dog motif charms, again enumerating their kills. Bar owners of Benidorm, though sympathising with Stockport's bereaved, were quietly upset butchers' bonuses were below initial projections.

In and around Stockport, sales of bamboo collapsed in all its forms, from plants to plant supports to even furniture and trays. Chinese Takeaways struggled to survive and had to drastically increase their free delivery radius from three miles to three and a half. Their hardships were not prolonged overmuch, as people quickly came to terms with the fact they too were victims along with everyone else. That and the fact their food is just too good to be without for long, and in the greater scheme of things, value for money, especially when they throw in some complimentary plawn a clacker.

On the other hand, trade immediately boomed for Riyad at his petrol station franchise. He was regarded locally as a freedom fighter. He even bought himself a Che Guevara style red beret beloved among starry eyed politically illiterate students. He binned it later after learning Che was a ruthless killer, who calmly murdered in cold blood anyone standing between him and his aims. Riyad became the go-to man for tinned dog meat and baked beans, and he made sure he gave the loose lipped shoe-shine boy on Shaw Heath a good slap too.

Jake Baretta aka Graham Barrett has long since dropped the false name, American accent, trilby and even Brylcream. He is also now one of Riyad's family's weekend drivers and has a cupboard at home absolutely rammed with baked beans.

The once murky brown and polluted River Mersey became an international symbol of liberty. From its humble beginnings, being barely able to host a medium-sized canoe club lesson, to its zenith at the 4-mile-wide estuary at Ellesmere Port, it became almost as famous as the Nile and the Danube. The source of the river and the slippery slidey stone were both designated as a Unesco World Heritage Sites. Hearing this the National Trust commandeered the Vernon Park car parks and the previously free parking is now £2 per hour.

The international response to Stockport's tragedy eventually turned into a flood, quenching a thirst for truth and refreshing nations. It washed away much greed and corruption, and the stench of oligarchy. PC Craig Brown eventually rose to become Chief Constable of Greater Manchester. His methods became a model for police forces across the land. Sir Robert Peel's vision was finally fulfilled. Big ex-army lads were hired by the thousand. A couple of six-foot plus burly ex-soldiers were found to de-escalate a conflict much quicker than ten five foot two eyes of blue graduates shouting calm down we're here to help. Success was measured by the lack of crime and vice versa. PC Danny Andrews eventually made a full recovery and progressed to become Detective Chief Inspector Andrews. He even became the British Police Arm Wrestling Champion, a title he held for six years, wrestling with either arm.

In the courts of heaven, Peel and Whittington became firm friends, regularly toasting the fortitude and stoicism of Stockport. Whittington still complained how those crafty conniving cockneys led him and his cat on a wild goose chase. On occasion they met with John Wesley to knock out a few of his hymns, and to pray for the still spiritually desolate village of Hazel Grove, where all manner of wickedness is still enacted.

The genuine Sooty and Sweep and friends returned for a special gala night at the town hall. Ticket sales for children were sluggish but were more than compensated for by starry-eyed adults, most of whom were now of pensionable age. Some even organised excursions to the standing stone in Vernon Park. This was followed by coffee and cake in the Pear Mill Vintage Emporium, where they discussed the discrepancy in the size of the stone between their memories and the reality.

The giant pear on Pear Mill was upgraded to one made of pure four-inch-thick green glass, illuminated from within, and clearly visible even to excited airline passengers. The wealthy weird island dweller Richard Branflakes even claimed to have seen it from space from one of his environmentally friendly rockets.

Incredibly (i.e. not credibly), one night when no one was on the premises, Wagger Mamas was destroyed. An off-course, heavily armed, presumed Russian military drone on manoeuvres accidentally crash-landed right on top of it, in an Emmerdale style far-fetched plotline.

In Greater Stockport it didn't take long for the dog population to begin its recovery as shelters and rescue centres nationally were quickly emptied. Whether the dogs or politicians will ever be fully trusted again, only time will tell.

As might be expected, along with the Song for Stockport, there was an explosion of books, films and documentaries about Stockport which eventually eclipsed even the Titanic tragedy. The latest Mission Implausible movie was entitled: "Catch 22 the Sequel" and was filmed in Stockport. It included dramatic scenes of a grey and balding Tom Crude flying an F16 in and out of the twenty-two yawning arches of the viaduct, and nobody could catch the elusive wee rascal. It also bumped up PM Fishy Shoe-rack's popularity ratings as he had the ideal stature to be Tom Crude's body double. Sadistic Khan applied but withdrew when told he would be fined £12.50 for each fly through and he couldn't put it on expenses. They also feared his hooter might confuse American viewers into thinking the F-16 had been merged with Concord.

Liam Knees-gone got in on the act, throwing baddies through train windows into the Mersey and onto the M60 carriageway from the viaduct, in his Commuter sequel. It was a stilted performance and critics said it lacked even the superficial appeal of the original. His reputation was restored however by his enthralling performance in his blockbuster, "The Scourge of the Scallies," in which he cleaned up the 192 late nighter single handedly. Critics agreed throwing baddies out of train windows had become stale and predictable. Throwing them from Stockport double deckers gave fresh impetus and vitality to the genre, thanks to the bus roof fight scenes being more precarious, due to all the frequent stopping and starting.

Long gone Frankie Vaughan enjoyed a posthumous revival with "Stockport That's Where It's At" going to number one where it remained for 17 weeks eclipsing Bryan Adams' Everything I do I do it for you. Adams briefly claimed his song was actually about Stockport before issuing a retraction in the face of public ridicule.

In time, the hype and money-making opportunities died down a little, but a legacy remained. Stockport, lowly Stockport, became a beacon of hope, an enduring promise of sunlit uplands. Even so, its skies remained grey and sullen, and the rain continued to fall, feeding the town's three rivers as it has for centuries.

**The End**